# The New
# Treasury of Great
# Racing Stories

ALSO PUBLISHED BY W. W. NORTON & COMPANY

*The Dick Francis Treasury of Great Racing Stories*
edited and introduced by Dick Francis and John Welcome

*Fools, Knaves and Heroes: Great Political Short Stories*
edited and introduced by Jeffrey Archer and Simon Bainbridge

*Great Law and Order Stories*
selected and introduced by John Mortimer

# The New
# Treasury of Great
# Racing Stories

---

# DICK FRANCIS
## and JOHN WELCOME, editors

W·W·NORTON & COMPANY
New York     London

Printed in the United States of America

Manufacturing by R. R. Donnelley & Sons Co.

Library of Congress Cataloging-in-Publication Data

The New Treasury of Great Racing Stories / Dick Francis and
John Welcome, editors. — 1st American ed.
    p.   cm.
Originally published under title: Classic lines:
more great racing stories.
1. Horse racing–Fiction.   2. Short stories, English.   3. Short
stories, American.     I. Francis, Dick.     II. Welcome, John. 1914–   .
PR1309.H64N4, 1992
823'.0108355–dc20

ISBN 0-393-03102-0

W.W. Norton & Company, Inc., 500 Fifth Avenue, New York, N.Y. 10110
W.W. Norton & Company Ltd., 10 Coptic Street, London WC1A 1PU

1 2 3 4 5 6 7 8 9 0

# CONTENTS

# Acknowledgements

Grateful acknowledgement is made to the following for permission to reprint the material in this volume:

The authors and Messrs John Johnson Ltd for the stories *Spring Fever* and *My First Winner*.

The Estate of Damon Runyon and Constable Publishers Ltd for the story *Pick The Winner* from *Furthermore, Runyon On Broadway*.

*The Dead Cert* by J. C. Squire is reprinted by permission of the Peters Fraser & Dunlop Group Ltd.

The author and Mr Murray Pollinger for the story *Pullinstown* from *Conversation Piece*, published in Virago Modern Classics in the Commonwealth and in the same series distributed by Penguin in the USA.

The story *Occasional Licences*, copyright E. Œ. Sommerville & Martin Ross, reproduced by permission of John Farquharson Ltd.

The author and David Higham Associates for the story *The Good Thing*.

The Richards Literary Agency for the story *The Losers* by Maurice Gee.

Whilst all reasonable attempts have been made to contact the original copyright holders, the Publishers would be happy to hear from those they have been unable to trace, and due acknowledgement will be made in future editions.

# INTRODUCTION

HE lot of those who compile collections such as this, happy
though it may be, is not without its hazards. The most
obvious is, of course, the accusation of omission, the sin of
leaving out fondly recalled favourites of whatever reader or critic
happens to pick up the collection. Avoidance of the hackneyed is
seldom accepted as an excuse; nevertheless it is suggested that
freshness and rediscovery must play a major part, especially in a
second selection. Perhaps, too, it may be pointed out that anthologies are of their very nature a matter of personal choice and for
better or worse must stand or fall as such. It has to be said,
however, that those who venture into the sphere of sporting
anthologies are facing a further obstacle to be surmounted. What
they select must be authentic. Nothing can be more damaging than
to include a story which, however compelling its narrative, fails
this test. One recalls how Ouida, beloved by the Victorians for
her bestsellers of high society featuring dashing guardsmen and
languorous ladies, made herself into a laughing-stock when she
wrote of the boatrace that all the Oxford crew rowed hard but
none rowed harder than stroke. This was almost as bad a gaffe as
the writer, who shall be nameless, who made his hero own a colt
who won the Derby in successive years!

That having been said, times they are a'changing in racing as in
everything else and one or two of the stories included here, accurate
when written, may appear to modern eyes to contain errors of
plot and procedure. However, when that explanation is borne in
mind, mistakes do nothing to derogate from the stories' strength
and effectiveness. The jockey in C. C. L. Browne's splendid tale
of the ups and downs of a run-of-the-mill steeplechase rider's day
would have been unlikely in these softer times to have been passed

by the doctor as fit to ride again. But in the sterner ethos of an earlier day the decision was his, he made it and got away with it. He would today also earn considerably more than £7 a ride.

Similarly in Donn Byrne's story, the rule in which nominations became void on death was abolished by the friendly test case of the Jockey Club versus Edgar Wallace decided in the late twenties, years after the time in which the story is set. And in *Occasional Licences* the race in which the immortal Flurry Knox with the connivance of the rascally Slipper cajoled the coachhorse, Sultan, to win at the gymkhana meeting would certainly nowadays rank as an illegal or flapping contest, bringing condign penalties down upon its participants. Only the pens of those two ladies could adequately have recorded Flurry's forceful comments on the same, had they done so.

Much has recently been written of Somerville and Ross and their position in literature, sporting and otherwise, and there is nothing further usefully to add to it here. Donn Byrne, however, immensely popular in his day but largely forgotten now, may be regarded as a rediscovery. Born in Brooklyn in 1899 of Irish-American parentage he was educated in Ireland and France. Later he roamed the continents in a variety of employments including that of a cowpuncher and, it is believed, a strapper in a racing stable, before he took to writing. Unashamedly romantic in his theme and outlook, as his novels and stories show, he struck a chord which matched the thinking of his time and enjoyed great success on both sides of the Atlantic. In 1928 at the age of thirty-nine he returned to Ireland, and purchased a castle in county Cork. Tragically he was killed in a motor accident soon after his arrival and just before the publication of his last collection, *Destiny Bay*, from which this story is taken.

Edgar Wallace was another romantic but of a very different sort. He fell in love with racing but, unfortunately for him, his enthusiasm, especially where his own horses were concerned, far outran his judgment. When he wrote of one of his characters, 'Sir Jacques was merely one of many racing people who harboured the illusion that they knew more than the bookmaker. It brought many a promising racing career to an untimely end', he might have been writing about himself.

He died suddenly in Hollywood in 1932 aged fifty-seven. Steve Donoghue, an old friend who was in America at the time, tells in his memoirs that it was he who made the arrangements for despatching the coffin back to England, and Wallace would have found it entirely appropriate that it was the greatest jockey of his time who was given this task. When the estate was marshalled by his executors it was found that there were precious few assets and debts amounting to £140,000, none of them, however, to the bookies with whom he had always settled promptly.

Wallace, although foolish in his betting and his ownership of bad horses he insisted on believing to be world-beaters, nevertheless knew racing. When he put his mind to it and was not dashing off bits and pieces in a hurry to keep the bookies quiet, he could write of it tellingly and well. The story which we have reproduced, improbable though it may appear at first sight, may well have been based on an actual incident in the Ascot Gold Cup some years before when the favourite, Tracery, nearly suffered the same fate. And Wallace did signal service to the sport he loved when he financed at his own expense the case we have mentioned above. We have already written about Wallace in our first collection and of several of the authors collected here, but a word needs to be said of certain of the others more especially the Americans, Damon Runyon, Gordon Grand and John Taintor Foote. With the exception of Runyon, little is known of them on this side of the Atlantic and even Runyon's popularity peaked over forty years ago. In their very diversity these three demonstrate the many facets of the sport's appeal.

Runyon was a newspaperman on the New York American who loved, above all, to write of racing and boxing. The genesis of the many stories he wrote of 'the bandits of Broadway', Harry the Horse, Sam the Gonoph, Dave the Dude and the rest is strange indeed. He was in despair, thinking he was written out, when suddenly the idea came to him of putting them all and their adventures into print as he saw them through the eyes of his comic genius. In so doing he invented and perfected a line of light literature as unique and original as that of Wodehouse. His end was tragic; he died of cancer in December 1946, having suffered terribly during the last two years of his life, but kept going only by his indomitable and buoyant spirit. To the end he never lost his love of racing. He was a versifier, too, of light verse and jingles, and the scribbled few lines sent across to a friend from the press box

of one of the last Kentucky Derbies he attended well describe how
he saw and loved it all:

> Say, have they turned the pages
> Back to the past once more?
> Back to the racin' ages
> An' a Derby out of the yore?
> Say, don't tell me I'm daffy,
> Ain't that the same ol' grin?
> Why, it's that handy
> Guy named Sande,
> Bootin' a winner in?

Earl Sande was the leading American jockey of the twenties.
Among a host of other winners he rode Zev in the famous Zev–Papyrus match at Belmont Park in October 1923. Papyrus had won
the Derby of that year and Zev was an American champion. The
match was made in an effort to start a series of international races
but it was long before its time and it failed dismally. The track
was dirt and saturated by a night's rain, and to handicap him
further Papyrus, who had had a hard season being narrowly
defeated in the St Leger the previous month, was wrongly plated.
He was beaten out of sight with Donoghue, who rode him, having
accepted the inevitable, virtually pulling him up. Runyon reported
the preliminaries and the race itself in his usual graphic style for
Sande was then and remained always one of his heroes.

Gordon Grand's background was very different. He was born
to a fox-hunting and racing family and saw his first day to hounds
in 1891 at the age of eight when he was warned by the Master to
'keep your pony where it belongs, in the Field, and not pretend
you can't hold him!' He later became president of that pack, the
Millbrook Hounds, and hunted, raced and bred horses all his life.
He was the amateur where Runyon was the professional. The story
of his which we include is from a collection called *The Silver Horn*.
Written to alleviate a long illness it only saw print almost as an
afterthought in America and later in England. Its success encouraged him to follow it up with more hunting and racing stories,
many featuring Colonel Weatherford. But when his editor at the
Derrydale Press, who had discovered and encouraged him, died,
'I put my pen away and employed the time formerly given over

to writing, to gardening, raising a colt or two on my farm, fox-hunting and business interests.'

Little appears to be known of John Taintor Foote save that he, too, truly loved racing and wrote of it with humour, understanding and knowledge of the American turf, its characters and character-istics. He was a playwright and screenwriter as well as novelist, several of his plays being produced on Broadway; his screen credits include *Kentucky* and *The Story of Sea Biscuit*. Born in Leadville, Colorado in 1891, he died in 1950 and will at least always be remembered for having coined the phrase, 'The look of eagles', which has been repeated all over the world as the hallmark of a true champion.

In contrast to the Americans, Sir John Squire was the quintessen-tial Englishman. He is little thought of now for in himself and his life he was the exemplar of an all but vanished type, the literary cove with sporting tastes. As editor of *The London Mercury* he had at one time immense influence on the London literary scene, he founded and captained an eccentric touring cricket team called 'The Invalids', he produced a very bad blank verse epic about an intervarsity rugby match, and he wrote some of the best verse parodies in the language. He knew little or nothing about the nuts and bolts of racing and would have cared less, but in *The Dead Cert* he showed that he knew all about how they talk and tip in pubs – he was something of an expert on pubs – and what happens when the conversation takes an unusual turn. The story is yet another instance of the many sides to the racing game and the diversity of those who interest themselves in it, and has a typical Squireish twist at its end.

If Squire exemplified one type of Englishman then A. B. 'Banjo' Paterson did the same for Australia. He was, like Runyon, a news-paperman and a versifier, one of the band of Bush Balladeers who sang of racing and riding on the outback and on city tracks, whose numbers included Adam Lindsay Gordon, Will H. Ogilvie and the tragic 'Breaker' Morant. He is best known in England as the author of *Waltzing Matilda* which the Anzacs adopted as their marching song, though he wrote many other stirring rhymes of the racetrack and those who rode it, all of them laced with humour. His *Riders In The Stand* is a classic and as true today as the day he wrote it, which, to quote only one short verse, will show:

They'll say Chevalley lost his nerve, and Regan lost his head;
They'll tell how one was 'livened up' and something else was 'dead' –
In fact, the race was never run on sea, or sky, or land,
But what you'd get it better done by riders in the Stand.

As well as being one of the poets of the sport he was a prolific
writer of racing journalism, and editor for some ten years of a
racing paper. Also to his credit was a racing novel *The Shearer's
Colt* and a parody of Nat Gould, whom he disliked both as a man
and an author. When he died he left behind an unfinished history
of Australian racing and numerous racing short stories of which
*The Oracle* is as good a description of a racing pest still extant as
one is ever likely to get.

Paterson and indeed all the authors represented here, with the
possible exception of Maurice Gee, whose *The Losers* is included
to show that the sport has its darker side, would have echoed the
words of Reginald Herbert, who in the early days of steeplechasing
wrote one of the most lively of all racing reminiscences, *When
Diamonds Were Trumps*. Red and white diamonds were his racing
colours and the title gives some idea of the flavour of the book.
'I may be said to know something about it,' he wrote, and indeed
he did having ridden over fences with success for upwards of thirty
years, 'And I unhesitantly affirm that, "there's nowt like racing".'

It is the editors' hope that the stories here included bear out that
testimony.

# The New
# Treasury of Great
# Racing Stories

# SPRING FEVER

## Dick Francis

LOOKING back, Mrs Angela Hart could identify the exact instant in which she fell irrationally in love with her jockey. Angela Hart, plump, motherly, and fifty-two, watched the twenty-four year old man walk into the parade ring at Cheltenham races in her gleaming pink and white colours, and she thought: how young he is, how fit, how lean . . . how *brave*.

He crossed the bright turf to join her for the usual few minutes of chit-chat before taking her horse away to its two-mile scurry over hurdles, and she looked at the way the weather-tanned flesh lay taut over the cheekbone and agreed automatically that yes, the spring sunshine was lovely, and that yes, the drier going should suit her Billyboy better than all the rains of the past few weeks.

It was a day like many another. Two racehorses having satisfactorily replaced the late and moderately lamented Edward Hart in Angela's affections, she contentedly spent her time in going to steeplechase meetings to see her darlings run, and in clipping out mentions of them from 'The Sporting Life', and in ringing up her trainer, Clement Scott, to enquire after their health. She was a woman of kindness and good humour, but suffered from a dangerous belief that everyone was basically as well-intentioned as herself. Like children who pat tigers, she expected a purr of appreciation in return for her offered friendship, not to have her arm bitten off.

Derek Roberts, jockey, saw Mrs Angela Hart prosaically as the middle-aged owner of Billyboy and Hamlet. A woman to whom he spoke habitually with a politeness born of needing the fees he was paid for riding her horses. His job, he reckoned, involved pleasing the customers before and after each race as well as doing his best for them in the event, and as he had long years ago discovered that most owners were pathetically pleased when a jockey praised their horses, he had slid almost without cynicism into a way of conveying optimism even when not believing a word of it.

When he walked into the parade ring at Cheltenham, looking for Mrs Hart and spotting her across the grass in her green tweed coat and brown fur hat, he was thinking that as Billyboy hadn't much chance in today's company he had better prepare the old duck for the coming disappointment and at the same time insure himself against being blamed for it.

'Lovely day,' he said, shaking her hand. 'Real spring sunshine.'

'Lovely.'

After a short silence, when she said nothing more, he tried again.

'Much better for Billyboy, now all that rain's drying out.'

'Yes, I'm sure you're right.'

She wasn't as talkative as usual, he thought. Not the normal excited chatter. He watched Billyboy plod round the ring and said encouragingly, 'He should run well today . . . though the opposition's pretty hot, of course.'

Mrs Hart, looking slightly vague, merely nodded. Derek Roberts, shrugging his mental shoulders, gave her a practised half-genuine smile and reckoned (mistakenly) that if she had something on her mind, and didn't want to talk, it was nothing to do with him.

A step away from them, also with his eyes on the horse, stood Billyboy's trainer, Clement Scott. Strong, approaching sixty, a charmer all his life, he had achieved success more through personality than any deep skill with horses. He wore good clothes. He could talk.

Underneath the attractive skin there was a coldness which was apparent to his self-effacing wife, and to his grown and married children, and eventually to anyone who knew him well. He was good company, but lacked compassion. All bonhomie on top; ruthlessly self-seeking below.

Clement Scott was old in the ways of jockeys and owners, and professionally he thought highly of the pair before him: of Derek because he kept the owners happy and rode well enough besides, and of Angela because her first interest was in the horses themselves and not in the prize-money they might fail to win. Motherly sentimental ladies, in his opinion, were the least critical and most forgiving of owners, and he put up gladly with their gushing telephone calls because they also tended to pay his bills on receipt. Towards Angela, nicely endowed with a house on the edge of Wentworth golf course, he behaved with the avuncular roguishness that had kept many a widow faithful to his stable in spite of persistent rumours that he would probably cheat them if given half a chance.

Angela, like many another lady, didn't believe the rumours. Clement, dear naughty Clement who made owning a racehorse such satisfying fun, would never in any case cheat *her*.

She stood beside Clement on the stands to watch the race, and felt an extra dimension of anxiety: not simply, as always, for the safe return of darling Billyboy, but also, acutely, for the man on his back. Such risks he takes, she thought, watching him through her binoculars; and before that day she had thought only of whether he'd judged the pace right, or taken an available opening, or ridden a vigorous finish. During that race her response to him crossed conclusively from objectivity to emotion, a change which at the time she only dimly perceived.

Derek Roberts, by dint of not resting the horse when it was beaten, urged Billyboy forwards into fourth place close to the winning post, knowing that Angela would like fourth better than fifth or sixth or seventh. Clement Scott smiled to himself as he watched. Fourth or seventh, the horse had won no prize-money; but that lad Derek, with his good looks and crafty ways, he sure knew how to keep the owners sweet.

Her raceglasses clutched tightly to her chest, Angela Hart breathed deeply from the release of pulse-raising tensions. She thought gratefully that fourth place wasn't bad in view of the hot opposition, and Billyboy had been running on at the end, which was a good sign . . . and Derek Roberts had come back safely.

With her trainer she hastened down to meet the returning pair, and watched Billyboy blow through his nostrils in his usual post-race sweating state, and listened to Derek talking over his shoulder to her while he undid the girth buckles on the saddle.

' . . . Made a bit of a mistake landing over the third last, but it didn't stop him . . . He should win a race pretty soon, I'd say . . . '

He gave her the special smile and a sketchy salute and hurried to weigh-in and change for the next race, looping the girths round the saddle as he went. Angela watched until he was out of sight and asked Clement when her horses were running next.

'Hamlet had a bit of heat in one leg this morning,' he said. 'And Billyboy needs a fortnight at least between races.' He screwed up his eyes at her, teasing. 'If you can't wait that long to see them again, why don't you come over one morning and watch their training gallops?'

She was pleased. 'Does Derek ride the gallops?'

'Sometimes,' he said.

It was on the following day that Angela, dreamily drifting around her house, thought of buying another horse.

She looked up Derek Roberts's number and telephoned.

'Find you another horse?' he said. 'Yeah . . . sure . . . I think another horse is a grand idea, but you should ask Mr Scott . . . '

'If Clement finds me a horse,' Angela said, 'Will you come with me to see it? I'd really like your opinion, before I buy.'

'Well . . . ' He hesitated, not relishing such a use of his spare time but realising that another horse for Angela meant more fees for himself.

' . . . All right, certainly I'll come, Mrs Hart, if I can be of use.'

'That's fine,' she said. 'I'll ring Clement straight away.'

'Another horse?' Clement said, surprised. 'Yes, if you like, though it's a bit late in the season. Why not wait . . . ?'

'No,' Angela interrupted. 'Dear Clement, I want him now.'

Clement Scott heard but couldn't understand the urgency in her voice. Four days later, however, when she came to see her existing two horses work, having made sure beforehand that Derek would be there to ride them, he understood completely.

Angela, fiftyish matronly Angela, couldn't keep her eyes off Derek Roberts. She intently watched him come and go, on horse and on foot, and scanned his face uninterruptedly while he spoke. She asked him questions to keep him near, and lost a good deal of animation when he finally went home.

Clement Scott, who had seen that sort of thing often enough before, behaved to her more flirtatiously than ever and kept his sardonic smile to himself. He had luckily heard of a third horse for her he said and he would take her to see it.

'Actually,' Angela said diffidently, 'I've already asked Derek to come with me . . . and he said he would.'

Clement, that evening, telephoned to Derek.

'Besotted with me?' said Derek astounded. 'That's bloody nonsense. I've been riding for her for more than a year. You can't tell me I wouldn't have noticed.'

'Keep your eyes open, lad,' Clement said. 'I reckon she wants this other horse just to give her an excuse to see you oftener, and that being so, lad, I've a little proposition for you.'

He outlined the little proposition at some length, and Derek discovered that his consideration of Mrs Hart's best interests came a poor second to the prospect of a tax-free instant gain equal to half his annual earnings.

He drove to her house at Wentworth a few days later, and they went on together in her car, a Rover, with Derek driving. The horse belonged to a man in Yorkshire, which meant, Angela thought contentedly, that the trip would take all day. She had rationalised her desire to own another horse as just an increase in her interest in racing, and also she had rationalised her eagerness for the Yorkshire journey as merely impatience to see what Clement had described as 'an exciting bargain, at sixteen thousand. A real smasher. One to do you justice, my dear Angela.'

She could just afford it, she thought, if she didn't go on a cruise this summer, and if she spent less on theatre tickets and clothes. She did not at any point admit to herself that what she was buying at such cost was a few scattered hours out of Derek Roberts's life.

Going North from Watford, Derek said, 'Mrs Hart, did Mr Scott tell you much about this horse?'

'He said you'd tell me. And call me Angela.'

'Er . . . ' He cleared his throat. 'Angela . . . ' He glanced at her as she sat beside him, plump and relaxed and happy. It couldn't be true, he thought. People like Mrs Hart didn't suffer from infatuations. She was far too old. Fifty . . . an unimaginable age to him at twenty-four. He shifted uncomfortably in his seat and felt ashamed (but only slightly) at what he was about to do.

'Mr Scott thinks the horse has terrific potential. Only six years old. Won a hurdle race last year . . . ' He went on with the sales talk, skilfully weaving in the few actual facts which she could verify from form books if she wanted to, and putting a delicately rosy slant on everything else. 'Of course the frost and snow has kept it off the racecourse during the winter . . . but I'll tell you, just between ourselves . . . er . . . Angela . . . that Mr Scott thinks he might even enter him for the Whitbread. He might even be in that class.'

Angela listened entranced. The Whitbread Gold Cup, scheduled for six weeks ahead, was the last big race of the season. To have a horse fit to run in it, and to have Derek Roberts ride it, seemed to her a pinnacle in her racing life that she had never envisaged. Her horizons, her joy, expanded like flowers.

'Oh, how lovely,' she said ecstatically; and Derek Roberts (almost) winced.

'Mr Scott wondered if you'd like me to do a bit of bargaining for you,' he said. 'To get the price down a bit.'

'Dear Clement is so thoughtful.' She gave Derek a slightly anxious smile. 'Don't bargain so hard that I lose the horse, though, will you?'

He promised not to.

'What is it called?' she said, and he told her 'Magic.'

Magic was stabled in the sort of yard which should have warned Angela to beware, but she'd heard often enough that in Ireland champions had been bought out of pigsties, and caution was nowhere in her mind. Dear Clement would certainly not buy her a bad horse, and with Derek himself with her to advise . . . She looked trustingly at the nondescript bay gelding produced for her inspection and saw only her dreams, not the mud underfoot, not the rotten wood round the stable doors, not the dry cracked leather of the horse's tack.

She saw Magic being walked up and down the weedy stable yard and she saw him being trotted round a bit on a lunging rein in a small dock-grown paddock; and she didn't see the dismay that Derek couldn't altogether keep out of his face.

'What do you think?' she said, her eyes still shining in spite of all.

'Good strong shoulder,' he said judiciously. 'Needs a bit of feeding to improve his condition, perhaps.'

'But do you like him?'

'He nodded decisively. 'Just the job.'

'I'll have him then.' She said it without the slightest hesitation, and he stamped on the qualms which pricked like teeth.

She waited in the car while Derek bargained with Magic's owner, watching the two men who stood together in the stable yard shaking their heads, spreading their arms, shrugging, and starting again. Finally, to her relief, they touched hands on it, and Derek came to tell her that she could have the horse for fifteen thousand, if she liked.

'Think it over,' he said, making it sound as if she needn't.

She shook her head. 'I've decided. I really have. Shall I give the man a cheque?'

'No,' he said. 'Mr Scott has to get a vet's report, and fix up transport and insurance and so on. He'll do all the paperwork and settle for the horse, and you can pay him for everything at once. Much simpler.'

'Darling Clement,' she said warmly. 'Always so sweet and thoughtful.'

Darling Clement entered Magic for the Whitbread Gold Cup at Sandown Park, and also for what he called a 'warm-up' race three weeks before the big event.

'That will be at Stratford-upon-Avon,' he told Angela. 'In the Pragnell Cup, first week of April.'

'How marvellous,' Angela said.

She telephoned several times to Derek for long cosy consultations about Magic's prospects and drank in his heady optimism like the word of God. Derek filled her thoughts from dawn to dusk. Dear Derek, who was so brave and charming and kind.

Clement and Derek took Magic out onto the gallops at home and found the 'exciting bargain' unwilling to keep up with any other horse in the stable. Magic waved his tail about and kicked up heels and gave every sign of extreme bad temper. Both Clement and Derek, however, reported to a delighted Angela that Magic was a perfect gentleman and going well.

When Angela turned up by arrangement at ten one morning to watch Magic work, he had been sent out by mistake with the first lot at seven, and was consequently resting. Her disappointment was mild, though, because Derek was there, not riding but accompanying her on foot, full of smiles and gaiety and friendship. She loved it. She trusted him absolutely, and she showed it.

'Well done, lad,' Clement said gratefully, as she drove away later. 'With you around our Angela wouldn't notice an earthquake.'

Derek, watching her go, felt remorse and regret. It was hardly fair, he thought. She was a nice old duck really. She'd done no one any harm. He belatedly began not to like himself.

They went to Stratford races all hoping for different things: Derek that Magic would at least get round, Angela that her horse would win, and Clement that he wouldn't stop dead in the first furlong.

Three miles. Fast track. Firm ground. Eighteen fences.

Angela's heart was beating with a throb she could feel as Magic, to the relief of both of the men, deigned to set off in the normal way from the start, and consented thereafter to gallop along steadily among the rear half of the field. After nearly two miles of this mediocrity both men relaxed and knew that when Magic ran out of puff and pulled up, as he was bound to do soon, they could explain to Angela that 'he had needed the race,' and 'he'll be tuned up nicely for the Whitbread'; and she would believe it.

A mile from home, from unconscious habit, Derek gave Magic the speeding-up signs of squeezing with his legs and clicking his tongue and flicking the reins. Magic unexpectedly plunged towards the next fence, misjudged his distance, took off too soon, hit the birch hard and landed in a heap on the ground.

The horse got to his feet and nonchalantly cantered away. The jockey lay still and flat.

'Derek,' cried Angela, agonised.

'Bloody fool,' Clement said furiously, bustling down from the stands, 'Got him unbalanced. What does he expect?'

Angela at first stayed where she was, in a turmoil of anxiety, watching through her binoculars as the motionless Derek was loaded slowly onto a stretcher and carried carefully to an ambulance; and then she walked jerkily round to the first aid room to await his return.

I should never have bought the horse, she thought in anguish. If I hadn't bought the horse, Derek wouldn't be . . . wouldn't be . . .

He was alive. She saw his hands move as soon as the blue-uniformed men opened the ambulance doors. Her relief was almost as shattering as her fear. She felt faint.

Derek Roberts had broken his leg and was in no mood to worry about Angela's feelings. He noticed she was there because she made little fluttery efforts to reach his side – efforts constantly thwarted by the stretcher-bearers easing him out – saying to him over and over, 'Derek, oh Derek, are you all right?'

Derek didn't answer. His attention was on his leg, which hurt, and on getting into the ambulance room without being bumped. There was always a ghoulish crowd round the door, pressing forward to look. He stared up at the faces peering down and hated their probing interest. It was a relief to him, as always on these occasions, when they carried him through the door and shut out the ranks of eyes.

Inside, waiting for the doctor and lying quietly on a bed, he reflected gloomily that his present spot of trouble served him right.

Angela, outside, wandered aimlessly about, not seeing anyone she knew and wondering whether to go for a drink on her own. Dear Clement, who would have sustained her, had been last seen hurrying down the course to help catch the riderless horse. She thought that she ought to worry about the horse, but she couldn't; she had room in her mind only for Derek.

'Never mind, missus,' a voice said cheerfully. 'Yon Magic is all right. Cantering round the middle there and giving them the devil's own job of catching him. Don't you fret none. He's all right.'

Startled, she looked at the sturdy man with the broad Yorkshire accent who stood confidently in her way.

'Came from my brother, did that horse,' he said, 'I'm down here special like, to see him run.'

'Oh,' said Angela vaguely.

'Is the lad all right? The one who rode him?'

'I think he's broken his leg.'

'Dear, oh dear. Bit of hard luck, that. He drove a hard bargain with my brother, did that lad.'

'Did he?'

'Aye. My brother said Magic was a flier but your lad, he wouldn't have it. Said the horse hadn't any form to speak of, and looked proper useless to him. My brother was asking seven thousand for it, but your lad beat him down to five. I came here, see, to learn which was right.' He beamed with goodwill. 'Tell you the truth, the horse didn't run up to much, did it? Reckon your lad was right. But don't you fret, missus, there'll be another day.'

He gave her a nod and a final beam, and moved away. Angela felt breathless, as if he had punched her.

Already near the exit gate, she turned blindly and walked out through it, her legs taking her automatically towards her car. Shaking, she sat in the driving seat, and with a feeling of unreality drove all the one hundred miles home.

The man must have got it wrong, she thought. Not seven and five thousand, but seventeen and fifteen. When she reached her house she looked up the address of Magic's previous owner, and telephoned.

'Aye,' he said. 'Five thousand, that's right.' The broad Yorkshire voice floated cheerfully across the counties. 'Charged you a bit more, did they?' He chuckled. 'Couple of hundred, maybe? You can't grudge them that missus. Got to have their commission, like. It's the way of the world.'

She put down the receiver, and sat on her lonely sofa, and stared into space. She understood for the first time that what she had felt for Derek was love. She understood that Clement and Derek must have seen it in her weeks ago, and because of it had exploited and manipulated her in a way that was almost as callous as rape.

All the affection she had poured out towards them . . . all the joy and fond thoughts and happiness . . . they had taken them and used them and hadn't cared for her a bit. They don't like me, she thought. Derek doesn't even like me.

The pain of his rejection filled her with a depth of misery she had never felt before. How could she, she wondered wretchedly, have been so stupid, so blind, so pathetically immature?

She walked after a while through the big house, which was so quiet now that Edward wasn't there to fuss, and went into the kitchen. She started to make herself a cup of tea: and wept.

Within a week she visited Derek in hospital. He lay halfway down a long ward with his leg in traction, and for an instant he looked like a stranger; a thin young man with his head back on the pillows and his eyes closed. A strong young man no longer, she thought. More like a sick child.

That too was an illusion. He heard her arrive at his bedside and opened his eyes, and because he was totally unprepared to find her there she saw quite clearly the embarrassment which flooded through him. He swallowed, and bit his lip; and then he smiled. It was the same smile as before, the outward face of treason. Angela felt slightly sick.

She drew up a chair and sat by his bed.

'Derek,' she said. 'I've come to congratulate you.'

He was bewildered. 'What for?'

'On your capital gain. The difference between five thousand pounds and fifteen.'

His smile vanished. He looked away from her. At anything but her. He felt trapped and angry and ashamed, and he wished above all things that she would go away.

'How much of it,' Angela said slowly, 'Was your share? And how much was Clement's?'

After a stretching silence of more than a minute, he said, 'Half and half.'

'Thank you,' Angela said. She got to her feet, pushing back the chair. 'That's all, then. I just wanted to hear you admit it.' And to find out for sure, she thought, that she was cured. That the fever no longer ran in her blood. That she could look at him and not care: and she could.

He still couldn't look at her, however. 'All?' he said.

She nodded. 'What you did wasn't illegal, just . . . horrid. I should have been more businesslike.' She took a step away. 'Good-bye, Derek.'

She had gone several more steps before he called after her, suddenly, 'Angela . . . Mrs Hart.'

She paused and came halfway back.

'Please,' he said. 'Please listen. Just for one moment.'

Angela returned slowly to his bedside.

'I don't suppose you'll believe me,' he said, 'But I've been lying here thinking about that race at Stratford . . . and I've a feeling that Magic may not be so useless after all.'

'No,' Angela said. 'No more lies. I've had enough.'

'I'm not . . . this isn't a lie. Not this.'

She shook her head.

'Listen,' he said. 'Magic made no show at Stratford because nobody asked him to, except right at the end, when I shook him up. And then he fell because I'd done it so close to the fence . . . and because when I gave him the signal he just shot forward as if he'd been galvanised.'

Angela listened, disbelieving.

'Some horses,' he said, 'won't gallop at home. Magic won't. So we thought . . . I thought . . . that he couldn't race either. And I'm not so sure, now. I'm not so sure.'

Angela shrugged. 'It doesn't change anything. But anyway, I'll find out when he runs in the Whitbread.'

'No.' He squirmed. 'We never meant to run him in the Whitbread.'

'But he's entered,' she said.

'Yes, but . . . well, Mr Scott will tell you, a day or two before the race, that Magic has a temperature, or has bruised his foot, or something, and can't run. He . . . we . . . planned it. We reckoned you wouldn't quibble about the price if you thought Magic was Whitbread class . . . that's all.'

Angela let out an 'Oh' like a deep sigh. She looked down at the young man who was pleating his sheets aimlessly in his fingers and not meeting her eyes. She saw shame and the tiredness and the echo of pain from his leg, and she thought that what she had felt for him had been as destructive to him as to herself.

At home, after thinking it over, Angela telephoned to Clement.

'Dear Clement, how is Magic?'

'None the worse, Angela, I'm glad to say.'

'How splendid,' she said warmly. 'And now there's the Whitbread to look forward to, isn't there?'

'Yes, indeed.' He chuckled. 'Better buy a new hat, my dear.'

'Clement,' Angela said sweetly, 'I am counting on you to keep Magic fit and well-fed and uninjured in every way. I'm counting on his turning up to start in the Whitbread, and on his showing us just exactly how bad he is.'

'*What?*'

'Because if he doesn't Clement dear, I might just find myself chattering to one or two people . . . you know, pressmen and even the taxman, and people like that . . . about you buying Magic for five thousand pounds one day and selling him to me for fifteen thousand the next.'

She listened to the silence travelling thunderously down the wire, and she smiled with healthy mischief. 'And Clement, dear, we'll both give his new jockey instructions to win if he can, won't we? Because it's got to be a fair test, don't you think? And just to encourage you, I'll promise you that if I'm satisfied that Magic has done his very best, win or lose, I won't mention to anyone what I paid for him. And that's a bargain, Clement dear, that you can trust.'

He put the receiver down with a crash and swore aloud. 'Bloody old bag. She must have checked up.' He telephoned to Yorkshire and found out that indeed she had. Damn and blast her, he thought. He was going to look a proper fool in the eyes of the racing world, running rubbish like Magic in one of the top races. It would do his reputation no damn good at all.

Clement Scott felt not the slightest twinge of guilt. He had, after all, cheated a whole succession of foolish ladies in the same way, though not perhaps to the same extent. If Angela talked – and she could talk for hours when she liked – he would find that the gullible widowed darlings were all suddenly suspicious and buying their horses from someone else.

Magic, he saw furiously, would have to be trained as thoroughly as possible, and ridden by the best jockey free.

On Whitbread morning, Angela persuaded a friend of hers to promise to back Magic for her: a hundred pounds each way on the Tote, just in case. 'Anything can happen in a handicap,' she said. 'All the good horses might fall – you never know.'

In the parade ring at Sandown Park Angela was entirely her old self, kind and gushing and bright-eyed.

She spoke to her new jockey, who was unlike Derek Roberts to a comfortable degree. 'I expect you've talked it over with darling Clement,' she said gaily. 'But I think it would be best, don't you, if you keep Magic just sort of back a bit among all the other runners for most of the way, and then about a mile from the winning post tell him it's time to start winning, if you see what I mean, and of course after that it's up to both of you to do what you can.'

The jockey glanced at the stony face of Clement Scott.

'Do what the lady wants,' Clement said.

The jockey, who knew his business, carried out the instructions to the letter. A mile from home he dug Magic sharply in the ribs and was astonished at the response. Magic, young, lightly-raced and carrying bottom weight, surged past several older, tireder contenders, and came towards the last fence lying fifth.

Clement could hardly believe his eyes. Angela could hardly breathe. Magic floated over the last fence and charged up the straight and finished third.

'There,' Angela said. 'Isn't that lovely?'

Since almost no one else had backed her horse, Angela collected a fortune in place money from the Tote; and a few days later, for exactly what she'd paid, she sold Magic to a scrap-metal merchant from Kent. He had offered her more, and couldn't understand why she wouldn't take it.

Angela sent Derek Roberts a get-well card. A week later she

sent him an impersonal case of champagne and a simple message, 'Thanks.'

I've learned a lot, she thought, because of him. A lot about greed and gullibility, about façades and consequences and the transience of love. And about racing . . . too much.

She sold Billyboy and Hamlet, and took up pottery instead.

# MY FIRST WINNER

## *John Welcome*

THE story I am about to relate happened in the far-off days
of the nineteen-thirties when I was a member of the Oxford
University Air Squadron. The aircraft in which we young
men disported ourselves across the skies of southern England were
called Avro Tutors. The Tutor was constructed of canvas stretched
across metal ribs, had two open cockpits, a radial Armstrong-
Siddeley air-cooled engine and a cruising speed of ninety m.p.h.
It was a biplane with an exciting mass of rigging between the
wings through which the winds sometimes sang, a fixed under-
carriage, and slots in the leading edges of its upper wings to lower
the stalling speed. It was also said to be indestructible, and that it
was almost impossible to kill yourself flying one.

It had need of both of these qualities when it was in the hands
of the young gentlemen from the dreaming spires. I can, myself,
bear witness to the truth of its reputation. One sunny morning at
Eastchurch, where we held our summer camp, I was coming in
to land for the mid-morning break. The sky at that time was
always, in the words of a Canadian member of the squadron,
'lousy with aircraft'. As I approached the fence, another cheerful
aviator flew so close across my bows that I could have thrown a
biscuit into his empty forward cockpit.

Instinctively and very foolishly I yanked back the stick. The
nose came up, and the slots fell forward. The Tutor then gave that
peculiar yawing motion which in any other aircraft betokened a
stall, an instant spin and subsequent severe contact with the earth.
Desperately I slammed the stick forward. As a result I flew straight
into the ground. The wheels hit the earth with a resounding bang
and I went up again. To stop stalling once more I pushed on the
stick and the whole performance was repeated. We covered the

length of the grass airfield at Eastchurch in what are called in Irish horsey circles 'standing leps'. At last, on the fourth bounce, I regained sufficient of my scattered senses to push the throttle forward. The engine fired and caught and I went round again. When I came in there was a reception committee of the top brass of the squadron and station waiting for me.

I prefer to gloss over the next few minutes. But an examination of the oleo legs of the aircraft found them to have suffered no damage. They must have been built like the Forth Bridge. No wonder we could not go fast.

All this, you may say, has little to do with riding winners but in my particular case it had, as I shall show. Because you were strapped into a Tutor, you could not fall out of it, unless you were to lose speed on the upward arc of a loop and hang on the top. Then you could have a fairly good try at falling out, and it was necessary to hope that your straps were secure.

Had it been possible I am sure that I would have fallen off, or out of, an aircraft. For, although I had lived with horses all my life, I seemed to be constitutionally incapable of sitting on one over a fence. This happens to a few unlucky people and I was one of them. In Ireland where I was born and brought up, it did not matter so much. You have an instant's grace on the top of a bank while the horse is changing legs. In that instant you can grab at something, the mane, the neckstrap, or even the front of the saddle. In England you go much faster, there is no moment's pause, and so the horse and I parted company.

My best friend at the University was a man called Brian Manson. His father was dead, and he had been left with more money than was good for him. In retrospect, undergraduates of those days appear to have been divided into two classes, those who had too much money, and those who had enough to buy drink but not enough to buy food. I belonged to the latter class and I sometimes wonder if my constitution has ever really recovered.

Brian kept a couple of hunters and a chaser or two with a man called Kerrell out Headington way. Kerrell ran a racing stable cum riding school cum livery establishment. The Warren Farm was its name and it was there that Brian spent most of his time instead of at his books. Not that his books would have made much difference to him, had he attended to them, for he was a member of what we called The Dung Club. In other words he read Agriculture, a school whose members did not expect to have to devote themselves to earning a living in later life.

Kerrell was a tall gaunt man with a long face and a look in his eyes in which roguery and humour were mixed. The years and a bad fall had stopped his riding career, so Brian used to ride his horses for him in amateur and sometimes professional races. They were as thick as thieves (and the analogy is not all that inapt) in getting the horses ready together, trying them, arguing and wrangling about placing them, and what to do with them when they ran. Frequently those arguments led to side bets between themselves and they kept some sort of running account in which Brian's livery and training fees, Kerrell's bets, their own side bets, entries, stakes and travelling expenses were all inextricably mixed. During the time I knew them, I do not believe one ever settled with the other.

Undergraduates who had too much money in those days ran sports cars. Brian's choice was an Aston Martin. This was not the gilded carriage of today, but a chunky, spartan vehicle with bicycle type mudguards and a snarl in its throat. Sometimes I was permitted to accompany Brian racing and, huddled in the tiny back seat, I would endure the rigours of winter wind and rain, for the spartan nature of his car extended to its lack of weather-proofing. Thus the three of us would storm along the all but empty roads, Brian hunched over the wheel and Kerrell's great nose jutting out over the vestigial windscreen like the prow of a pirate ship. Once on the racecourse I would be sent off on mysterious errands clutching bundles of pound notes which I invested, according to instructions, with the ready money bookmakers in Tatts.

One February afternoon, having finished flying at Abingdon, I returned to my rooms to find Brian in an armchair in front of the fire reading *Horse and Hound*.

'Well, Baron von Richthofen,' he said; 'How many did you shoot down today?'

'Ten before breakfast,' I answered, putting my flying helmet with the headphones attached (we rather fancied ourselves walking about with them) onto a chair and taking off my coat.

'Rather below average, Baron. Something wrong with the Spandaus?'

'I'm afraid so. Not spitting correctly.' (There was just then a fashion for flying magazines containing highly-coloured stories of the First World War, and a favourite cliché of their contributors was to describe the machine-guns of German aircraft as 'spitting Spandaus'.)

'I've been looking at *Horse and Hound*,' he said. 'There's an Air Squadron race at the Bullingdon Grind. You should go in for that. You could just about win it.'

'Nonsense. I'd be jumped off at the first fence.'

'Not this time, you won't. Kerrell's just bought a horse that could have been made for you. Even you won't be able to fall off him.'

'I could fall off a gym horse standing still.'

'Not this one. Anyway, come out tomorrow and try him. It can't do you any harm.'

'I still won't ride him in that race.'

'It isn't a race. The man who won it last year had only been riding for three weeks. No one else got round. He was jumped off twice and remounted.'

Of course I went. The horse was a big gentle chestnut called Friar Tuck. He looked like a high-class Leicestershire hunter but in those days you could still ride that type in point-to-points.

Kerrell had a series of schooling fences and I went over them at half-speed, in company with Brian. I only fell off once but, as I pointed out when we came in, once, in a race, is enough.

'Not in this sort of a race,' Brian said. 'What did I tell you about last year's winner?'

'You'll be all right, sir,' Kerrell said. 'Besides, the faster they go, the easier it is to sit on.'

Now it cannot be denied that somewhere inside me was the desire to ride in a race and, even more, to win one. I was getting tired of being a standing joke where horses and aeroplanes were concerned, and I knew that if ever I was to win a race, this presented the best possible chance. Here I had better explain that the conditions of those undergraduate races were so framed that you could enter and ride a horse you had hired from a livery stable provided you paid the entry money and insurance yourself.

'We'll do a fast school over the course tomorrow,' Kerrell said.

'The course' was a series of birch fences Kerrell had built into the existing fences round his farm. You made a circuit of, I suppose, a mile to a mile-and-a-half and jumped six fences in doing it.

The following morning saw us preparing to go out over these fences. Kerrell decided to come along too. He sat up on a big black horse on which Brian had won two 'chases; Brian was on some hot thing of his own that they were getting ready.

'Now, remember,' Kerrell counselled me. 'Don't hang on to his head going into the fences, or you'll get pulled off. You've lost your confidence. This fellow knows it all. Let him have his head and hold on by the neck-strap.'

'What are you two coffee-housing about?' Brian said sourly. 'Come on. I'm off.'

We seemed to go into the first fence very fast indeed. I remembered what I'd been told. The fence disappeared beneath me and I was still there. In fact I survived two circuits despite a bump and a curse from Brian towards the end.

'There now,' Kerrell said. 'You're all right now. You're home and dried.'

I thought Brian looked pensive, but as I was so jubilant, I put it down to his preoccupation over his own mount.

Two days later he said to me in his offhand way, 'Now you're sitting on like Billy Stott, you'd better get some experience riding upsides with a few others, just like a race. I've arranged to go round the course tomorrow. Tim Maitland and Mike Rashley will come along.'

Tim and Mike were horsey acquaintances of ours. Mike was a gay spark from the Pytchley. He had a couple of useful horses and often crossed swords with Brian. He was nothing like as good a rider as Brian but he had, I think, rather more money and resources. They were on good enough terms off the racecourse. On it they were at daggers drawn.

The school seemed a good idea until we got to the Warren Farm. There Brian flatly announced he was not going to allow Friar Tuck to risk getting hurt so soon before the race, and that we were to draw lots for our rides. He held the straws. I drew the hot thing he had been riding in the earlier school. Kerrell had gone off somewhere to look for oats.

'This is bloody silly,' I said.

'Nonsense. Now you've got your confidence you want a bit of experience on other horses.'

The hot thing kicked and sidled and played up as we went down to the start. It jumped the first fence so fast that I did not have time to fall off. At the second it went straight into the air and turned itself into a fair imitation of a corkscrew. I went sailing away. The ground came up to meet me with an almighty bang.

I got up slowly and observed the riderless horse pursuing the others. There was nothing to do but walk back to the yard. At the gate I met Kerrell who, it seemed, had returned sooner than expected. He was watching the finish of the school. 'Been down, sir? You're all right, sir?' he said with a heavy scowl.

They came back in, Brian leading the riderless horse which he had caught. Kerrell produced a bottle of whisky. The scowl had disappeared and had been replaced by the expression he wore when he was thinking furiously. Brian had a glint in his eye and seemed to be savouring some secret joke. Before we left I thought I heard them having words.

The following Saturday I drove to the course with Brian. I knew Mike Rashley had a horse in our race but Brian said he thought he was going in an earlier one. There were four other runners. Two of them I did not know at all. They were in different flights of the Squadron from mine. One was riding a horse of his own, the other something hired from a livery stable which, Brian assured me, could not gallop enough to warm itself. The others were a conceited chap who flew very well indeed but who had only recently taken to point-to-pointing, and a man in The House I knew slightly who assured me he was only having a bump around. Friar Tuck was fit enough and he could jump. If I could only stay on top I must have a chance, or so I told myself.

The college kitchen had put up a lavish lunch in a hamper for Brian – he was not himself riding at the meeting – and he pressed me to salmon mousse, tinned asparagus, cold pheasant, chicken, white wine, port and brandy. I nibbled a biscuit, and surreptitiously poured away behind the car the beakers of port and brandy which he handed to me. So many times did he ask me how I was feeling that I snapped at him. He looked into the middle distance and grinned.

Kerrell was bringing the horses over. Tim Maitland was riding one of his in another race. Somehow the time dragged by. I changed and passed through the scales as in a dream. My shaking fingers could not tie my cap properly and I had to get Brian to do it for me. Then I was standing in the ring with Brian beside

me. Kerrell seemed to have disappeared. I wondered why everything had taken on a strange ethereal dimension as if there was a
haze suspended between me and reality.

Then something happened to jerk me out of my trance. A
smiling undergraduate walked past wearing a racing jersey and
white breeches. He wished me luck. 'That's Mike,' I said. 'I
thought he was going before.'

'He's changed his mind,' Brian said shortly. 'Says this is an
easier one to win.'

A faint suspicion as to what might be going on crossed my
mind for the first time. 'When did he tell you that?' I said.

'Oh, a little while ago.'

'You and Mike have got very confiding all of a sudden, haven't
you?'

Somebody shouted, 'Riders, get up, please.' In the bustle and
flurry I did not hear his answer, if he made one.

It would be idle to pretend that after a lapse of over thirty years
I remember every detail of that race. I do, however, recall the first
fence very vividly. It was approached down a fair slope and there
was a small stream in front of it. Friar Tuck had become a bit
excited and the thud of hooves round him as we went down to
that fence set him going. He caught hold of his bit and went on.
True to my instructions I slipped my reins and gripped the neck-
strap. It was as well that I did. Friar Tuck, feeling his head free,
shortened his stride, popped and jumped off his hocks with a
fiendish upward thrust. I went straight into the air. But my hands
on the neck-strap kept me, if not in contact, at least within reasonable flying distance of my mount. I came down into the saddle
with a bang, having been airborne alone for what seemed like
several long seconds. We were over in more or less one piece, and
I had the satisfaction of seeing the conceited chap describing a
graceful parabola beside me as a result of being well and truly
jumped off.

Somehow we survived the next few fences and then approached
the one where I felt sure I was bound to go. It was a small fence
with a stiffish drop on landing from which the ground sloped
sharply away. Friar Tuck was galloping on strongly now and
appeared to be enjoying himself even if his rider was not.

At this fence his whole shoulder and front simply disappeared
underneath me and I became airborne once more, but even the

neck-strap could not save me this time. As I hit the ground I thought, 'Well, there it goes. I've done it again. It's all over.' I also remember using some exceedingly bad language about myself.

Then, suddenly, out of nowhere a familiar voice was saying: 'Get up, sir. You're all right. Nothing wrong with you, sir.' Kerrell was standing over me. In some miraculous way he had caught Friar Tuck. His hand went under my leg and I was shot into the saddle again. 'Go on, sir. Go on!' he adjured me. 'They're all stone cold in front of you. You'll catch them easy. You've got it won. Leave him alone. Let him stride on!'

With these stirring words in my ears I went off in pursuit. I had lost my crash helmet and my whip but it did not matter. Friar Tuck entered into the spirit of the race. He put his head down and slogged along as hard as he could go. He was moving so easily and meeting each fence so exactly that even I could hardly fall off him. I began to enjoy myself.

As we passed the hill where the spectators were, only Mike and the chap who was having a bump around were in front of me. The second circuit was a sort of inner one with only three fences in it. At the first of these, the 'bump around' ended with an inglorious refusal. And then only Mike and I were left in the race.

Fired with the lust of battle and the chase, I began to close the gap. At the last fence we were all but level. It had to be jumped out of plough, and my antics in the saddle must have taken more out of Friar Tuck than three ordinary races. He hit the top of the fence and burst his way through it. I went up his neck. Friar Tuck did not fall but he all but came to a standstill on the other side.

Mike Rashley should have won the race by five lengths. But he was not really a very good or experienced race-rider. Instead of sitting down to ride, he kept looking over his shoulder to see where I was and what was happening.

I was on the flat now with no more of these infernal obstacles to surmount. I had, after all, ridden horses all my life. I pulled Friar Tuck together and gave him a kick. He snorted, got himself going – I was precious little help to him – and began to gallop. He was a game old brute. I've never forgotten him.

Mike, startled at this capless, whipless apparition bearing down on him, pulled out his own whip and began to use it. That completed his undoing. Rolling round in the saddle, flailing about with his whip he succeeded in stopping his horse instead of driving him on.

Friar Tuck came at him and caught him. I knew Mike was stopping. I threw everything I had, heart, head, legs and lungs, into those last three strides. We got up by a neck.

'Where did you come from, damn you?' Mike said as we rode in. 'Brian said you were bound to fall off.' Then, being Mike, he slapped me on the back. 'Well done, anyway, you old devil,' he said.

The reception by my best friend was scarcely so happy. He was standing waiting for us with a look of thunder on his face.

'You idiot,' he said. 'I had fifty quid with Kerrell you wouldn't finish. And I had a pony on Mike to win. Why didn't you fall off?'

'Oh, but he did, sir,' came from Kerrell who had suddenly materialised beside us. 'At the drop fence. I thought he might. I put him on again.'

For a second Brian was speechless, a state to which he was very seldom reduced. 'Fancy losing that on someone who couldn't ride a donkey on Margate sands,' he said, looking at me in fury. But that night he stood me dinner – and a magnum of champagne – in The George.

# THE MAN WHO SHOT THE 'FAVOURITE'

## *Edgar Wallace*

'THERE always will be a certain percentage of mysteries turnin' up, that simply won't untwist themselves, but the mystery that I'm thinkin' of particularly is the Wexford Brothers' Industrial Syndicate, which unravelled itself in a curious fashion,' said PC Lee.

If you don't happen to know the Wexford Brothers, I can tell you that you haven't missed much. It was a sort of religious sect, only more so, because these chaps didn't smoke, an' didn't drink, or eat meat, or enjoy themselves like ordinary human bein's, an' they belonged to the anti-gamblin', anti-Imperial, anti-life-worth-livin' folks.

The chief chap was Brother Samsin, a white-faced gentleman with black whiskers. He was a sort of class leader, an' it was through him that The Duke started his Wexford Brothers' Industrial Society.

The Duke wasn't a bad character, in spite of his name, which was given to him by the lads of Nottin' Dale. He was a bright, talkative, an' plausible young feller, who'd spent a lot of time in the Colonies, an' had come back to London broke to the world owin' to speculation.

'Why I know so much about him is that he used to lodge in my house. He was a gentleman with very nice manners, an' when Brother Samsin called on me one afternoon an' met The Duke, the Brother was so impressed with the respect an' reverence with which the Duke treated him that he asked him home to tea.

★　★　★

'To cut a long story short, this bright young man came to know all the brothers and sisters of the society an' became quite a favourite.

'I thought at first he had thoughts of joinin' the Brotherhood, but he soon corrected that.

' "No, Lee," ses he, "that would spoil the whole thing. At present I'm attracted to them because I'm worldly and wicked. If I became a brother, I'd be like one of them. At present they've no standard to measure me by, an' so I'm unique.'

'What interested the brothers most was the Duke's stories of his speculations in the Colonies, of how you can make a thousand pounds in the morning, lose two thousand in the evening, an' wake up next mornin' to find that you've still got a chance of makin' all you've lost an' a thousand besides.

'Well, anyway, he got the brothers interested, an' after a lot of palaver an' all sorts of secret meetin's, it was decided to start the Industrial Society, an' make the Duke chief organiser an' secretary.

'The idea was to subscribe a big sum of money, an' allow the Duke to use it to the best of his ability "on legitimate enterprises" – those were the words in the contract.

'The Duke took a little office over a barber's shop near the Nottin' Hill Gate Station, an' started work. Nothin' happened for a month. There were directors' meetin's an' money was voted, but in the second week of April, two months after the society was formed, the Duke said the society was now flourishin' an' declared a dividend of twenty per cent. What is more, the money was paid, an' you may be sure the brothers were delighted.

'A fortnight later, he declared another dividend of 30 per cent, an' the next week a dividend of 50 per cent, an' the brothers had a solemn meetin' an' raised his salary. Throughout that year hardly a week passed without a dividend bein' declared and paid.

'Accordin' to his agreement the Duke didn't have to state where the money came from. On the books of the society were two assets:

Gold mine . . .  £1,000
Silver mine . . .  £500

an' from one or the other the dividends came.

'All went well to the beginning of this year. You would think that the brothers, havin' got their capital back three times over, would be satisfied to sit down an' take their "divvies," but of all true sayin's in this world the truest is that "the more you get, the more you want".'

'From what I hear, the Duke paid no more dividends at all from the end of November to the end of February, an' only a beggarly ten per cent in March. So the directors had a meetin' an' passed a vote of censure on the secretary.

'He wasn't the kind of man to get worried over a little affair like that, but he was annoyed.

' "What these perishers don't understand," he ses to me, "is that the gold mine doesn't work in the winter."

' "Where is it?" I asked.

'He thought a bit. "In the Klondike," he ses, thoughtful.

' "An' where's the silver mine?"

' "In the never-never land," he ses, very glib.

'He got the brothers quiet again by the end of March, for he declared a dividend of twenty per cent, but somehow or other all those weeks of non-payment got their backs up, an' they wasn't so friendly with him as they used to be.

'Mr Samsin asked me to call round an' see him, an' I went.

'When I got to his house, I was shown into the parlour, an' to my surprise, I found about a dozen of the brothers all sittin' round a table very solemn an' stern.

' "We've asked you to come, Mr Lee," ses Samsin, "because bein' a constable, an' acquainted with law, an' moreover," he ses with a cough, "acquainted with our dear young friend who's actin' as secretary to our society, you may be able to give us advice."

' "You must know," he ses, mysteriously, "that for three months no dividends have been forthcomin' to our society."

'I nodded.

' "We have wondered why," he ses, "but have never suspected one whom we thought was above suspicion."

' "Meanin', the Duke?" I ses.

' "Meanin' Mr Tiptree," ses Brother Samsin. Tiptree was the Duke's private name.

' "We have made a discovery," ses Samsin, impressively, "an' when I say 'we' I mean our dear Brother Lawley."

'A very pale gent in spectacles nodded his head.

' "Brother Lawley," ses Samsin, "was addressin' a meetin' on

Lincoln racecourse – he bein' the vice-president of the Anti-Race-course League – an' whilst runnin' away from a number of mis-guided sinners, who pursued him with contumely – "

' "An' bricks," ses Brother Lawley.

' "An' bricks," Samsin went on, "he saw Tiptree!"

'He paused, and there was a hushed silence.

' "He was bettin'!" ses Brother Samsin.

' "Now," he adds, "I don't want to be uncharitable, but I've got an idea where our dividends have gone to."

' "Stolen," ses I.

' "Stolen an' betted," ses the brother, solemnly.

' "Well," ses I, "if you report the matter to me, an' you've got proof, an' you'll lay information, I'll take it to my superior, but if you ask me anythin' I'll tell you that you haven't much of a case. It's no offence to bet – "

' "It's an offence against our sacred principles," ses Brother Samsin.

The upshot of this conversation was – they asked me to watch the Duke an' report any suspicious movement, an' this I flatly refused to do.

'An' with that I left 'em. I don't know what they would have done, only suddenly the society began to pay dividends. Especially the Gold Mine, which paid a bigger dividend every week.

'So the brothers decided to overlook the Duke's disgraceful con-duct, especially in view of the fact that Brother Lawley was prepa-rin' for one of the most terrible attacks on horse-racin' that had ever been known.

'I got to hear about it afterwards. Brother Lawley was all for bein' a martyr to the cause. He said he wanted to draw attention to the horrible gamblin' habits of the nation, but there were lots of people who said that the main idea was to call attention to Brother Lawley.

'Be that as it may, he thought out a great plan, an' he put it into execution on the day before Derby Day.

'A number of our fellows were drafted down for the races and I went with them.

'On the Monday as I went down on the Tuesday, I saw the Duke. He still lodged in my house, although he was fairly prosper-ous, an' happenin' to want to borrow the evenin' paper to see what young Harry Bigge got for a larceny I was interested in, I went to his room.

'He was sittin' in front of a table, an' was polishin' up the lenses of a pair of race-glasses, an' I stopped dead when I remembered my conversation with the brothers.

' "Hullo!" I ses, "you an' me are apparently goin' to the same place."

' "Epsom? Yes," ses he, coolly. "An' if you take my tip you'll back Belle of Maida Vale in the second race."

' "I never bet," I ses, "an' I take no interest in horse-racing' an', moreover," I ses, "she can't give Bountiful Boy seven pounds over a mile an' a quarter."

'When I got downstairs I went over her "form". She was a consistent winner. The year before she'd won eight races at nice prices, an' I decided to overcome my aversion to bettin' an' back her, although I'd made up my mind to have my week's salary on Bountiful Boy.

'There was the usual Tuesday crowd at Epsom, an' I got a glimpse of Brother Lawley holdin' his little meetin'. He was on his own. It wasn't like the racecourse Mission, that does its work without offence, but Lawley's mission was all brimstone an' heat.

'We cleared the course for the first race, an' after it was over I casually mentioned to Big Joe France, the Bookmaker, that if Belle of Maida Vale was 20 to 1 I'd back her.

' "I'm very sorry, Mr Lee," he ses, "but you'll have to take a shorter price – I'll lay you sixes."

'I took the odds to 30s and laid half of it off with Issy Jacobs a few minutes later at threes.

'The course was cleared again for the second race, an' it was whilst the horses were at the post that I saw Brother Lawley leanin' over the rails near the winnin' post. He looked very white an' excited, but I didn't take much notice of him, because that was his natural condition.

'In the rings the bookies were shoutin' "Even money on Belle of Maida Vale," an' it looked as if somebody was havin' a rare gamble on her.

'The bell rang, an' there was a yell. "They're off!" '

'I was on the course, near the judge's box, an' could see nothin' of the race till the field came round Tattenham Corner with one horse leadin' – and that one the Belle.

'Well out by herself she was, an' there she kept right along the straight to the distance. There was no chance of the others catchin' her, an' they were easin' up when suddenly from the rails came a report like the snap of a whip, an' the Belle staggered, swerved, an' went down all of a heap.

'For a moment there was a dead silence, an' then such a yell as I've never heard before.

'They would have lynched Brother Lawley, with his smokin' pistol in his hand, but the police were round him in a minute.

' "I've done it!" he yelled. "I've drawn attention to the curse – "

' "Shut up!" I said, "an' come along before the people get you."

'Next day there was a special meetin' of the Wexford Brothers' Industrial Society, an' the Duke attended by request.

'Brother Samsin was in the chair.

' "We are gathered," he ses, "to consider what can be done for the defence of our sainted Brother Lawley, who's in the hands of the myrmidons of the law. I propose that we vote a sum out of the society – "

' "Hold hard," ses the Duke, roughly, "you can't vote any money – because there ain't any."

' "Explain yourself," ses Brother Samsin. "What of the gold mine?"

' "The gold mine," ses the Duke sadly, "was a horse called Belle of Maida Vale, that I bought out of the society's funds – she's dead."

' "An' the silver mine?" faltered Samsin.

' "That was the Belle of Maida Vale, too," ses the Duke. "A good filly, she was. She won regularly every month at a nice price – but she won't win any more dividends." '

# PICK THE WINNER

## *Damon Runyon*

WHAT am I doing in Miami associating with such a character as Hot Horse Herbie is really quite a long story, and it goes back to one cold night when I am sitting in Mindy's restaurant on Broadway thinking what a cruel world it is, to be sure, when in comes Hot Horse Herbie and his everloving fiancée, Miss Cutie Singleton.

This Hot Horse Herbie is a tall, skinny guy with a most depressing kisser, and he is called Hot Horse Herbie because he can always tell you about a horse that is so hot it is practically on fire, a hot horse being a horse that is all readied up to win a race, although sometimes Herbie's hot horses turn out to be so cold they freeze everybody within fifty miles of them.

He is following the races almost since infancy, to hear him tell it. In fact, old Captain Duhaine, who has charge of the Pinkertons around the race tracks, says he remembers Hot Horse Herbie as a little child, and that even then Herbie is a hustler, but of course Captain Duhaine does not care for Hot Horse Herbie, because he claims Herbie is nothing but a tout, and a tout is something that is most repulsive to Captain Duhaine and all other Pinkertons.

A tout is a guy who goes around a race track giving out tips on the races, if he can find anybody who will listen to his tips, especially suckers, and a tout is nearly always broke. If he is not broke, he is by no means a tout, but a handicapper, and is respected by one and all, including the Pinkertons, for knowing so much about the races.

Well, personally, I have nothing much against Hot Horse Herbie, no matter what Captain Duhaine says he is, and I certainly have nothing against Herbie's ever-loving fiancée, Miss Cutie Singleton. In fact, I am rather in favour of Miss Cutie Singleton, because in all the years I know her, I wish to say I never catch Miss Cutie Singleton out of line, which is more than I can say of many other dolls I know.

She is a little, good-natured blonde doll, and by no means a crow, if you care for blondes, and some people say that Miss Cutie Singleton is pretty smart, although I never can see how this can be, as I figure a smart doll will never have any truck with a guy like Hot Horse Herbie, for Herbie is by no means a provider.

But for going on ten years, Miss Cutie Singleton and Hot Horse Herbie are engaged, and it is well known to one and all that they are to be married as soon as Herbie makes a scratch. In fact, they are almost married in New Orleans in 1928, when Hot Horse Herbie beats a good thing for eleven C's, but the tough part of it is the good thing is in the first race, and naturally Herbie bets the eleven C's right back on another good thing in the next race, and this good thing blows, so Herbie winds up with nothing but the morning line and is unable to marry Miss Cutie Singleton at this time.

Then again in 1929 at Churchill Downs, Hot Horse Herbie has a nice bet on Naishapur to win the Kentucky Derby, and he is so sure Naishapur cannot miss that the morning of the race he sends Miss Cutie Singleton out to pick a wedding ring. But Naishapur finishes second, so naturally Hot Horse Herbie is unable to buy the ring, and of course Miss Cutie Singleton does not wish to be married without a wedding ring.

They have another close call in 1931 at Baltimore when Hot Horse Herbie figures Twenty Grand a standout in the Preakness, and in fact is so sure of his figures that he has Miss Cutie Singleton go down to the city hall to find out what a marriage licence costs. But of course Twenty Grand does not win the Preakness, so the information Miss Cutie Singleton obtains is of no use to them, and anyway Hot Horse Herbie says he can beat the price on marriage licences in New York.

However, there is no doubt but what Hot Horse Herbie and Miss Cutie Singleton are greatly in love, although I hear rumours that for a couple of years past Miss Cutie Singleton is getting somewhat impatient about Hot Horse Herbie not making a scratch as soon as he claims he is going to when he first meets up with her in Hot Springs in 1923.

In fact, Miss Cutie Singleton says if she knows Hot Horse Herbie is going to be so long delayed in making his scratch she will never consider becoming engaged to him, but will keep her job as a manicurist at the Arlington Hotel, where she is not doing bad, at that.

It seems that the past couple of years Miss Cutie Singleton is taking to looking longingly at the little houses in the towns they pass through going from one race track to another, and especially at little white houses with green shutters and yards and vines all around and about, and saying it must be nice to be able to live in such places instead of in a suitcase.

But of course Hot Horse Herbie does not put in with her on these ideas, because Herbie knows very well if he is placed in a little white house for more than fifteen minutes the chances are he will lose his mind, even if the house has green shutters.

Personally, I consider Miss Cutie Singleton somewhat ungrateful for thinking of such matters after all the scenery Hot Horse Herbie lets her see in the past ten years. In fact, Herbie lets her see practically all the scenery there is in this country, and some in Canada, and all she has to do in return for all this courtesy is to occasionally get out a little crystal ball and deck of cards and let on she is a fortune teller when things are going especially tough for Herbie.

Of course Miss Cutie Singleton cannot really tell fortunes, or she will be telling Hot Horse Herbie's fortune, and maybe her own, too, but I hear she is better than a raw hand at making people believe she is telling their fortunes, especially old maids who think they are in love, or widows who are looking to snare another husband and other such characters.

Well, anyway, when Hot Horse Herbie and his ever-loving fiancée come into Mindy's, he gives me a large hello, and so does Miss Cutie Singleton, so I hello them right back, and Hot Horse Herbie speaks to me as follows:

'Well,' Herbie says, 'we have some wonderful news for you. We are going to Miami,' he says, 'and soon we will be among the waving palms, and revelling in the warm waters of the Gulf Stream.'

Now of course this is a lie, because while Hot Horse Herbie is in Miami many times, he never revels in the warm waters of the Gulf Stream, because he never has time for such a thing, what with hustling around the race tracks in the daytime, and around the dog tracks and the gambling joints at night, and in fact I will lay plenty of six to five Hot Horse Herbie cannot even point in the direction of the Gulf Stream when he is in Miami, and I will give him three points, at that.

But naturally what he says gets me to thinking how pleasant it is in Miami in the winter, especially when it is snowing up north, and a guy does not have a flogger to keep himself warm, and I am commencing to feel very envious of Hot Horse Herbie and his ever-loving fiancée when he says like this:

'But,' Herbie says, 'our wonderful news for you is not about us going. It is about you going,' he says. 'We already have our railroad tickets,' he says, 'as Miss Cutie Singleton, my ever-loving fiancée here, saves up three C's for her hope chest the past summer, but when it comes to deciding between a hope chest and Miami, naturally she chooses Miami, because,' Herbie says, 'she claims she does not have enough hope left to fill a chest. Miss Cutie Singleton is always kidding,' he says.

'Well, now,' Herbie goes on, 'I just run into Mr Edward Donlin, the undertaker, and it seems that he is sending a citizen of Miami back home tomorrow night, and of course you know,' he says, 'that Mr Donlin must purchase two railroad tickets for this journey, and as the citizen has no one else to accompany him, I got to thinking of you. He is a very old and respected citizen of Miami,' Herbie says, 'although of course,' he says, 'he is no longer with us, except maybe in spirit.'

Of course such an idea is most obnoxious to me, and I am very indignant that Hot Horse Herbie can even think I will travel in this manner, but he gets to telling me that the old and respected citizen of Miami that Mr Donlin is sending back home is a great old guy in his day, and that for all anybody knows he will appreciate having company on the trip, and about this time Big Nig, the crap shooter, comes into Mindy's leaving the door open behind him so that a blast of cold air hits me, and makes me think more than somewhat of the waving palms and the warm waters of the Gulf Stream.

So the next thing I know, there I am in Miami with Hot Horse Herbie, and it is the winter of 1931, and everybody now knows that this is the winter when the suffering among the horse players in Miami is practically horrible. In fact, it is worse than it is in the winter of 1930. In fact, the suffering is so intense that many citizens are wondering if it will do any good to appeal to Congress for relief for the horse players, but The Dancer says he hears Congress needs a little relief itself.

Hot Horse Herbie and his ever-loving fiancée, Miss Cutie Single-ton, and me have rooms in a little hotel on Flagler Street, and while it is nothing but a fleabag, and we are doing the landlord a favour by living there, it is surprising how much fuss he makes any time anybody happens to be a little short of the rent. In fact, the landlord hollers and yells so much any time anybody is a little short of the rent that he becomes a very great nuisance to me, and I have half a notion to move, only I cannot think of any place to move to. Furthermore, the landlord will not let me move unless I pay him all I owe him, and I am not in a position to take care of this matter at the moment.

Of course I am not very dirty when I first come in as far as having any potatoes is concerned, and I start off at once having a little bad luck. It goes this way a while, and then it gets worse, and sometimes I wonder if I will not be better off if I buy myself a rope and end it all on a palm tree in the park on Biscayne Boulevard. But the only trouble with the idea is I do not have the price of a rope, and anyway I hear most of the palm trees in the park are already spoken for by guys who have the same notion.

And bad off as I am, I am not half as bad off as Hot Horse Herbie, because he has his ever-loving fiancée, Miss Cutie Single-ton, to think of, especially as Miss Cutie Singleton is putting up quite a beef about not having any recreation, and saying if she only has the brains God gives geese she will break off their engage-ment at once and find some guy who can show her a little speed, and she seems to have no sympathy whatever for Hot Horse Herbie when he tells her how many tough snoots he gets beat at the track.

But Herbie is very patient with her, and tells her it will not be long now, because the law of averages is such that his luck is bound to change, and he suggests to Miss Cutie Singleton that she get the addresses of a few preachers in case they wish to locate one in a hurry. Furthermore, Hot Horse Herbie suggests to Miss Cutie Singleton that she get out the old crystal ball and her deck of cards, and hang out her sign as a fortune teller while they are waiting for the law of averages to start working for him, although personally I doubt if she will be able to get any business telling fortunes in Miami at this time because everybody in Miami seems to know what their fortune is already.

Now I wish to say that after we arrive in Miami I have very little truck with Hot Horse Herbie, because I do not approve of some of his business methods, and furthermore I do not wish Captain Duhaine and his Pinkertons at my hip all the time, as I never permit myself to get out of line in any respect, or anyway not much. But of course I see Hot Horse Herbie at the track every day, and one day I see him talking to the most innocent-looking guy I ever see in all my life.

He is a tall, spindling guy with a soft brown Vandyke beard, and soft brown hair, and no hat, and he is maybe forty-odd, and wears rumpled white flannel pants, and a rumpled sports coat, and big horn cheaters, and he is smoking a pipe that you can smell a block away. He is such a guy as looks as if he does not know what time it is, and furthermore he does not look as if he has a quarter, but I can see by the way Hot Horse Herbie is warming his ear that Herbie figures him to have a few potatoes.

Furthermore, I never know Hot Horse Herbie to make many bad guesses in this respect, so I am not surprised when I see the guy pull out a long flat leather from the inside pocket of his coat and weed Herbie a bank-note. Then I see Herbie start for the mutuels windows, but I am quite astonished when I see that he makes for a two-dollar window. So I follow Hot Horse Herbie to see what this is all about, because it is certainly not like Herbie to dig up a guy with a bank roll and then only promote him for a deuce.

When I get hold of Herbie and ask him what this means, he laughs, and says to me like this:

'Well,' he says, 'I am just taking a chance with the guy. He may be a prospect, at that,' Herbie says. 'You never can tell about people. This is the first bet he ever makes in his life, and furthermore,' Herbie says, 'he does not wish to bet. He says he knows one horse can beat another, and what of it? But,' Herbie says, 'I give him a good story, so he finally goes for the deuce. I think he is a college professor somewhere,' Herbie says, 'and he is only wandering around the track out of curiosity. He does not know a soul here. Well,' Herbie says, 'I put him on a real hot horse, and if he wins maybe he can be developed into something. You know,' Herbie says, 'they can never rule you off for trying.'

Well, it seems that the horse Herbie gives the guy wins all right and at a fair price, and Herbie lets it go at that for the time being, because he gets hold of a real good guy, and cannot be bothering with guys who only bet deuces. But every day the professor is at the track and I often see him wandering through the crowds, puffing at his old stinkaroo and looking somewhat bewildered.

I get somewhat interested in the guy myself, because he seems so much out of place, but I wish to say I never think of promoting him in any respect, because this is by no means my dodge, and finally one day I get to talking to him and he seems just as innocent as he looks. He is a professor at Princeton, which is a college in New Jersey, and his name is Woodhead, and he has been very sick, and is in Florida to get well, and he thinks the track mob is the greatest show he ever sees, and is sorry he does not study this business a little earlier in life.

Well, personally, I think he is a very nice guy, and he seems to have quite some knowledge of this and that and one thing and another, although he is so ignorant about racing that it is hard to believe he is a college guy.

Even if I am a hustler, I will just as soon try to hustle Santa Claus as Professor Woodhead, but by and by Hot Horse Herbie finds things getting very desperate indeed, so he picks up the professor again and starts working on him, and one day he gets him to go for another deuce, and then for a fin, and both times the horses Herbie gives him are winners, which Herbie says just goes to show you the luck he is playing in, because when he has a guy who is willing to make a bet for him, he cannot pick one to finish fifth.

You see, the idea is when Hot Horse Herbie gives a guy a horse he expects the guy to bet for him, too, or maybe give him a piece of what he wins, but of course Herbie does not mention this to Professor Woodhead as yet, because the professor does not bet enough to bother with, and anyway Herbie is building him up by degrees, although if you ask me, it is going to be slow work, and finally Herbie himself admits as much, and says to me like this:

'It looks as if I will have to blast,' Herbie says. 'The professor is a nice guy, but,' he says, 'he does not loosen so easy. Furthermore,' Herbie says, 'he is very dumb about horses. In fact,' he says, 'I never see a guy so hard to educate, and if I do not like him personally, I will have no part of him whatever. And besides liking him personally,' Herbie says, 'I get a gander into that leather he carries the other day, and what do I see,' he says, 'but some large, coarse notes in there back to back.'

Well, of course this is very interesting news, even to me, because large, coarse notes are so scarce in Miami at this time that if a guy runs into one he takes it to a bank to see if it is counterfeit before he changes it, and even then he will scarcely believe it.

I get to thinking that if a guy such as Professor Woodhead can be going around with large, coarse notes in his possession, I make a serious mistake in not becoming a college professor myself, and naturally after this I treat Professor Woodhead with great respect.

Now what happens one evening, but Hot Horse Herbie and his ever-loving fiancée, Miss Cutie Singleton, and me are in a little grease joint on Second Street putting on the old hot tripe à la Creole, which is a very pleasant dish, and by no means expensive, when who wanders in but Professor Woodhead.

Naturally Herbie calls him over to our table and introduces Professor Woodhead to Miss Cutie Singleton, and Professor Woodhead sits there with us looking at Miss Cutie Singleton with great interest, although Miss Cutie Singleton is at this time feeling somewhat peevish because it is the fourth evening hand running she has to eat tripe à la Creole, and Miss Cutie Singleton does not care for tripe under any circumstances.

She does not pay any attention whatever to Professor Woodhead, but finally Hot Horse Herbie happens to mention that the professor is from Princeton, and then Miss Cutie Singleton looks at the professor, and says to him like this:

'Where is this Princeton?' she says. 'Is it a little town?'

'Well,' Professor Woodhead says, 'Princeton is in New Jersey, and it is by no means a large town, but,' he says, 'it is thriving.'

'Are there any little white houses in this town?' Miss Cutie Singleton asks. 'Are there any little white houses with green shutters and vines all around and about?'

'Why,' Professor Woodhead says, looking at her with more interest than somewhat, 'you are speaking of my own house,' he says. 'I live in a little white house with green shutters and vines all around and about, and,' he says, 'it is a nice place to live in, at that, although it is sometimes a little lonesome, as I live there all by myself, unless,' he says, 'you wish to count old Mrs Bixby, who keeps house for me. I am a bachelor,' he says.

Well, Miss Cutie Singleton does not have much to say after this, although it is only fair to Miss Cutie Singleton to state that for a doll, and especially a blonde doll, she is never so very gabby, at that, but she watches Professor Woodhead rather closely, as Miss Cutie Singleton never before comes in contact with anybody who lives in a little white house with green shutters.

Finally we get through with the hot tripe à la Creole and walk around to the fleabag where Hot Horse Herbie and Miss Cutie Singleton and me are residing, and Professor Woodhead walks around with us. In fact, Professor Woodhead walks with Miss Cutie Singleton, while Hot Horse Herbie walks with me, and Hot Horse Herbie is telling me that he has the very best thing of his entire life in the final race at Hialeah the next day, and he is expressing great regret that he does not have any potatoes to bet on this thing, and does not know where he can get any potatoes.

It seems that he is speaking of a horse by the name of Breezing Along, which is owned by a guy by the name of Moose Tassell, who is a citizen of Chicago, and who tells Hot Horse Herbie that the only way Breezing Along can lose the race is to have somebody shoot him at the quarter pole, and of course nobody is shooting horses at the quarter pole at Hialeah, though many citizens often feel like shooting horses at the half.

Well, by this time we get to our fleabag, and we all stand there talking when Professor Woodhead speaks as follows:

'Miss Cutie Singleton informs me,' he says, 'that she dabbles somewhat in fortune telling. Well,' Professor Woodhead says, 'this is most interesting to me, because I am by no means sceptical of fortune telling. In fact,' he says, 'I make something of a study of the matter, and there is no doubt in my mind that certain human beings *do* have the faculty of foretelling future events with remarkable accuracy.'

Now I wish to say one thing for Hot Horse Herbie, and this is that he is a quick-thinking guy when you put him up against a situation that calls for quick thinking, for right away he speaks up and says like this:

'Why, Professor,' he says, 'I am certainly glad to hear you make this statement, because,' he says, 'I am a believer in fortune telling myself. As a matter of fact, I am just figuring on having Miss Cutie Singleton look into her crystal ball and see if she can make out anything on a race that is coming up tomorrow, and which has me greatly puzzled, what with being undecided between a couple of horses.'

Well, of course, up to this time Miss Cutie Singleton does not have any idea she is to look into any crystal ball for a horse, and furthermore, it is the first time in his life Hot Horse Herbie ever asks her to look into the crystal ball for anything whatever, except to make a few bobs for them to eat on, because Herbie by no means believes in matters of this nature.

But naturally Miss Cutie Singleton is not going to display any astonishment, and when she says she will be very glad to oblige, Professor Woodhead speaks up and says he will be glad to see this crystal gazing come off, which makes it perfect for Hot Horse Herbie.

So we all go upstairs to Miss Cutie Singleton's room, and the next thing anybody knows there she is with her crystal ball, gazing into it with both eyes.

Now Professor Woodhead is taking a deep interest in the proceedings, but of course Professor Woodhead does not hear what Hot Horse Herbie tells Miss Cutie Singleton in private, and as far as this is concerned neither do I, but Herbie tells me afterwards that he tells her to be sure and see a breeze blowing in the crystal ball. So by and by, after gazing into the ball a long time, Miss Cutie Singleton speaks in a low voice as follows:

'I seem to see trees bending to the ground under the force of a great wind,' Miss Cutie Singleton says. 'I see houses blown about by the wind,' she says. 'Yes,' Miss Cutie Singleton says, 'I see pedestrians struggling along and shivering in the face of this wind, and I see waves driven high on a beach and boats tossed about like paper cups. In fact,' Miss Singleton says, 'I seem to see quite a blow.'

Well, then, it seems that Miss Cutie Singleton can see no more, but Hot Horse Herbie is greatly excited by what she sees already, and he says like this:

'It means this horse Breezing Along,' he says. 'There can be no doubt about it. Professor,' he says, 'here is the chance of your lifetime. The horse will be not less than six to one,' he says. 'This is the spot to bet a gob, and,' he says, 'the place to bet it is downtown with a bookmaker at the opening price, because there will be a ton of money for the horse in the machines. Give me five C's,' Hot Horse Herbie says, 'and I will bet four for you, and one for me.'

Well, Professor Woodhead seems greatly impressed by what Miss Cutie Singleton sees in the crystal ball, but of course taking a guy from a finnif to five C's is carrying him along too fast, especially when Herbie explains that five C's is five hundred dollars, and naturally the professor does not care to bet any such money as this. In fact, the professor does not seem anxious to bet more than a sawbuck, tops, but Herbie finally moves him up to bet a yard, and of this yard twenty-five bobs is running for Hot Horse Herbie, as Herbie explains to the professor that a remittance he is expecting from his New York bankers fails him.

The next day Herbie takes the hundred bucks and bets in with Gloomy Gus downtown, for Herbie really has great confidence in the horse.

We are out to the track early in the afternoon and the first guy we run into is Professor Woodhead, who is very much excited. We speak to him, and then we do not see him again all day.

Well, I am not going to bother telling you the details of the race, but this horse Breezing Along is nowhere. In fact, he is so far back that I do not recollect seeing him finish, because by the time the third horse in the field crosses the line, Hot Horse Herbie and me are on our way back to town, as Herbie does not feel that he can face Professor Woodhead at such a time as this. In fact, Herbie does not feel that he can face anybody, so we go to a certain spot over on Miami Beach and remain there drinking beer until a late hour, when Herbie happens to think of his ever-loving fiancée, Miss Cutie Singleton, and how she must be suffering from lack of food, so we return to our fleabag so Herbie can take Miss Cutie Singleton to dinner.

But he does not find Miss Cutie Singleton. All he finds from her is a note, and in this note Miss Cutie Singleton says like this: 'Dear Herbie,' she says, 'I do not believe in long engagements any more, so Professor Woodhead and I are going to Palm Beach to be married tonight, and are leaving for Princeton, New Jersey, at once, where I am going to live in a little white house with green shutters and vines all around and about. Goodbye, Herbie,' the note says. 'Do not eat any bad fish. Respectfully, Mrs Professor Woodhead.'

Well, naturally this is most surprising to Hot Horse Herbie, but I never hear him mention Miss Cutie Singleton or Professor Woodhead again until a couple of weeks later when he shows me a letter from the professor.

It is quite a long letter, and it seems that Professor Woodhead wishes to apologise, and naturally Herbie has a right to think that the professor is going to apologise for marrying his ever-loving fiancée, Miss Cutie Singleton, as Herbie feels he has an apology coming on this account.

But what the professor seems to be apologising about is not being able to find Hot Horse Herbie just before the Breezing Along race to explain a certain matter that is on his mind.

'It does not seem to me,' the professor says, as near as I can remember the letter, 'that the name of your selection is wholly adequate as a description of the present Mrs Professor Woodhead's wonderful vision in the crystal ball, so,' he says, 'I examine the programme further, and finally discover what I believe to be the name of the horse meant by the vision, and I wager two hundred dollars on this horse, which turns out to be the winner at ten to one, as you may recall. It is in my mind,' the professor says, 'to send you some share of the proceeds, inasmuch as we are partners in the original arrangement, but the present Mrs Woodhead disagrees with my view, so all I can send you is an apology, and best wishes.'

Well, Hot Horse Herbie cannot possibly remember the name of the winner of any race as far back as this, and neither can I, but we go over to the Herald office and look at the files, and what is the name of the winner of the Breezing Along race but Mistral, and when I look in the dictionary to see what this word means, what does it mean but a violent, cold and dry northerly wind.

And of course I never mention to Hot Horse Herbie or anybody else that I am betting on another horse in this race myself, and the name of the horse I am betting on is Leg Show, for how do I know for certain that Miss Cutie Singleton is not really seeing in the crystal ball just such a blow as she describes?

# A NIGHT AT THE OLD BERGEN COUNTY RACE-TRACK

## Gordon Grand

I HAD arranged to meet Colonel Weatherford at his club at four o'clock, motor to the country with him and hunt in the morning. Upon reaching the club I found a note advising me that the Colonel would be detained, but telling me to take his car and that he would be up on the seven o'clock train. I was to give his man, Albert, whom I would find in the car, a message about having the Colonel met at the train, and regarding the horse he wished to hunt in the morning. I located the car and started for the country.

I had bought an afternoon paper, which I read while we were motoring through Central Park. The sporting page contained one of those disagreeable accounts from the race-track telling of a sponge having been found in a horse's nostril. This incident reminded me of something about which I rather wanted to learn. Albert was sitting in the back of the car with me, the front seat having been given over to a steamer trunk, so I said, 'Albert, an old friend of Colonel Weatherford whom I met the other day asked me if I had ever heard about a little run-in which the Colonel had years ago with some bookmakers over at the old Bergen County track in New Jersey. What was the story?' 'Well, Sir,' said Albert, 'it's not a thing I like to talk about, because it puts me in a very bad light, Sir, but it was so long ago I guess it doesn't matter now.' Albert then told me the story.

A few years after I took service with Colonel Weatherford, he became interested in flat racing. At the time you speak about, Sir, he had four horses in training over at the old Bergen County track in New Jersey. There were some very rough characters around that track in those days, and the gambling was pretty heavy.

One of the Colonel's horses was a brown colt he had imported from France called *Le Grand Chên* by the English horse, *White Oak*. You know how the Colonel is, Sir, about certain of his horses and hunting dogs. Every once in a while he takes a very particular liking to some animal, and when he does he puts great store by him. Well, *Le Grand Chên* was one of them, and you couldn't blame the Colonel for feeling the way he did about that colt. Of course, Sir, I'm not a horseman, but it didn't take a horseman to admire that horse. He was a big seal-brown three-year-old with white on three of his legs, a white star on his forehead, and the largest, finest eye I ever saw on any horse. When you opened his box he would turn his head, look you square in the eye like some people do, then walk up and visit and stand looking at you as long as ever you stayed with him. The boys who took care of the colt were very sweet on him because he seemed to be always trying to do just what you wanted him to do.

There was one big important stake to be run for at that meeting called the North Jersey Stakes, and the Colonel was a deal set on winning it with this colt. He had come down from Massachusetts and was staying a fortnight at the old Holland House in New York, and had brought me down with him. He thought a powerful lot of that hotel, and even now says there was never a hotel like it.

Well, it came along to a Friday morning. The stake was to be run the next day. The Colonel had spent Thursday at the track, and said to me when he came home that the colt was tight, should win in a canter, and that a pot of money had been wagered on him to win. The Colonel was in fine spirits about his chances. I had never seen him so enthusiastic about anything as he was about that colt that evening.

About eight o'clock Friday morning he sent for me. I bought a morning paper for him, went to his room, found what he wanted for breakfast, ordered it, and was laying out his clothes when he said, 'Albert, what is that on the floor over by the door.' I went over to the door, picked up a soiled, mussy-looking envelope, looked at it, saw the Colonel's name scrawled across it in lead pencil and handed it to him. I returned to the bureau and was starting to pull out a drawer, when I heard the Colonel jump out of bed. As he did so he said, 'I'm in a hurry. Telephone about breakfast,' and went in the bathroom where I heard a big commotion going on. All the spigots in the place must have been turned on at once. He was out in jig time and into his clothes. He paid little attention to his breakfast, and as soon as he had finished he gathered up his hat, gloves and stick, said he was going to the track, and started out of the door. Then he turned and told me to stay in the hotel and be where the telephone operator could reach me. I was a good deal troubled, Sir, for the Colonel had acted quite upset. While he was dressing he had walked over to the window and stood looking out over Fifth Avenue with his hands behind his back, and kept tapping the floor with his foot. They weren't just taps, Sir, for his foot came down hard and deliberate like. I put things to rights and went downstairs.

As I was passing the head porter's desk he called me over, took me into his back office, shut the door and said, 'Albert, what's gone wrong with your Governor's horse? I have a bet on him and all the boys in the house are on him. Come on now – be a good fellow – what's up?' I told him I hadn't heard a thing except that the Colonel was very sweet on the colt and had told me only the night before that he expected to win with him. Then it was my turn, so I said, 'Jim, now you come across.' He sort of fiddled about and then said, 'Well, Albert, all I know is that a pretty smart guy who doesn't often get burned, went out of his way to send word to me at six o'clock this morning to lay off, or if it was too late, then to hedge and take care of myself.'

I stayed in the hotel all day, but nothing happened. Then at four o'clock a call came, a voice I didn't recognise said I was to come to the track right away, meet the Colonel at his stable and get supper on the way.

Our four horses were in a small, detached stable at the end of a long line of boxes. When I arrived I found the Colonel entirely alone and sitting on a bale of hay which he had placed in front of the box where *Le Grand Chên* always stood. There was no one else in or around the stable. He asked me if I had had supper. I told him I had. Then he said, 'Albert, I want you to sit here and watch these four stalls and stay here until either Pat Dwyer or I come to relieve you. You are not to permit anyone to enter any

part of the stable or even approach the stall doors. I have telephoned Dwyer to catch the first train from Boston, and he will
be here in the morning. (Pat Dwyer was the Colonel's head groom
then as he is now.) I will rely on you not to fall asleep nor to
leave the place for an instant. I have discharged every one connected
with the stable.' He started to move away, but came back and,
handing me a pistol, said, 'Should you be molested, this may be
serviceable in summoning assistance. Do not use it for any other
purpose if you can avoid it, and Albert, I don't think I would turn
my back to that swamp. Good night.'

As I said, our stable was off by itself. In the rear a dreary-
looking field strewn with rocks and bushes stretched away to the
west. To the north and about three hundred feet away lay a patch
of woods with a lane running through it leading to some shanties
where they said a good deal of gambling and other things went
on. In front of the stable the ground sloped down to a swamp
with cat-tails and alder bushes growing in it. The nearest other
stable was three or four hundred feet to the south. It was close to
dusk when the Colonel left me, for it was the Fall Meeting and
the days were short. I made myself as comfortable as might be on
the bale of hay and sat there watching it grow dark. Pretty soon
lanterns began to show at the different stables and I could hear
box stalls and tack room doors being closed, and saw the lights
moving up and down the long rows of stables. Before long the
lanterns became fewer and fewer as the boys went away to their
suppers and for the night. It became very quiet. After about an
hour I saw a lantern coming down the long line of boxes. It
stopped at the stable next to ours and I knew from the sounds that
followed that some of the swipes had started a crap game in the
tack room. I was glad of it, for the place didn't seem so lonesome.
They played a long time. Once I heard a horse coughing, and one
of the boys took the lantern and went into the horse's box. The
game ended about midnight. The boys came out, closed the tack
room door, and the lantern slowly disappeared. I sat a few minutes
staring into the dark, then walked to the end of our stable and
looked over towards the track and the rest of the stabling. Everything was dark except for one light away off, maybe half a mile
away, and as I watched even it disappeared. I climbed back on the
bale of hay and sat there. Once I heard a horse in a distant stable
kicking the side of his box, and it sounded sort of good to me. I

kept wishing our horses would move about or do something. I took the pistol out of my pocket and turned it over in my hand the way you do.

Of a sudden I heard something moving in the swamp. The sound was so faint I could hardly hear it and couldn't have told anyone what kind of a sound it was, yet I knew something was moving. I slipped off the bale and tip-toed slowly towards the edge of the swamp. Sometimes I couldn't hear anything, then there would be the sound of feet moving in the soft ground. Once or twice I heard the dry stems of the cat-tails clicking against each other. I started to take a step backward, when a clump of cat-tails rustled so close to me that I instinctively raised the pistol. Something was coming straight towards me. I didn't know whether to stand steady or move back towards the stable, when a goat walked out of the swamp and went off towards one of the stables.

I returned to the stable and was laying the pistol down when I saw something white on the hay. Putting my hand on it I found it to be a piece of paper. I had had no paper in my pocket and I knew there had been nothing on the hay when I walked over to the edge of the swamp.

I don't know how it was, Sir, but that piece of paper gave me sort of a turn. I didn't like to strike a match, but it seemed like I just had to find out what the paper was, so I crept up to the far end of the stable, went maybe ten feet around the corner, turned my back on the swamp, unbuttoned my coat, ducked my head down like you see people trying to light a match in a wind, struck a match right close to me, looked at the paper and read, 'Get out of here while you can.' I blew out the match, listened a minute, then went back to the hay. A clock away off somewhere struck two o'clock. I heard the brown colt get up on his feet and walk around his box. The handle of the water pail rattled, so I knew he was taking a drink.

It's odd, Sir, isn't it, the sort of things that come into your head at times like those. I got to thinking of the games of cribbage I used to play every night at the Holland House with Jim the porter in his snug little office. I hadn't rightly thought much of that office before, but sitting out there in the dark it seemed a cosy, safe kind of place. Then I got to thinking of the Colonel's fine home away up in Massachusetts where he lived.

Of a sudden I felt a cold damp blast of air on my face. A fresh east wind had blown up and was driving big clouds of fog in from the sea. In less than a minute it turned dreadful cold. Mr Pendleton, Sir, I've been cold lots of times, but never anything like I was then. I didn't have any overcoat and only a light suit. I began to shake and my teeth to chatter. It didn't seem like I could stand it. I wanted to go in with one of the horses, but the Colonel had said he didn't want any of the boxes opened or the horses disturbed. I tried our tack room thinking maybe to find a blanket, but the door was locked. All of a sudden I remembered that before it had grown dark I had seen some blankets or coolers hanging on a line back of the stable next to ours, and hoped that maybe they had been left out all night. It was pitch dark, but I thought I could walk right to 'em even in the fog, so started. I walked with my hands out in front of me and had good luck, for pretty soon I touched a corner of the stable and knew that the line was about thirty feet to the rear of the building. It took a good deal of groping about to find the line, but I finally brushed up against the blankets, took two of them and started back. Mr Pendleton, Sir, I don't know whatever I did to get twisted about after that. I thought I was headed straight for our stable, but after walking a short way the ground started to slope down very steep like. I stopped a second, then took a couple of more steps, but the footing felt soft and slippery. I had gotten twisted around and had walked straight for the swamp. I stood and listened a spell, but there was no sound from our stable. Then I figured out that if I walked along the edge of the swamp about three hundred feet, then turned sharp to the left, and could walk a straight line, I would hit some part of the stable. I have never seen anything like the dark of that night. It seemed as though you had to shove the fog away before you could move. I started walking, feeling my way every step and trying to keep on the edge of the swamp.

It's an odd thing, Sir, how for no reason that you know about, you can tell when things aren't right. I had been pretty good up to then, but all of a sudden I began to feel jumpy. I had walked maybe half the distance along the swamp and had stopped to calculate about where I should be, when of a sudden I heard a footstep and someone crossed right in front of me. I froze where I stood and reached for the pistol. It was on the bale of hay. Whoever had been moving had stopped. A horse over at our stable struck the side of his box the way they do sometimes when getting to their feet in a hurry. It didn't seem like I could walk straight ahead knowing that someone was standing there waiting, so I made a quarter-turn to the left and trusted to luck to hit the stable. I raised my foot, took a step and was just raising the other foot when I heard a pistol being cocked. I stopped short. The ground was sticky, and pretty soon I heard someone shifting his weight from one foot to another. Then I heard a low whistle from somewhere out in the swamp. That settled it. I knew then that I had to get to our stable no matter what happened. I gulped and started. I walked maybe ten paces right smart then stopped short to listen. Someone was following close behind me. I dropped the blankets and stepped quickly to one side. Someone tripped over the blankets but went on. I couldn't stand the thing any longer. I knew where the stable ought to be, so I clenched my fists and ran for it as fast as ever I could run. I had gone maybe a hundred feet, when something struck me a blow on the head that knocked me to the ground. I tried to get to my feet but was sick and dizzy like. I knew I would be hit again and should get up but couldn't. Then I heard a noise near me and listened. It was a horse getting upon his feet. I had hit my head on one of the posts of our stable. I reached out my hand, took hold of the post, got to my feet and listened. There was not a sound to be heard. I walked over to the bale of hay, found it against the colt's box, and the pistol where I had left it. Everything seemed all right. I picked up the pistol, cocked it and sat bolt upright listening and staring into the fog.

The half-hours and hours tolled off but I never heard another sound from the swamp or any place else. Finally it commenced to grow light and I could see people moving about at the different stables, and saw a colt being led over to the track for an early trial. I was mighty glad, Sir, to see the end of that night.

At a quarter to eight the Colonel and Pat Dwyer drove up in a cab. Pat whipped off his coat and started feeding and watering, while the Colonel inspected the horses. I was lending Pat a hand when of a sudden I heard the Colonel call me. He was standing at *Le Grand Chên*'s box. He closed the box and walked over to meet me. Never before nor since, Sir, have I seen him look as he did that moment. He started to speak to me, but instead called to Dwyer and pointed to the colt's box, then turned his back on me and walked off a few paces. Finally he turned, came back and faced me. It's wonderful, Sir, how he can hide what he is feeling and thinking. His face had entirely changed from what it was when he stood at the colt's box. Then I heard Pat Dwyer come out of the colt's box and say, 'Good God a'mighty, Mr John.'

The Colonel looked at me for what seemed an age, then said in a quiet voice, 'Albert, did you leave the stable last night?' 'Yes, Sir,' I said, 'I walked over to that clothes line over there back of that stable. It was very cold, Sir, and I wanted a blanket. It was about three o'clock.' He turned and studied the clothes line. 'How long did it take you?' 'Well, Sir,' I said, 'I didn't think it would take more than three or four minutes, but it was very dark and I couldn't find the blankets right away, then when I did find them I got some mixed up and twisted around in trying to get back. It might have taken me ten minutes or maybe fifteen.'

He didn't say anything for perhaps half a minute, then continued more to himself than to me, 'Three or four minutes to get a horse blanket if you were cold. Who the devil wouldn't? They thought he had left for good. If he had come back sooner they would have got him. If he hadn't gone they might have got him. I had no right to leave him here alone.' He walked over to the edge of the swamp and stood a long time examining the ground, then he deliberately stepped into the soft clay at the fringe of the swamp with one foot, held his foot there a while, came back to the stable, sat down on the bale, and went to studying the muddy shoe. He called Dwyer to him and they had a serious talk about the colt. It struck me as wonderful the way the Colonel took the whole thing. Dwyer asked him for a piece of paper and wrote out a prescription. Then the Colonel again sat looking at the mud on his shoe as though he had nothing else in the world to think about. He handed me the prescription and told me to get it filled. I asked him if I might look at the colt, but he said he did not want him disturbed.

When I got back to the stable with the medicine Pat Dwyer was doing up the horses, while the Colonel sat on the bale reading the morning paper.

About half-past eleven I heard someone come up and speak to the Colonel. I turned around and saw it to be a man by the name of Jake Katz. This Katz was one of the best-known gamblers around the track in those days, but nobody half-way respectable would be seen speaking to him. I don't guess there are any of his kind around these days. He was the leader of a group of book-makers who had made a pile of money through being mixed up with a chain of pool rooms and in other ways. This Katz was the brains of the outfit. I was surprised to see him down at our stable talking to the Colonel. They were standing outside of the tack room where I was cleaning a bridle for Pat, and I heard Katz say, 'Well, Colonel, and how is that grand colt of yours? I declare he is the best-looking three-year-old I've seen out in ten years and he moves just as sweet as he looks. He is the kind of a horse I like to have a look at once in a while just to keep my eye in. Could I have a peek at him?'

The Colonel smiled at him as though he was his very best friend and said, 'I'd be delighted to have you look at him, Mr Katz. I appreciate the complimentary things you have said about the colt. We are a bit short-handed today but, of course, we will show him to you. Albert, slip the blanket off the brown colt.' I went to the colt's box, opened the door and removed his blanket. Mr Pendleton, Sir, I couldn't understand how the Colonel could ever do such a thing. That was the first time I had seen the colt that morning and there he was standing in one corner with his head down pretty near to his knees, his eyes glassy, and when I took the blanket off I could see that he was having a hard time to breathe. I wished I had never seen him.

The Colonel and Katz stood at the door looking into the box. Neither of them spoke. Then I suppose Katz felt that he ought to say something as long as he had asked to see the colt, so he said, 'That's one of the best-balanced colts that ever looked through a bridle,' and continued to look at him. Then I saw the Colonel do a very queer thing, Sir. On the excuse of lighting his pipe he stepped back of Katz, struck a match, but did not use it, then rejoined Katz. You see, Sir, I was looking at the Colonel because I was hoping he would signal me to put the blanket back, for never in my life had I seen such a sick animal. As soon as he had rejoined Katz he said, 'Mr Katz, I suppose I should have some sort of a wager on my horse for this afternoon's race. I understand the talent doesn't think as much of him as they did. They don't approve of my discharging my trainer just before an important race. I am told that the odds have lengthened very much on the colt this morning. I admit the horse does not look as fit as I would wish him, but still I am sentimental about him. What are you quoting on him, or rather what will you quote me on him?' Katz cleared his throat. This was not what he had expected. 'Well, Mr

Weatherford,' he said, 'I don't know. They say the colt has a turn of speed and can go the route. On the other hand it looks like there would be a big field. I could make it 6 to 1.' 'No,' said the Colonel. 'That would not interest me.' Katz turned and looked at the colt again and stood looking at him, then said, 'Mr Weatherford, I have never had the pleasure of doing any business with you. I would like to make a start. I will make it 10 to 1.' Without a second's hesitation the Colonel took out his wallet and handed Katz four five-hundred-dollar bills. There was no mistake about Katz being taken back by the size of the wager. He held the bills in his hand, turned around, looked closely at the colt, folded the bills, put them in his pocket, said, 'All right, Mr Weatherford, much obliged,' and went off. I had been putting the blanket back on the colt while they were talking, and came out of the box just as Katz started away. The Colonel was standing with his feet apart, swinging his walking-stick behind his back, and following Katz with his eye. I also looked and there on the back of each of Katz's heels was a dab of light yellow clay. When Katz was out of sight the Colonel put his stick in a corner of the stable, sat down on the bale of hay, asked me if I would get something which would take the clay off his heels, took a magazine out of his pocket, and started to read.

Mr Pendleton, Sir, it seemed like I had enough to worry about and feel bad about that morning without the Colonel making that $2000 bet. To be game was all right, but I couldn't see the use of fighting after you were licked. Next to being sore at myself, I was most sore at Pat Dwyer. I knew he must have told the Colonel that he could fix the colt up in an hour or two so he could run. It seemed to me just like one of those Irish superstitions. You know, Sir, one of those quack remedies he most likely got from a witch and all that. He was in the colt's box fussing with him every ten minutes. Why, I had brought enough stuff and paraphernalia from the drug store to start a horse hospital with. I couldn't see how a man like the Colonel could be fooled by such rubbish, because even if the colt did get all right before the race, he was bound to be right weak.

At noon time the Colonel told me I would not be needed until just before our race, so to go to lunch, and gave me some telegrams to send for him. As I was about to start he called me and handed me a hundred dollar bill saying, 'Albert, put this on our colt for

Pat and yourself, but mind you lay it only with one of these four bookmakers.' He handed me a corner torn from the morning newspaper with four names written on it. One of them was Katz.

I never spent three such bad hours in my life. The only thing I could think of was that fine colt over at our stable. How sick he looked, how bad he must feel. Then of the Colonel and Dwyer trying to cure him in time to race, of how much the Colonel thought of the colt, how his heart had been sure set on winning this big stake, but worst of all I was thinking of my going off in the fog to get those blankets. I didn't feel good when I was at the stable, but it seemed like I felt worse when I was away from it.

I went back to the stable just before it was time for the horses entered in the stake to start for the saddling paddock. As I approached the stable I saw Dwyer leading *Le Grand Chên* up and down all covered up with a cooler. Certainly Dwyer seemed to have done him some good, for he looked brighter in the eye and walked free, but even so I couldn't understand why the Colonel, who didn't need the money, would ever ask a horse he was fond of to run in that condition. He wasn't my horse, but it didn't seem like I could watch him strain and struggle the way they have to. I heard the Colonel tell Dwyer they would wait until the last minute because he didn't want the colt standing in the paddock any longer than he could help. When time was up we started, Dwyer leading the colt, the Colonel and I following. As we approached the paddock the Colonel called me over close to him and said, 'Albert, this horse may look a little better to some people when we take his cooler off than they are expecting. I am going to hold him and Dwyer saddle him. The instant the cooler comes off you look sharp. Stand back of me and keep your eyes open. I don't want anyone coming within arm's length of this colt. Don't worry about insulting anyone or getting arrested. I will take care of you.'

Dwyer found a corner in the paddock where we could be off by ourselves, slipped the cooler off and started to saddle. It wasn't half a minute before I saw a small group of people huddled together and looking our way. Four or five hard-looking customers were even pointing at the colt. Then one of them slipped under the rail and went up to two men who were saddling a horse and pretty soon they all began to edge up towards us. The Colonel had seen the whole thing and immediately led *Le Grand Chên* away. Then the bugle blew. On the way to the track the Colonel took one side of the colt's bridle and Dwyer the other. As soon as the colt was safe on the track I hurried off to get a seat.

I couldn't rightly make up my mind whether I wanted to watch the race or not, but anyway I went on with the crowd. There were twelve starters and the distance was a mile and a quarter. The field got off to a prompt start, but for the first quarter I couldn't find our colt, then the field commenced to string out and I found him. There were three horses out front, then came a horse called *St Anthony*, a good horse that won a lot of races after that. He was running alone right back of the leaders. A couple of lengths back of *St Anthony* were four horses bunched together. Then *Le Grand Chên* running by himself and three horses trailing him. I didn't know a lot about horses in those days, but it seemed to me we must have had the gamest colt in the world, for even in the condition he was in he was out-running three horses. At the end of the next quarter one of the leading horses had dropped back. *St Anthony* had moved up and there were now four horses back of our brown colt. They ran this way until the three-quarter pole, then our horse moved up a little closer to the horses right in front of him and they started around the turn. There was a man standing next to me with a pair of field-glasses. He must have seen that I was mighty interested in that race, for he said, 'Have a look,' so I took the glasses. As I was saying, Sir, they were rounding the turn. The horses in front of our colt ran wide. Then I could hardly believe what I saw through the glasses. Of a sudden the boy on *Le Grand Chên* took him close to the rail and shot him through. It was wonderful, Sir. I was returning the glasses to the man when I heard someone back of me say, 'What the h— is that brown colt doing?' and someone whispered, 'Shut up, it's all right, I tell you.' I couldn't help turning around. The first speaker was the man I had seen slip under the paddock fence when we were saddling. The horses had passed the mile and were well started on the last quarter. *St Anthony* in front by three lengths, then a chestnut colt and *Le Grand Chên* at the chestnut's quarters. Then something happened that made me so mad, Sir, that I could hardly look at the race, for the boy on our colt drew his whip and went to it, and he did go to it. It was terrible, for I was just thinking how fine and game the colt had been, and to see anyone hit him seemed more than I could stand. The boy hadn't more than touched the colt when he shot past the chestnut horse as though he had been tied. Why, Mr Pendleton, he overhauled *St Anthony* like he was standing still. But *St Anthony* had a lot in reserve. You see his jockey had been caught napping. Our colt caught him in a couple of strides, but then the race started. Both boys were at their bats. They fought it out inch by inch. The crowd was roaring and everywhere around me I kept hearing, 'Come on you, *Anthony*, come on you, *Anthony*.' Neither colt would give up. They were a couple of lions to take punishment and the boys knew it and kept sailing into them. When they were three strides from the finish you couldn't tell which was in front. Neither colt could gain, and they finished just that way. No one in the stand knew who had won. There were about 15,000 people at the race and they all stood up watching the board, then I saw our colt's number put up. Think of it, Sir.

I hurried as fast as ever I could to get to the Colonel and the colt and Pat Dwyer. I've heard, Sir, about people throwing their arms around horses' necks and all that. Well, I don't know but what if there had been nobody around maybe I would have done the same. I wanted to go back to our stable with them all, but the Colonel handed me a note he had written to one of the stewards and told me to find him and give it to him. I knew the gentleman well by sight but it took me half an hour to find him, then I went to the stable. I didn't walk, Sir, I ran. When I got there the colt's box was open, the Colonel was standing at the door looking in, and Pat Dwyer was in the box and down on his knees doing something to the colt's legs. Mr Pendleton, after seeing the way that horse ran, it was pitiful to see what the race had taken out of him. He was standing there absolutely exhausted, with his head way down, and you could see the blanket going up and down as he tried to breathe. It struck me that human beings didn't have any right to do such things with animals. As I said, Dwyer was working on the horse's legs. He had a can of something and a roll of cotton. He would wet the cotton and rub it up and down the leg. I stood beside the Colonel watching Dwyer, but not paying much attention to what he was doing. Of a sudden something happened that made me doubt whether I was in my right senses. As I stood watching Dwyer swabbing the colt's off front leg that was white half-way to the knee, it turned brown. I started to say something then checked myself. The Colonel and Dwyer never said a word. When Dwyer had finished with that leg, he dried it with a towel, then started on the two white hind legs. In no time at all some sticky substance began to come off and the colt had two brown hind legs. Then Dwyer stood up, took his can and cotton, walked in front of the horse and stood looking at him. He turned to the Colonel and said, 'Mr John, it's yourself is a grand animal painter. There is no more illigant star on any horse in County Limerick than yourself has painted on this one.' Then he removed the star. As he was drying the horse's forehead he said, 'Albert, would you be going up to the end box and bringing the winner of this here North Jersey stake down to his own box? He'll rest better the night.' I said nothing, but went up to the tack room, found a halter shank, went to the end box and brought a beautiful brown colt down to his own box that looked as fresh as a daisy and as though he had never run a mile and a quarter. As I was leading him in, the Colonel said, 'Albert, find me a cab. I am going back to the Holland House to a particularly good dinner.' Mr Pendleton, Sir, if I may say so, Sir, Jim the porter and I had a right smart snack of dinner that night and a game of cribbage. Thank you, Sir.

# BLISTER

## *John Taintor Foote*

How my old-young friend 'Blister' Jones acquired his remarkable nickname, I learned one cloudless morning late in June.

Our chairs were tipped against number 84 in the curving line of box stalls at Latonia. Down the sweep of white-washed stalls the upper doors were yawning wide, and from many of these openings, velvet black in the sunlight, sleek snaky heads protruded.

My head rested in the center of the lower door of 84. From time to time a warm moist breath, accompanied by a gigantic sigh, would play against the back of my neck; or my hat would be pushed a bit farther over my eyes by a wrinkling muzzle – for Tambourine, gazing out into the green of the center field, felt a vague longing and wished to tell me about it.

The track, a broad tawny ribbon with a lacework edging of white fence, was before us; the 'upper-turn' with its striped five-eighths pole, not fifty feet away. Some men came and stretched the starting device across the track at this red-and-white pole, and I asked Blister what it meant.

'Goin' to school two-year-olds at the barrier,' he explained. And presently – mincing, sidling, making futile leaps to get away, the boys on their backs standing clear above them in the short stirrups – a band of deerlike young thoroughbreds assembled, thirty feet or so from the barrier.

Then there was trouble. Those sweet young things performed, with the rapidity of thought, every lawless act known to the equine brain. They reared. They plunged. They bucked. They spun. They surged together. They scattered like startled quail. I heard squeals, and saw vicious shiny hoofs lash out in every direction; and the dust spun a yellow haze over it all.

'Those jockeys will be killed!' I gasped.

'Jockeys!' exclaimed Blister contemptuously. 'Them ain't jockeys – they're exercise boys. Do you think a jock would school a two-year-old?'

A man who Blister said was a trainer stood on the fence and acted as starter. Language came from this person in volcanic blasts, and the seething mass, where infant education was brewing, boiled and boiled again.

'That bay filly's a nice-lookin' trick, Four Eyes!' said Blister, pointing out a two-year-old standing somewhat apart from the rest. 'She's by Hamilton 'n' her dam's Alberta, by Seminole.'

The bay filly, I soon observed, had more than beauty – she was so obviously the outcome of a splendid and selected ancestry. Even her manners were aristocratic. She faced the barrier with quiet dignity and took no part in the whirling riot except to move disdainfully aside when it threatened to engulf her. I turned to Blister and found him gazing at the filly with a far-away look in his eyes.

'Ole Alberta was a grand mare,' he said presently. 'I see her get away last in the Crescent City Derby 'n' be ten len'ths back at the quarter. But she come from nowhere, collared ole Stonebrook in the stretch, looked him in the eye the last eighth 'n' outgamed him at the wire. She has a hundred 'n' thirty pounds up at that.

'Ole Alberta dies when she has this filly,' he went on after a pause. 'Judge Dillon, over near Lexington, owned her, 'n' Mrs Dillon brings the filly up on the bottle. See how nice that filly stands? Handled every day since she was foaled, 'n' never had a cross word. Sugar every mawnin' from Mrs Dillon. That's way to learn a colt somethin'.'

At last the colts were formed into a disorderly line.

'Now, boys, you've got a chance – come on with 'em!' bellowed the starter. 'Not too fast . . . ' he cautioned. 'Awl-r-r-right . . . let 'em go-o-!'

They were off like rockets as the barrier shot up, and the bay filly flashed into the lead. Her slender legs seemed to bear her as though on the breast of the wind. She did not run – she floated – yet the gap between herself and her struggling schoolmates grew ever wider.

'Oh, you Alberta!' breathed Blister. Then his tone changed.

'Most of these wise Ikes talk about the sire of a colt, but I'll take a good dam all the time for mine!'

Standing on my chair, I watched the colts finish their run, the filly well in front.

'She's a wonder!' I exclaimed, resuming my seat.

'She acts like she'll deliver the goods,' Blister conceded. 'She's got a lot of step, but it takes more'n that to make a race hoss. We'll know about *her* when she goes the route, carryin' weight against class.'

The colts were now being led to their quarters by stable boys. When the boy leading the winner passed, he threw us a triumphant smile.

'I guess she's bad!' he opined.

'Some baby,' Blister admitted. Then with disgust: 'They've hung a fierce name on her though.'

'Ain't it the truth!' agreed the boy.

'What *is* her name?' I asked, when the pair had gone by.

'They call her Trez Jolly,' said Blister. 'Now, ain't that a hell of a name? I like a name you can kinda warble.' He had pronounced the French phrase exactly as it is written, with an effort at the 'J' following the sibilant.

'Très Jolie – it's French,' I explained, and gave him the meaning and proper pronunciation.

'Traysyolee!' he repeated after me. 'Say, I'm a rube right. Tra-aysyole-e in the stretch byano-o-se!' he intoned with gusto. 'You can warble that!' he exclaimed.

'I don't think much of Blister – for beauty,' I said. 'Of course, that isn't your real name.'

'No; I had another once,' he replied evasively. 'But I never hears it much. The old woman calls me "thatdam-brat," 'n'the old man the same, only more so. I gets Blister handed to me by the bunch one winter at the New Awlin' meetin'.'

'How?' I inquired.

'Wait till I get the makin's 'n' I'll tell you,' he said, as he got up and entered a stall.

'One winter I'm swipin' fur Jameson,' he began, when he returned with tobacco and papers. 'We ships to New Awlins early that fall. We have twelve dogs – half of 'em hopheads 'n' the other half dinks.

'In them days I ain't much bigger 'n a peanut, but I sure thinks

I'm a clever guy. I figger they ain't a gazabo on the track can hand it to me.

'One mawnin' there's a bunch of us ginnies settin' on the fence at the wire, watchin' the workouts. Some trainers 'n' owners is standin' on the track rag-chewin'.

'A bird owned by Cal Davis is finishin' a mile-'n'-a-quarter, under wraps, in scan'lous fast time. Cal is standin' at the finish with his clock in his hand lookin' real contented. All of a sudden the bird makes a stagger, goes to his knees 'n' chucks the boy over his head. His swipe runs out 'n' grabs the bird 'n' leads him in a-limpin'.

'Say! That bird's right-front tendon is bowed like a barrel stave!

'This Cal Davis is a big owner. He's got all kinds of kale – 'n' he don't fool with dinks. He gives one look at the bowed tendon.

' "Anybody that'll lead this hoss off the track, gets him 'n' a month's feed," he says.

'Before you could spit I has that bird by the head. His swipe ain't goin' to let go of him, but Cal says: "Turn him loose, boy!" 'N' I'm on my way with the bird.

'That's the first one I ever owns. Jameson loans me a stall fur him. That night a ginnie comes over from Cal's barn with two bags of oats in a wheelbarrow.

'A newspaper guy finds out about the deal, 'n' writes it up so everybody is hep to me playin' owner. One day I see the starter point me out to Colonel King, who's the main squeeze in the judge's stand, 'n' they both laugh.

'I've got all winter before we has to ship, 'n' believe me I sweat some over this bird. I done everythin' to that tendon, except make a new one. In a month I has it in such shape he don't limp, 'n' I begins to stick mile gallops 'n' short breezers into him. He has to wear a stiff bandage on the dinky leg, 'n' I puts one on the left fore, too – it looks better.

'It ain't so long till I has this bird cherry ripe. He'll take a-holt awful strong right at the end of a stiff mile. One day I turns him loose, fur three-eights, 'n' he runs it so fast he makes me dizzy.

'I know he's good, but I wants to know *how* good, before I pays entrance on him. I don't want the clockers to get wise to him, either!

'Joe Nickel's the star jock that year. I've seen many a good boy on a hoss, but I think Joe's the best judge of pace I ever see. One day he's comin' from the weighin' room, still in his silks. His valet's with him carryin' the saddle. I steps up 'n' says:

' "Kin I see you private a minute, Joe?"

' "Sure thing, kid," he says. 'N' the valet skidoos.

' "Joe," I says, "I've got a bird that's right. I don't know just how good he is, but he's awful good. I want to get wise to him before I crowds my dough on to the 'Sociation. Will you give him a work?"

'It takes an awful nerve to ask a jock like Nickel to work a hoss out, but he's the only one can judge pace good enough to put me wise, 'n' I'm desperate.

' "It's that Davis cripple, ain't it?" he asks.

' "That's him," I says.

'He studies a minute, lookin' steady at me.

' "I'm your huckleberry," he says at last. "When do you want me?"

' "Just as she gets light tomorrow mawnin'," I says quick, fur I hasn't believed he'd come through, 'n' I wants to stick the gaff into him 'fore he changes his mind.

'He give a sigh. I knowed he was no early riser.

' "All right," he says. "Where'll you be?"

' "At the half-mile post," I says. "I'll have him warmed up fur you."

' "All right," he says again – 'n' that night I don't sleep none.

'When it begins to get a little gray next mawnin' I takes the bird out 'n' gallops him a slow mile with a stiff breezer at the end. But durin' the night I gives up thinkin' Joe'll be there, 'n' I nearly falls off when I comes past the half-mile post, 'n' he's standin' by the fence in a classy overcoat 'n' kid gloves.

'He takes off his overcoat, 'n' comes up when I gets down, 'n' gives a look at the saddle.

' "I can't ride nothin' on that thing,' he says. 'Slip over to the jocks' room 'n' get mine. It's on number three peg – here's the key."

'It's gettin' light fast 'n' I'm afraid of the clockers.

' "The sharpshooters'll be out in a minute," I says.

' "I can't help it," says Joe. "I wouldn't ride a bull on that saddle!"

'I see there's no use to argue, so I beats it across the center field, cops the saddle 'n' comes back. I run all the way, but it's gettin' awful light.

' "Send him a mile in forty-five 'n' see what he's got left," I says, as I throws Joe up.

' "Right in the notch – if he's got the step," he says.

'I click Jameson's clock on them, as they went away – Joe whisperin' in the bird's ear. The backstretch was the stretch, startin' from the half. I seen the bird's mouth wide open as they come home, 'n' Joe has double wraps on him. "He won't beat fifty under that pull!" I says to myself. But when I stops the clock at the finish it was at forty-four-'n'-three-quarters. Joe ain't got a clock to go by neither – that's judgin' pace! – take it from me!

' "He's diseased with speed," says Joe, when he gets down. "He's oil in the can. Thirty-eight fur him – look at my hands!"

'I does a dance a-bowin' to the bird, 'n' Joe stands there laughin' at me, squeezin' the blood back into his mitts.

'We leads the hoss to the gate, 'n' there's a booky's clocker named Izzy Goldberg.

' "You an exercise boy now?' he asks Joe.

' "Not yet," says Joe. "M'cousin here owns this trick, 'n' I'm givin' him a work."

' "Up kinda early, ain't you? Say! He's good, ain't he, Joe?" says Izzy; 'n' looks at the bird close.

' "Naw, he's a mutt," says Joe.

' "What's he doin' with his mouth open at the end of that mile?" Izzy says, 'n' laughs.

' "He only runs it in fifty," says Joe, careless. "I takes hold of him 'cause he's bad in front, 'n' he's likely to do a flop when he gets tired. So long, Bud!" Joe says to me, 'n' I takes the bird to the barn.

'I'm not thinkin' Izzy ain't wise. It's a cinch Joe don't stall him. Every booky would hear about that workout by noon. Sure enough the *Item's* pink sheet has this among the tips the next day:

' "Count Noble" – that was the bird's name – "a mile in forty-four. Pulled to a walk at the end. Bet the works on him; his first time out, boys!"

'That was on a Saturday. On Monday I enters the bird among a bunch of dogs to start in a five-furlong sprint Thursday. I'm savin' every soomarkee I gets my hands on 'n' I pays the entrance to the secretary like it's a mere bag of shells. Joe Nickel can't ride fur me – he's under contract. I meets him the day before my race.

' "You're levelin' with your hoss, ain't you?" he says. "I'll send my valet in with you, 'n' after you get yours on, he'll bet two hundred fur me."

' "Nothin' doin', Joe!' I says. "Stay away from it. I'll tell you when I gets ready to level. You can't bet them bookies nothin' – they're wise to him."

' "Look-a-here, Bud!" says Joe. "That bird'll cakewalk among them crabs. No jock can make him lose, 'n' not get ruled off."

' "Leave that to me," I says.

'Just as I figgers – my hoss opens up eight-to-five in the books.

'I gives him all the water he'll drink afore he goes to the post, 'n' I has bandages on every leg. The paddock judge looks at them bandages, but he knows the bird's a cripple, 'n' he don't feel 'em.

' "Them's to hold his legs on, ain't they?" he says, 'n' grins.

' "Surest thing you know," I says. But I feels some easier when he's on his way – *there's seven pounds of lead in each of them bandages*.

'I don't want the bird whipped when he ain't got a chance.

' "This hoss backs up if you use the bat on him," I says to the jock, as he's tyin' his reins.

' "He backs up anyway, I guess," he says, as the parade starts.

'The bird gets away good, but I'd overdone the lead in his socks. He finished a nasty last – thirty len'ths back.

' "Roll over, kid!" says the jock, when I go up to slip him his feel. "Not fur ridin' that hippo. It'ud be buglary – he couldn't beat a piano!"

'I meets Colonel King comin' out of the judge's stand that evenin'.

' "An owner's life has its trials and tribulations – eh, my boy?" he says.

' "Yes, sir!" I says. That's the first time Colonel King ever speaks to me, 'n' I swells up like a toad. "I'm gettin' to be all the gravy 'round here," I says to myself.

'Two days after this they puts an overnight mile run fur maidens on the card, 'n' I slips the bird into it. I knowed it was takin' a chance so soon after his bad race, but it looks so soft I can't stay 'way from it. I goes to Cal Davis, 'n' tells him to put a bet down.

' "Oh, ho!" he says. "Lendin' me a helpin' hand, are you?" Then I tells him about Nickel.

' "Did Joe Nickel work him out for you?" he says. "The best is good enough fur you, ain't it? I'll see Joe, 'n' if it looks good to him I'll take a shot at it. Much obliged to you."

' "Don't never mention it," I says.

' "How do you mean that?" he says, grinnin'.

' "Both ways," says I.

'The mawnin' of the race, I'm givin' the bird's bad leg a steamin', when a black swipe named Duckfoot Johnson tells me I'm wanted on the phone over to the secretary's office, 'n' I gets Duckfoot to go on steamin' the leg while I'm gone.

'It's a feed man on the phone, wantin' to know when he gets sixteen bucks I owe him.

' "The bird'll bring home your coin at four o'clock this afternoon," I tells him.'

' "Well, that's lucky," he says. "I thought it was throwed to the birds, 'n' I didn't figure they'd bring it home again."

'When I gets back there's a crap game goin' on in front of the stall, 'n' Duckfoot's shootin'. There's a hot towel on the bird's leg, 'n' it's been there too long. I takes it off 'n' feel where small blisters has begun to raise under the hair – a little more 'n' it 'ud been clear to the bone. I cusses Duckfoot good, 'n' rubs vaseline into the leg.'

I interrupted Blister long enough to inquire:

'Don't they blister horses sometimes to cure them of lameness?'

'Sure,' he replied. 'But a hoss don't work none fur quite a spell afterwards. A blister, to do any good, fixes him so he can't hardly raise his leg fur two weeks.

'Well,' he went on, 'the race fur maidens was the last thing on the card. I'm in the betting-ring when they chalks up the first odds, 'n' my hoss opens at twenty-five-to-one. The two entrance moneys have about cleaned me. I'm only twenty green men strong. I peels off ten of 'em 'n' shoved up to a booky.

' "On the nose fur that one," I says, pointin' to the bird's name.

' "Quit your kiddin'," he says. "What'ud you do with all that money? This fur yours." 'N' he rubs to twelve-to-one.

' "Ain't you the liberal gink?" I says, as he hands me the ticket.

' "I starts fur the next book, but say! – the odds is just meltin' away. Joe's 'n' Cal's dough is comin' down the line, 'n' the gazabos, thinkin' it's wise money, trails. By post time the bird's a one-to-three shot.

'I've give the mount to Sweeney, 'n' like a nut I puts him hep to the bird, 'n' he tells his valet to bet a hundred fur him. The bird has on socks again, but this time they're empty, 'n' the race was a joke. He breaks fifth at the getaway, but he just mows them dogs down. Sweeney keeps thinkin' about that hundred, I guess, 'cause he rode the bird all the way, 'n' finished a million len'ths in front.

'I cashes my ticket, 'n' starts fur the barn to sleep with that bird, when here comes Joe Nickel.

' "He run a nice race," he says, grinnin', 'n' hands me six hundred bucks.

' "What's this fur?" I says. "You better be careful . . . I got a weak heart."

' "I win twelve hundred to the race," he says. "'N' we splits it two ways."

' "Nothin' doin'," I says, 'n' tries to hand him back the wad.

' "Go awn!" he says, "I'll give you a soak in the ear. I bet that money fur you, kiddo."

'I looks at the roll 'n' gets wobbly in the knees. I never see so much kale before – not at one time. Just then we hears the announcer sing out through a megaphone:

' "The o-o-owner of Count Nobul-l-l-l is wanted in the judge's stand!"

' "Oy, oy!" says Joe. "You'll need that kale – you're goin' to lose your happy home. It's Katy bar the door fur yours, Bud!"

' "Don't worry – watch me tell it to 'em," I says to Joe, as I stuffs the roll 'n' starts fur the stand. I was feelin' purty good.

' "Wait a minute," says Joe, runnin' after me. "You can't tell them people nothin'. You ain't wise to that bunch yet, Bud – why, they'll kid you silly before they hand it to you, 'n' then change the subject to somethin' interestin', like where to get pompono cooked to suit 'em. I've been up against it," he says, "'n' I'm tellin' you right. Just keep stallin' around when you get in the stand, 'n' act like you don't know the war's over."

' "Furget it," I says. "I'll show those big stiffs where to head in. I'll hypnotise the old owls. I'll give 'em a song 'n' dance that's right!"

'As I goes up the steps I see the judges settin' in their chairs, 'n' I takes off my hat. Colonel King ain't settin', he's standin' up with his hands in his pockets. Somehow, when I sees *him* I begins to wilt – he looks so clean. He's got a white mustache, 'n' his face is kinda brown 'n' pink. He looks at me a minute out of them blue eyes of his.

' "Are you the owner of Count Noble, Mr – er – ?"

' "Jones, sir," I says.

' "Jones?" says the colonel.

' "Yes, sir," I says.

' "Mr Jones," says the colonel, "how do you account for the fact that on Thursday Count Noble performs disgracefully, and on Saturday runs like a stake horse? Have the days of the week anything to do with it?"

'I never says nothin'. I just stands there lookin' at him, foolin' with my hat.

' "This is hell," I thinks.

' "The judges are interested in this phenomenon, Mr Jones, and we have sent for you, thinking perhaps you can throw a little light on the matter," says the colonel, 'n' waits fur me again.

' "Come on . . . get busy!" I says to myself. "You can kid along with a bunch of bums, 'n' it sounds good – don't get cold feet the first time some class opens his bazoo at you!" But I can't make a noise like a word, on a bet.

' "The judges, upon looking over the betting sheets of the two races in which your horse appeared, find them quite interesting," says the colonel. "The odds were short in the race he did *not* win; they remained unchanged – in fact, rose – since only a small amount was wagered on his changes. On the other hand, these facts are reversed in today's race, which he *won*. It seems possible that you and your friends who were pessimists on Thursday became optimists today, and benefited by the change. Have you done so?"

'I see I has to get some sorta language out of me.'

' "He was a better hoss today – that's all I knows about it," I says.

' "The *first* part of your statement seems well within the facts," says the colonel. "He was, apparently, a much better horse today. But these gentlemen and myself, having the welfare of the American thoroughbred at heart, would be glad to learn by what method he was so greatly improved."

'I don't know why I ever does it, but it comes to me how

Duckfoot leaves the towel on the bird's leg, 'n' I don't stop to think.

' "I blistered him," I says.

'Of course any dope knows that after you blister a hoss fur a sore tendon he can't more 'n' walk around in his stall fur the next thirty days.

' "You – *what?*" says the colonel. I'd have give up the roll quick, sooner'n spit it out again, but I'm up against it.

' "I blisters him," I says.

'The colonel's face gets red. His eyes bung out 'n' he turns 'round 'n' starts to cough 'n' make noises. The rest of them judges does the same. They holds on to each other 'n' does it. I know they're givin' me the laugh fur that fierce break I makes.

' "You're outclassed, kid!" I says to myself. "They'll tie a can to you, sure. The gate fur yours!"

'Just then Colonel King turns round, 'n' I see I can't look at him no more. I looks at my hat, waitin' fur him to say I'm ruled off. I've got a lump in my throat, 'n' I think it's a bunch of bright conversation stuck there. But just then a chunk of water rolls out of my eye, 'n' hits my hat – pow! It looks bigger'n Lake Erie, 'n' 'fore I kin jerk the hat away – pow! – comes another one. I knows the colonel sees 'em, 'n' I hopes I croak.

' "Ahem – ," he says.

' "Now I get mine!" I says to myself.

' "Mr Jones," says the colonel, 'n' his voice is kinda cheerful. "The judges will accept your explanation. You may go if you wish."

Just as I'm goin' down the steps the colonel stops me.

' "I have a piece of advice for you, Mr Jones," he says. His voice ain't cheerful neither. It goes right into my gizzard. I turns and looks at him. "*Keep that horse blistered from now on!*" says the colonel.

'Some ginnies is in the weighin' room under the stand, 'n' hears it all. That's how I gets my name.'

# THE DEAD CERT

## J. C. Squire

EVERY Wednesday night, from eight o'clock until closing time, Mr William Pennyfeather was to be found sitting on a high stool at the counter in the Saloon Bar of The Asparagus Tree. He had other ports of call in various quarters of London. But gradually, almost without intention, over a period of years, he had drifted into the one methodical habit of his life: at the same hour on the same day he was almost always to be found in the same public-house. All his haunts had this much in common: they were none of them very riotous, and they were none of them frigidly quiet. Even those which were in the middle of the glaring West End were tucked away up side streets and depended more on regular frequenters than on casual droppers-in. Otherwise they differed, their customers ranging from the auctioneers, solicitors, doctors and prosperous tradesmen of his favourite resort at Ealing, to the dockers and draymen with whom he consorted in the Butchers' Arms near the southern end of the Rotherhithe Tunnel. Geographically and socially, The Asparagus Tree split the difference between these extremes: it was within five minutes of Waterloo Station, it had a Saloon Bar, and the tone of that aristocratic *enclave* was set by shabby-respectable members of the vaudeville and racing fraternities. The reader may have guessed by now that Mr Pennyfeather was a student of mankind. If so, the reader has guessed right. He was even a professional student of mankind. His novels did not sell very well, but they kept him in comfortable celibacy: as all the reviewers said in unison once a year: 'Whatever the changing fashions of the market, there is always room for the genuine novel of Cockney life, and no man knows his Londoners, with their irrepressible humour, indomitable courage, and racy idiom, better than the author of *Battersea Bill*.'

Things, at eight o'clock, were quiet. Two cadaverous, shaggy and grubby actors, at the other end of the bar, were earnestly discussing something in voices at once husky and subdued. Mr Pennyfeather, comfortably sheltered from the November night in stuffy warmth with a pipe and a pint, was talking to the landlord. The landlord had known him for two or three years, but probably did not know his name: this place was very unlike the 'hotel' at Ealing, where not merely his name but his profession were known, and where he frequently played billiards with certain cronies. Here people were incurious: willing to enjoy a talk with a stranger and ask no questions, to develop a gradual semi-intimacy and still refrain from inquiry. They might, he thought, when he had left the bar, sometimes say to each other, 'I wonder what that chap does: might be a lawyer's clerk, perhaps, or something to do with the railway.' He could even hear Mr Porter, the septuagenarian ex-bookmaker, shrewdly observing to his pals, 'Shouldn't be surprised if 'e 'ad a bit of money of 'is own.' Well, if he ever did achieve that desirable condition, it would be partly due to Mr Porter, who had already appeared in three of his books under three different names, with many of his conversations reported as nearly verbatim as might be – for Mr Pennyfeather was a realist, and could not invent conversations anything like as good as those which he overheard.

'Quiet, this evening!' remarked Mr Pennyfeather.

'Oh, I dessay some of 'em 'll be in presently,' replied the land-lord.

At this moment he was called to the jug-and-bottle department by the tapping of a coin on wood; the swing door of the Saloon Bar groaned, and there entered Mr Porter himself, beaming and buttonholed, with a grey soft hat and a new suit of checks: he was the Croesus of The Asparagus Tree, and a man who had three prosperous sons in the old business. 'Took the Missus to the Zoo,' he said, explaining his especial grandeur: then, to the dark minx of a barmaid who had suddenly appeared, 'Guinness, me dear.'

No one else had come in, Mr Pennyfeather observed with satis-faction; there was a chance, therefore, that Mr Porter might become confidential, which usually meant that he divulged deeds of peculiar rascality, with a jolly Falstaffian frankness that made his worst swindles appear the innocent pranks of a child. Tonight, however, the sight of the two actors in the corner switched him in a more edifying direction. He jerked his thumb towards them, gave an upward fling of his head, and whispered: 'Pore devils, ruinin' theirselves.'

'How?' asked Pennyfeather.

'Bettin', o' course. Lot o' babies, that's what they are. Comes 'ere for tips – from each other! Hinside hinformation!'

'Stupid, isn't it?'

'Yes. But there, we're all of us mugs sometimes. W'y, on'y larst year I'll be jiggered if I didn't back a 'orse meself on a tip I got 'ere.'

'What made you do it?'

'Off me chump, I s'pose. Just like the rest of 'em, when it came to the point! Said to meself, 'Nah this one *is* all right.' Jockey it come from; at least, he used to be. Little Dicky 'Arris. Come in 'ere with 'is precious tip, an' I went an' believed 'im. 'Orse called Absalom. Down at the first 'urdle. Come in last!'

'But you've always been so funny about jockeys' tips.'

'Don't rub it in. I'm a mug, that's what I am. I thought this was different. You see, this little Dicky 'Arris – believe it or not – he's straight.'

The dramatic revelation of this eccentricity demanded another couple of drinks. The calamity was shelved, and Mr Porter entered on a long story of how he had suborned, and for some years virtually employed, several police constables, and finally a sergeant, to protect his street betting operations. With a sigh over the fallibility of human nature, he took a deep draught, then looked round the room, which had been filling up. 'Why, blimey!' he exclaimed, with pleasure on his face, 'if there isn't the very little chap that I was talkin' about!'

'D'you mean the sergeant?' inquired Pennyfeather.

'Garn, that old skunk?' frowned Mr Porter. 'No! it's Dicky 'Arris, the little boy from Epsom. Dicky!' he called; and there stepped towards them a minute horsy man, with very sharp features but an agreeable smile, a blue-eyed, sunburnt, wrinkled man with white eyelashes, like an unsophisticated and even kindly weasel.

''Allo, Dicky! 'aven't seen you for months!' Mr Porter cheerily greeted him. 'Pint, please, me dear.' Then, nudging each companion with an elbow, ''Ow's Absalom? Near broke me over that, you did, you villain!'

Little Harris threw back his head in mock weariness. Then he spoke, in a Cockney thick beyond phonetic rendering.

'Cheese it, Mr Porter! D'you know, sir, 'e's bin raggin' me about thet there 'orse for twelve munce.'

'Dead cert?' inquired Pennyfeather, with a knowing twinkle.

'Lumme! I can see you know all abaht it. All the sime, I give 'im some good 'uns in me time, and 'e knows it.'

'So you 'ave, Dicky, so you 'ave,' admitted Mr Porter. His eyes wandered; he caught sight of some friends, and with a hearty apology he left the novelist and the jockey together.

Mr Pennyfeather liked Dicky Harris's face, and before long he liked Dicky Harris himself, very much. It wasn't long before the little man pulled out of his inside coat pocket a picture of a trim wife and a healthy baby, and it wasn't much longer before he was pouring out, to the most sympathetic listener he had ever met, the story of his life. He was forty, and, until recently, had been a jockey – at one time particularly successful on the flat. Then, he said – and Pennyfeather looked down on a figure which was like the skeleton of a small rat – he had put on too much weight, and obtained a job around a training stable. 'A bit of 'ard luck; boss give up': for three months he had been out of work, though another job was now promised. Meanwhile he had got into debt: that he hadn't saved anything, he accounted for by the disarming explanation, 'But then, lumme, jockeys never do! Give a jockey the Benk of England, and it'll be gorn before you can wink.' It would be different now he'd got a missus and a kid. But here he was, work beginning next week, he hadn't been able to keep up the instalments on his furniture – including a pianner which his missus's sister Mabel sometimes come in and played – and the men were arriving to fetch it away tomorrow. 'Nice little 'ome it was, too!' He sighed.

Pennyfeather lit a fresh pipe, and looked around the bar. It had filled up: numerous picturesque characters were babbling in groups, Mr Porter laughing lustily in the middle of one of them; but their own corner was still their own. He looked at the profile of the ex-jockey, who was gazing sadly at his own reflection in his tankard. 'Poor plucky little sparrow!' he thought: then, clearing his throat awkwardly and trying to look nonchalant, he asked: 'How much are they dunning you for?'

'Might as well be a thousand,' was the gloomy and evasive reply.

'But what is it?'

'Ten pahnd, guv'nor.'

The tide of impulse was now running strong. It came to Penny-feather two or three times a year on odd occasions, and he had so regularly failed to regret his wanton generosities, that he could almost have budgeted so much a year for the purchase of happiness by absurd prodigality.

'Look here, I say,' he remarked, gazing earnestly into the little man's eyes, 'please don't take offence, but couldn't I lend it to you?'

Harris gaped at the prodigy; and he went on:

'I can't bear to see a chap done down by such rotten luck as this. It wouldn't in the least matter when you paid it back.'

'Thenks all the sime, mister,' Harris mumbled, 'but I caunt tike it.'

'But you simply must. Look here,' hurriedly fumbling under the counter, 'here it is. It's nothing at all to me. I've got tons.'

He had his way. 'My Gawd, sir, you're a peach!' stammered the little man. For half a minute he was on the verge of tears. Then he pulled himself together and grinned. He refused another drink, saying candidly, 'I'm goin' 'ome before it burns a nole in me pocket.'

He moved as to go, and then came back and put his face very close to the novelist's. 'Look 'ere, sir, do you ever 'ave anythink on a 'orse?'

'Not often,' replied Pennyfeather, with a gross understatement.

'Well, once in a way's enough,' said Harris. 'But Mangel-Wurzel for the 3.30 tomorrow. It's all right. Lad 'oo's ridin' 'er's a pal o' mine.'

'Thanks for the tip,' said Pennyfeather, 'and good night, if you must be going. Your wife can cheer up now. I'm always here on Wednesday evenings, and I hope we shall meet again.'

He resumed his original solitude. No, he did not bet 'often'. In youth he had tried four several infallible betting systems, and each one had left in his mind's eye a panorama of disastrous scenes, the last of which was himself receiving from a pawnbroker an inadequate sum for his grandfather's gold watch.

Conversation grew noisier, the passage of drinks was speeded

up, friends began departing with affectionate salutations, there was
a general welter of 'Just one more!' 'Well, goo' night, Tom !' 'Goo'
night, Bill!' 'Till tomorrow, then!' 'Goo' night', and smashing clean
through this tissue of sound the landlord's blaring 'Time now,
gentlemen! Time, please, gentlemen! Long past time!'

He went out in the wet street, started out for his Tube station,
and by the time he reached his lodgings in Paddington had completely forgotten, for he made no effort to remember, even the
name of the horse for tomorrow, much less the time of the race.

Dicky Harris appeared in The Asparagus Tree the very next Wednesday night. He peered round the door, then rushed up, snatched
Pennyfeather away from Mr Porter (who had been talking about
horse-doping) and began chattering eagerly in an undertone. He
had only a few minutes, he said, having a train to Epsom to catch,
but he couldn't miss a chance of seeing his benefactor.

'I 'hope you were On, sir!' he whispered.

'On?' inquired the benefactor, rather stupidly.

'Why, the filly, sir! Mangel-Wurzel. The tip I give you. Fifteen
to one.'

Pennyfeather blushed with shame, having now no option but to
confess. He assumed an expression of exasperation at his own folly.
'Ass that I was,' he said. 'I searched the papers for all I was worth
in the morning, and I simply couldn't remember the name of the
damned horse.'

Harris was chapfallen to the point of misery.

'Fifteen to one!' he repeated. 'Why, with only a fiver that 'ud
a' bin seventy-five quid. Look 'ere, sir,' he went on pathetically,
'I won't give you no duds, I promise you I won't. I can tell yer
when they're bahnd to win, and when they're almost bahnd to
win.' Pennyfeather, he said, could put his shirt on horses in the
former category, and a modicum on the latter. 'Friday, nah,' said
Harris, 'it ain't quite what yer'd call a cert, but next door to it.
One of our own 'orses. Ten bob wouldn't do you no 'arm, would
it?'

Assured on this point, he made Pennyfeather promise, honour
being involved, to take a chance on 'Flibbertigibbet'. (This horse,
as it happened, fell at the last hurdle when leading.) Harris's tip
had not been bad; but there you were, that was racing; and Pennyfeather, who had not the slightest intention of ever backing another

horse for the rest of his life, congratulated himself on saving his ten shillings.

Harris, the following week, was full of apologies; it had been miles the best horse running, but the jockey was a fool.

'That's all right,' observed Pennyfeather with easy sportsmanship, 'one must take the rough with the smooth'; and he agreed to recoup his losses and a bit over by backing a runner in the four o'clock at Salisbury, twelve days later, this runner being in the cert class.

So it proved, and when he met his 'Epsom Correspondent', he admitted with bold mendacity to having made nine pounds on the race. A wild thought even crossed his mind to clinch conviction by offering to dock his winnings from the ten-pound loan; but he realised at once how such a suggestion would wound his little friend.

Harris went away happy: one good turn had not only deserved but received another; and if he did not make his noble helper's fortune, he was no stable lad but a Dutchman.

During the next three months Harris appeared seven times with seven tips – not to mention new photographs of his family, of his sister-in-law playing the piano, and of strings of cavalry galloping over the Downs. Of the seven horses five won and two lost; and Pennyfeather managed so to manipulate the amounts he alleged himself to have put on as to give the impression that he was winning very moderately. The only money that, so far as he was responsible, actually passed on these races was not his own.

One evening in February he happened to go, being engaged on a chapter in which a fast young clerk embezzled money, to one of his places, which was a billiard-saloon-cum-drinking-den at the back of Shaftesbury Avenue. Here, in his efforts to produce really free conversation from three young bucks, with whom he had made recent acquaintance, he consumed so many more whiskies than was his wont, that his own tongue became unloosed. Temporarily the experienced man-about-town, and speaking with the off-hand air of one who Knew the Owner (in this case a chilled meat baronet), he impressed upon his young friends the necessity, if they wished to make their futures safe, of putting all they possessed on the tip that Dicky Harris had given him for the next day. In the morning, as he held his head over the desk which bore the half-written chapter about the wastrel clerk, he remembered his indiscretion and cursed himself for it: in the afternoon, when the evening paper informed him that the disgusting animal had crawled in last, he felt quite sick: and for weeks afterwards he took circuitous routes round Shaftesbury Avenue.

Dicky's abject apologies after that occasion drew from him a wry smile which bewildered Dicky. But next week the run of success was resumed.

There came at last the week before the Grand National, and with it the visitor from Epsom, who had not been seen at The Asparagus Tree for three weeks. The tavern was very full: the names of at least twenty probable winners were excitedly handed about, whilst a procession of anxious-looking men sought a private word with Mr Porter and others who were supposed to be authorities.

Pennyfeather, watching the scene with amusement, and occasionally catching an augur's wink from Mr Porter, had been wondering which of the twenty dead certs would be Dicky's, when, with a hist-and-finger-to-lip air, the little figure stole in at the door, stealthily approached him, and took him to a plush-covered bench in a far corner, as one who had momentous tidings to communicate. He had.

Having fetched drinks, he opened, with an unprecedented solemnity of expression and a clenched right fist: 'Have you got twenty pounds to play with, mister?'

For an instant Pennyfeather was chilled by the thought that more borrowing was proposed, but the phraseology, as the sentence was repeated, made the situation clear. A mammoth bet was going to be suggested; and doubtless on the Grand National. Well, it didn't matter: it wouldn't go on, anyhow.

'Yes, yes; I think I have,' he said.

'That's the stuff!' resumed the Man on the Spot. 'It's for next week's big race. I've got *the* absolute cert. Can't lose!'

'But,' the novelist ventured, 'isn't the National always uncertain? Can anybody ever know the winner of it beforehand?'

'Yus, and no; once in a while the thing's a cert, and this 'orse next week's a cert.'

'What's its name?'

Harris looked around; then leaned forward, and putting his hand over his mouth hoarsely muttered 'Absalom'.

The name rang uneasily in Pennyfeather's head. Absalom? Absalom? Harris? Then he remembered, with amazement: it was the very tip the little man had given old Porter a year ago, and the esteemed Absalom had come in last. Fidelity was doubtless a fine quality, but Harris was, perhaps, carrying it too far.

'Didn't that horse,' he inquired in a tentative way, 'run last year?'

'Yus, boss, it did; come in nowhere. All the jockey's fault. Boss, you got to believe me. Took 'im hover the sticks meself larst week. 'E *cawn't* lose. 'E'll leave the rest standin'. S'welp me, bob, 'e's bahnd to! . . . An' nobody knows. Only the stible and the howner. Kep it dark – you'll get *any* price. Mister, never speak to me again if it's a wrong 'un this time.'

Pennyfeather did not hesitate long. After all, it would cost nothing to humour the grateful little expert. 'All right,' said he, 'I'll back him.'

'For the twenty pahnds wot you promised?'

'I'll take your word for it.'

'Boss, I'll put it on for you meself, if you like.'

Pennyfeather hastily disclaimed any desire to give Mr Harris trouble. As a matter of fact, he improvised; his few small commissions were always put through a West End firm of which a cousin was a director.

'Can you ring him up nah? persisted Harris, touchingly determined that the glorious good thing should not be missed.

'Sheep as a lamb!' shot through Pennyfeather's brain. 'I will,' he declared with resolution; 'there's always somebody there late.' Then went to the telephone box behind the curtains, carefully closed the door, got his club number, asked the porter whether there were any letters for him, and returned with a thoroughly plausible rubbing of the hands. 'So that's that,' he observed with hearty finality. 'What's yours?'

'Since it's tonight,' replied Dicky, 'I'll have a double Scotch . . . And here's to you, and here's,' in a gleeful undertone, 'to Absalom.'

On the homeward bus he made up his mind that this must be the end of his career of kindly hypocrisy. Fake telephone calls were really too elaborate. He should have to announce his intention, when he next saw Dicky, of resting on his laurels.

The week passed. Pennyfeather did a good deal of work, and

contrived to bring into his book what he thought a satisfactory
picture of a thoroughly innocent jockey; he worked so well, indeed,
that he 'cut out' most of his social life, and only once remembered
the existence of the Grand National, then humorously thanking his
stars that he was old enough not to risk his bank balance on
anything with four legs. On the Wednesday, as he did once every
six months or so, he took a train to Guildford to have tea with a
comfortable aunt. They fell to playing cribbage, and he stayed to
early supper: by the time he reached Waterloo it was half-past
nine, and dark, and the station almost deserted. Turning over in
his mind the scene of the country parlour, the old lady, the lamp,
the woolwork, as possible material, he walked down the sloping
roadway impatiently waving away a vaguely clamorous newsboy.
Then he automatically turned left; and in five minutes reached the
accustomed lights and din of The Asparagus Tree. Pushing open
the door against pressure, he found himself in a dense mob, and
with difficulty struggled through to his accustomed corner. He
shouted for a drink, then felt a clutch at his sleeve and, turning,
saw beside him Dicky Harris, whose eyes gleamed with unusual
excitement from a face preternaturally white and drawn. The small
man gulped and then stammered: 'Gawd forgive me, I thought
you was off somewheres else and wasn't goin' to come to see me!'
and then clutched at his hand and grasped it feverishly. 'If only I
could explain how unnecessary his anguish is!' thought Pennyfeather.

'Nonsense, Dicky!' he said, 'we can none of us always win. I
can afford to lose that twenty.'

'Stroike me pink!' gasped Harris incredulously. 'D'yer mean yer
don't *know*!'

'What is it?' asked Pennyfeather weakly, the fear that he might
have, hypothetically, won quite a large sum flashing across his
mind.

'Why, you've won!' shouted Harris, forgetting his habitual secrecy so entirely that half the crowd turned round and craned its
necks to see who had won what.

'By Gad, I'm grateful to you,' cried Pennyfeather, with fine
aplomb, slapping the other on the shoulder. 'What was the price?'

'Well, I'm damned!' said Dicky slowly, his eyes blazing, his face
wrinkled in a rigid smile. 'To be on a 'undred to one 'orse an' not
know it! Yer've won two thousand bloomin' quid!'

The figure was staggering. Pennyfeather felt faint; then he was aghast as the clamour swelled around him and finally cheer after cheer broke out. Half those present knew him; the other half were resolved to be in on anything good that was going. 'Hip! Hip! Hip!' they yelled, and the nearest swarmed round him, cramming him painfully against the bar, and fought for the privilege of wringing him by the hand, forearm or biceps. He was completely dazed; and scarcely conscious of what was happening, when 'Silence! Silence!' rose above the tumult in the voice of Mr Porter, which had roared the odds on the Epsom Hill for forty years. Mr Porter had mounted a chair.

'Silence! Silence!' repeated Mr Porter. 'Give the gentleman a chance.'

Silence was secured. People from the street were gaping through every crevice and every unfrosted patch of glass; the landlord, the august landlady with her golden chignon, the little barmaid with a look in her eyes that offered Mr Pennyfeather a lifelong devotion, were clustered in front of the hero.

'We are all delighted,' proceeded the aged rascal, 'that our friend Mr – er – our old friend has had such a stroke of good luck, and 'as honoured us with 'is presence 'ere tonight.' (Loud cheers.) 'I know our old friend well enough to know that 'e's a real sportsman and one of the best.' (Loud cheers.) 'Sir,' as he raised his glass in the air, 'your 'ealth and many of 'em!'

The cheering was terrific. Great roars of it now came from even the remotest of the more plebeian compartments in the background. Then the ham-like hand of Mr Porter commanded silence again. There was a pause of agony. Mr Pennyfeather realised that he was expected to reply. No; there was no way out. He had to play the man. He set his jaw and stared at Mr Porter.

'Mr Porter,' he said, in a voice that sounded very remote to himself, 'I thank you all very much and I hope that everybody present will take a drink with me!'

There was a new outbreak of hurrahing, mingled with mild cat-calling. Somebody far away started the National Anthem on a mouth organ; the whole concourse took it up with great enthusiasm and in several keys. While the ovation was at its height, the landlord leant across the bar and took hold of his coat.

'Champagne, sir?' he asked hoarsely.

'Of course,' said Mr Pennyfeather, with patrician calm.

They didn't all drink champagne, but the gold-necked bottles arrived by the case, nevertheless. Feeling like a visitor from another planet, Mr Pennyfeather stood in the centre of the pandemonium and waited patiently for time, pretending to drink with dozens of men, and occasionally clasping the overjoyed Dicky by the hand. . . .

Time came, and with it a beckoning from the landlord. In a back parlour he was presented with a bill, written with a blunt pencil, for £57 10s 0d. He wrote a cheque, said good night, and passed, with a gruff greeting, through a crowd of his more proletarian admirers who still lingered around the darkened doorway.

Next day he rose gloomily and faced his loss. An idea came to him. He could recover some of it, at any rate, if he wrote the story down.

# THE INSIDE VIEW

## C. C. L. Browne

Few of the crowd that passes ceaselessly up and down the busy street ever notice the little alley that runs between the chemist's and the draper's shops. It is no more to them than a black gap, an absence of a shop-front and therefore a negation of attraction. Their gaze automatically skips it to fasten on the next window with its calculated, eye-trapping display. Concentrating on the plate-glass cages which hold so much that is covetable, they seldom see the faded sign over the mouth of the alley which reads:

J. BOSSINGTON
Turf Accountant

Mr Bossington would have to think twice before he recognised that such a mode of address referred to him. For thirty years he has made a reasonable living by catering for those who like to put something on a horse, and for as long as he can remember he has been known to all as 'Jem'. He has not visited a racecourse for a quarter of a century, for he is too busy as a shopkeeper, selling money. The reason why his trade makes him a living is that he charges more than the value of the money he offers; and that, in essence, is how a Starting-Price bookmaker flourishes.

His overheads are small. He has a large room for his clients with, for their greater comfort, a coal-stove and a dozen collapsible chairs ranged along one wall. Opposite is a huge blackboard ruled in lines, on which his man, Steve, lists the runners by races, marks the ever-fluctuating odds against each horse, and ultimately records which ones are placed, together with their official starting-prices. The third wall has two copies of the day's *Sporting Life* drawing-pinned to it so that punters can read up form and study the prophecies of the experts before plunging. The fourth wall is peculiarly Jem's own. Along it is built a narrow room, not unlike a railway station ticket-office, with one small *guichet* through which he both receives bets and pays out any winnings. There he lives from noon to five p.m. on every day when there is racing, ceaselessly receiving scraps of paper stating that someone (for initials only are used) is eager to wager 2s 6d on Blue Moon in the two-thirty p.m. race at Wye.

Finally, there is the most important feature of the room. High up on a shelf stands a dusty and old-fashioned loudspeaker, and from it at intervals comes a dispassionate and rather metallic female voice. It is the Blower, that means of racecourse communication by which are announced over hired telephone-lines such matters as the runners, changes in riders, moment-by-moment odds, the 'OFF', a brief commentary, the result and the starting-prices of the placed horses.

It is the link between the man on the course, ceaselessly recording how the money is being staked, and the little group in Jem's office wondering how best to place their shillings. That old loudspeaker is the very Voice of Racing.

Let us momentarily insert ourselves in spirit among the thirty or so of Jem's clients, some talking together, others brooding over the race-sheets, a few sitting silently on chairs. There is a click and the Voice speaks.

'Three-thirty race at Lingfield,' it says. 'Cross out numbers 2, 7, 11, 14, 17 and 20. Numbers 2, 7, 11, 14, 17 and 20. Thirteen runners in all.'

Steve picks up his rag and rubs out the names of the non-runners. What he had previously written on the board was the list of likely starters from the morning's paper, but seldom do they all come to the post. One has lamed himself in his horse-box, another has been withheld from an encounter with a rival who is thought to be too good for him at the weights, and a third is not going because he is known to be unable to act in the heavy going produced by the morning's rain.

The group study the reduced list with interest. They have now only to find the best horse among thirteen; not, as a few minutes ago, among nineteen. But the Voice interrupts them again. Two hundred miles away a frame has been hoisted opposite the stands and a pair of binoculars studies the list of runners and riders.

Click! 'No. 8 will be ridden by D. Garnham,' it announces,

'No. 13 by Mr R. Widnes.' Click! Steve chalks in the names against their mounts. There is a moment's pause and then the Voice of Racing speaks again.

'Kilbrennan – five to two, two and a half,' it says in its level monotone. 'Beggars' Roost – three to one, Sultan IV – five to one, Porphyry – eight to one.' Steve chalks the odds against the horses named. He stands no truck with arithmetical niceties, and when the price is a hundred to eight or a hundred to six he firmly writes up twelve or sixteen. After all, it is only a guide and will shortly be amended. A few minutes later the Voice announces fresh odds. The old ones are lightly crossed out and the onlookers study the new quotations.

All that the Voice is saying in several thousand bookies' offices scattered over the United Kingdom comes from a lynx-eyed gentleman with a flair for race-reading developed by years of practice. High in the stands he watches the busy scene below him. Little escapes his gaze, and his asides to the Lady of the Microphone are relayed nationwide. Thousands of pounds will be placed as a result of his commentary.

But even he cannot see everything.

At three-thirty-one p.m. on a certain dirty winter's day Ted Frisby was conscious only of gross discomfort. He was one of a dozen riders sitting their restless horses in front of the starting-gate. Normally, National Hunt horses are reasonably sedate at the post. They are not excitable two-year-olds, ready to swerve at the flap of an umbrella as they canter past the crowd. They are older and more experienced, and they know that their work does not begin until they form line and wait for the release that will send them off on the journey some of them will not complete. But this was a hurdle-race and the hurdler is usually a younger horse. He may be a cast-off from flat-racing or a would-be chaser being smartened up. Anyhow, the four-year-olds in this race were uneasy. They were being required to face into driving sleet, and they twisted and sidled to try to take the wind on a flank rather than straight into their eyes.

Ted Frisby had ridden in all the three previous races that afternoon, two steeplechases and another hurdle-race, and his luck had not been with him. In the first race a horse had jumped across him at the last but one fence and his mount had done well to get over with no more than a sprawl. He had lost two or three lengths by the incident and had never made them up in the run-in, so that when he rode his horse into the second pen in the unsaddling enclosure he was aware of a furious owner waiting to catch him on his way to the scales.

'Sorry, Mr Nicholls,' said Ted, 'I thought we had it, but that cow of a chestnut came right across me and we were as near as a touch down. If it hadn't been for that we'd have walked it.'

The fat, angry owner was in a difficult mood. 'None of your damned excuses,' he said. 'You're paid to ride and not to get boxed in. Why the hell can't you keep out of trouble? Anyone with the wit of a duck would have got himself a clear view instead of riding in another horse's pocket. Don't expect any more rides from me. In future I'll get me a jockey who can use his loaf.'

For a moment Ted was tempted to speak his mind and tell the owner that he ought to try it himself instead of always criticising what he could neither understand nor do. But he remembered in time that owners were few and riders a-plenty, and that he needed the £7 amount that he got. The trainer would see the owner later and would tell him that he ought to be grateful to his rider for getting him even-place money. In a week or two it would all be forgotten and he'd get another mount. Meanwhile he had to weigh-in and get ready for the next race. So he made as mollifying an answer as he could contrive and thanked his stars that there was no question of an objection. He hated them, and he knew that the circumstances in this case did not permit of one being lodged.

'I'm real sorry, Mr Nicholls,' he repeated, 'but I'd got the inside and he was crowding me. There was nothing I could do except try to get ahead, and he was keeping half a length in front of me all the time.'

He touched his cap and went to the changing-room. After he had weighed-in he took his new colours and warmed himself by the fire for a few precious moments. Then he presented himself at the scales, weighed-out and gave the saddle and weight-cloth to the trainer of his next horse. Five minutes later he was standing in the parade-ring, talking with forced confidence to the owner. The rain was lashing down with a cold, relentless fury that discouraged hope. It increased the hazards while diminishing the enthusiasm. On a day like this only the stout-hearted won races. They had to conquer their own feelings as well as their horses' before they could begin to think about besting the others. And even that was insufficient, for luck played a bigger part than on a dry day. A hoof-full of mud in your face or a slip-up on landing and where were you? Blinded or down!

As it turned out, that race was wasted effort. Ted kept his horse wide of the turns, where there was only torn turf, and brought him with a run between the last two hurdles. He was no more than a length behind the leaders when his horse suddenly faltered with that horrible little dip and lurch that tells of a tendon gone; and that was that. Ted pulled him up to a walk and they made their sad, limping progress back to the stables, Ted to get ready for the next race and the horse to pass out of the racing-scene, for a season if it was lucky and for ever if it was not.

He had had an undistinguished ride in the third race, a two-mile steeplechase for novices. His horse was just not good enough, and after driving him into fourth place as the last fence loomed ahead, he had eased him up the finishing straight when he saw that he had no hope of improving his position. He was a conscientious man like all his profession, with an intuitive feeling of what the horse might be thinking in its simple mind.

'No good pushing him,' he thought, as he eased the reins, 'only give him a rotten taste in his mouth for racing. Why they jump and why we ride them in filthy weather like this beats me! Some day this one will win but not today,' and he turned off the course up the cinder path that led back to the stables.

The same ritual was observed. Change silks, into clean breeches, weigh-out, keep under cover until the last possible moment and then out to talk to yet another owner. One had to give an owner a strong feeling of confidence in oneself if there were to be more rides. And so Ted talked with that cheerful ring in his voice that was so comforting to an owner who, having backed his horse too heavily, had begun to see with uneasy clarity that the vile conditions were upsetting form.

Ted did not know this horse. He had been offered the ride an hour before when the stable-jockey had broken a collar-bone. The trainer told him that it was running better and improving with every race. 'But keep him back,' he said; 'he takes a fair hold and burns himself out. He does best when held up for a late run.'

Ted nodded and glanced at the plaited reins. Privately he thought, 'Takes a fair hold, does he? Pulls your guts out, I suppose!

I would get a tearaway sort in weather like this!' Aloud, he said, 'What's he called?'

'Tornado,' said the other. 'Own brother to Four Winds,' and Ted recognised the latter name. It was that of an older horse that had won several two-mile chases.

The time came to mount and he was given his leg-up into the little saddle. Within thirty seconds he was soaked to the skin, his silks clinging to him. It was misery to face into the half-sleet, and when he turned right on to the course and started to canter, Tornado took such a hold that, with the wind behind him urging him on, he was near to being unstoppable. They were past the starting-gate before Ted could check him. He turned him eventually and took him back very steadily, circling him round at a trot and finally at a walk once they had rejoined the others. Tornado was upset, sidling and plunging and fretting until it was all Ted could do to get him to go up to the others. One rider was late, having delayed to tighten a breast-girth, and the moments of waiting seemed like hours.

Ted humoured his restless mount almost automatically. The conscious part of his mind was reviewing the financial future and was not best pleased with what it saw. By National Hunt rules he got £7 a ride, and if he won a race most owners gave him a present. He himself was not allowed to bet lest it affected the honesty of his riding, but it was an understood thing that the riders of winners were treated by owners as though they had put £5 on themselves. If, thought Ted, you got only one ride at a meeting you barely made money. Expenses and paying the valet for producing your kit ate into it. Two or more rides showed a good profit on the day, and there was also the regular wage that he got from his trainer for riding-work. But if you could get a win you were well up. Yet, how often could you? He'd had twenty-odd in the last six months and he'd been lucky. No damaging falls had come his way and no meetings had been lost through frost. These were the two ever-present hazards in his career, and there was nothing much he could do about them. And his riding-life was not long. Few National Hunt riders continued much after they were thirty. Flesh and blood could not take indefinitely the battering that came their way, and eventually, when you had broken a dozen bones and been concussed several times you lost the art of riding Berlin-or-Bust. Once that happened your winners became few and far between and then you were offered rides less often and people began to talk behind your back about your nerve, and once that occurred you'd had it.

No, if you were lucky you had twelve years of it, and you must make all you could in the time and hope for some long-priced winners. Only two months before, he'd taken the ride that had been refused by two better jockeys on a flashy brute that had fallen in the three previous races, and after nearly being on the floor twice had got him up in the last few strides to snatch a victory by a neck. Twenty to one he had started at and Lord Castlethorpe had put him a tenner on. But he was a real gentleman who had ridden a lot himself when younger and knew how hard was the life of a N.H. 'jock'. That was one reason why the professionals like himself never looked sideways at an amateur. He'd once been asked by a reporter if he did not resent G.R.'s taking the bread out of the mouths of the professionals, so to speak, but he'd never seen it that way. The more amateurs that rode and enjoyed it the more there would be who would keep horses in training when they grew too old to ride themselves, and that was where the likes of him would benefit.

The missing rider appeared and Ted had one last thought before he lined up with the others. He was chilled to the bone and tired, but if thrust would win a race he would not lose this one. He badly needed a win. He wanted the money for a TV set for his wife. Little he saw of her when the jumping-season was on. She lived in their cottage in the shadow of the Berkshire Downs and could not but be lonely. She was a good wife to him and he knew that her days were drab now that their boy was away at school morning and afternoon. With all his heart he longed for the win that would let him give her a television set. It had to be that way because she would have no truck with hire-purchase.

The Starter called over the names of the runners, his mackintosh collar turned up and rain dripping off the brim of his bowler on to the paper in his hand. He climbed up to the platform and watched them come forward. Tornado backed out of the line and the gap closed so that Ted had no option but to take him up on the outside. For an instant the shifting, wavering line was fairly straight and in that instant the Starter released the catch, the wire whipped upwards and they were off. He stood for a moment watching them thunder away before descending to ground level and getting back into his car. 'God help all jockeys!' said the Starter.

High in the Stand, the Blower's race-reader tried to make out the runners. He called the two leaders by name, then cursed and hurriedly wiped the object-glasses of his big binoculars. He swung on to them again, confirmed the two leaders and was then forced to say 'They're out of sight.' They were not, but their colours were indistinguishable in the driving rain while they were on the far side of the course. He waited for them to come nearer, and two hundred miles away the crowd in Jem's office waited also, silently eyeing the list of runners as though to will their chosen horses into the lead.

Tornado had not been mentioned; for he was deep in the bunch on the rails with horses all round him. Ted had taken him straight across to the inside of the course in order to prevent him from pulling into the van prematurely, and now he lay tucked in behind the leaders and boxed round by other runners. His position was much better than it looked. Shut in he might be, but presently gaps would occur and horses would make their way forward or drop back. Ted foresaw little difficulty in extricating himself when the moment came. For the time being all he had to do was to keep in touch with the leaders and try to restrain Tornado without fighting him too much. When they had gone a little farther he would be able to judge the pace and decide if the race was being truly run and when he should start turning on the tap.

The flights of hurdles came sliding towards him in quick succession. Tornado was taking them easily and Ted had a half-thought that at any rate he had been well schooled. There was no check, no measuring of distance unless it was to take off a stride earlier if in doubt. This was no place for the putting in of a short one as the clever chaser does when something goes wrong and he finds he is going to take off underneath the fence. Above all things the hurdler must not check. Gallop he must; jump he should. The rider's seat over hurdles showed that. Catch the horse short by the head, keep your seat on the plate and crouch so that your face is in your horse's mane. There must be no dwelling on landing. Your horse must be really galloping and you must be in that attitude which will best help him to keep up his momentum. And that means having your weight forward all the time.

They rounded the last bend and turned downwind. There were

only two more flights of hurdles and then the run-in to the finishing-post. Ted still sat quiet but he could see his plan clearly now. There were four or five horses ahead of him: before the last flight he would move out and give Tornado a clear view. He wanted to start his run before they reached the last hurdles. A horse could not quicken sharply on a day like this. He must work up gradually to the top-speed of his final burst.

The leaders were accelerating perceptibly as they came at the penultimate flight, and Ted felt his horse strong under him. And then, even as he dared to be hopeful, disaster struck.

A tired horse ahead of him failed to rise sufficiently and hit the hurdle hard. He got over with a lurch and a stagger but the hurdle sprang back and struck Tornado's fore-legs as he was in mid-air. Whether it was that they were knocked from under him or whether the pain of the blow dulled his mount's reactions Ted never knew, but the result was the same; for the pair of them were down in the mud even as other horses took off behind them. From as far away as the stands watchers could see the horrible impact of a following horse which, brought down by Tornado's struggles, struck Ted's body with such force as to turn him over and over like a doll pitched along a floor, a sprawl of arms and legs.

The ambulance, its engine already running, needed no signal to send it to the spot. It whirled down the course, and the doctor in the front jumped off even before it stopped and ran to the muddy, motionless figure. 'It could be anything,' he thought as he ran, 'legs, arms, ribs; even his neck if he's unlucky.' But, to his surprise, Ted slowly sat up. To the doctor's question he made no reply but sat, sobbing for breath as a badly winded man does, and pressing with shaking hands on his ribs. Rain poured down on them as the doctor made his first quick examination. Within thirty seconds he had satisfied himself that there were no major breaks and that Ted could be moved, and quickly the men had him on a stretcher and into the ambulance. They took him back and by the time the ambulance stopped Ted was able to walk out of it. The doctor led him into the little surgery and examined him. He found Ted shaken and slow to answer, but there were no fractures and no concussion, and in the end he said, 'You're lucky. You've no bones broken but you'll be very stiff tomorrow. Have you anyone to see you home?'

Ted did not really answer him. He stood up slowly, felt his

neck, moved his head about gingerly, retrieved his cap and whip from a chair, said 'Thank you, sir,' vaguely, and limped out of the door and down the passage to the changing-room. There he sat on a bench and rested his face in his hands, waiting for his head to clear. The others looked at him curiously but left him alone. They knew all too well the brain-loosening jar that a heavy fall can give and how that after such a shock a man craves solitude. They were anything but unsympathetic, but they knew from their own experience, even if they had never formulated it in words, that a man can grapple for and recover his fortitude only by himself. So they went about their own business and left him to his.

Two minutes later Ted felt a touch on his shoulder and looked up to find the trainer for whom he worked bending over him.

'Are you fit to ride, Ted?' he asked. 'If you're not, there's Tim Parks that'll take the mount. How do you feel?'

Ted considered it. It never occurred to him that he had heard the trainer the first time only because he was bending over him, but then it had equally never occurred to him that he had burst his right ear-drum in the concussion of the last fall.

'I'm all right, Mr Skipwith,' he answered. 'That was a dirty one I had, but it's passing,' and he put his hand up to feel his neck. Again, he was not aware that he had torn some of the muscles at the base of it. All he knew was that so long as people wanted him to ride he was ready to ride. His very living depended on it.

The valet helped him to change, saw him weigh-out and then started to clear up in the changing-room.

Luckily for Ted, the owner of the mount did not come into the parade-ring and he was spared the effort of making cheerful conversation. He stood in the centre, a small, undistinguished figure looking at the horses as they filed round. When the time came to mount, he watched the trainer draw off the rug and look to the girth before he himself slipped out of his big coat and took the leg-up. He knew the horse, which had been in training with them for some months. He was honest enough and a reasonable jumper, but he lacked that touch of class that would make him notable. There were lots like him about. If he was placed right and had a bit of luck he would win an occasional race, but he had not done so up to date. He had a depressing name, Mediocrity, and even the lad who 'did' him found it hard to enthuse over his charge.

The Voice of the Blower spoke to the crowd in Jem's room. 'Parson's Pleasure,' it said, 'two to one; Verification – seven to two, three and a half; Cosmopolis – four to one; Poisson d'Avril – six to one; The Firefly – seven to one; Sporting Sam – ten to one.' It did not mention Mediocrity or half a dozen of the other runners because there was little money being wagered on them. Individually, their chances of winning were perhaps one in twenty, though the layers would have been the first to admit that horses did not run true to form in such vile weather. They were not quoted simply because the public was not supporting them.

The hinged rail was lifted and the runners filed out on to the track that led down to the course. Ordinarily, there would have been crowds within a few feet of them out of which would have come cheery remarks from friends, but there were few today. The spectators had placed their bets and were back in the shelter of the stands. Ted missed the calls. They heartened a man with their implied suggestion that someone cared how he did. As it was, he could only mop his streaming face on his sleeve, and as he did so he winced. Nothing broken, the doctor had said, but all the same his neck was somewhat painful. Still, it was the last race of the day and in ten minutes it would be over, one way or another. He turned on to the course and shook his horse up. He would need to move smartly if he were to be warmed and loosened up by the time they reached the start.

He let Mediocrity stride out, conscious only at first of the relief of moving downwind. He did not try to check him until he was nearing the start, and when he did take a pull he nearly cried out with pain. He felt as if red-hot pincers had gripped the muscles low down on one side of his neck and it was agony to pull with his right arm. He overshot the start and careered on for two or three furlongs before he could turn his horse. The other riders had preceded him down to the start and so the whole field had to wait for him. He dared not go back too quickly, and with his left hand gripping both reins and taking most of the pull he made his way back at a steady trot. There were angry looks to meet as he rejoined the others, but no one said anything. All that everyone wanted was to get going. They were too cold to realise that Mediocrity was the only horse that was truly warmed-up. He had benefited by his overshoot while they were having to wait for him.

Back in Jem's office the Blower said unemotionally, 'the flag's up.' They had come under Starter's Orders.

The twelve horses came up in a rough line, broke dressing and were turned away. The Starter brought them up again and this time caught them in a reasonable line for an instant. The gate went up and they were gone.

('They're off!' said the Blower.)

Mediocrity went straight into the lead. It was no wish of Ted's but he just could not hold him back. He loathed waiting in front. You could not see where the danger would come from. Another horse could get the first run on you and by the time you had yours moving too you could be a few strides to the bad with inadequate time in which to catch up. Provided a race was truly run he preferred to lead only at the finish. But there was no option here. Ted's side hurt at every breath and he had not the power to take a real pull at Mediocrity. All he could do was to keep the steady tension on the reins that a horse requires if it is to lean on the bit.

('Mediocrity leading by four lengths from The Firefly, Cosmopolis and Poisson d'Avril.')

He took two plain fences in succession without incident, and the field entered the bend towards the far side of the course. They were travelling almost directly away from the stands and only the tail horses could be identified. All down the far side Mediocrity led the field, jumping freely and easily, and Ted wondered what was happening behind him. The wind was across them and no sound of hoofs reached him from behind as he crouched over his horse's withers. The Open Ditch came and went, two more plain fences followed and then they were going at the water. Ted wondered if the landing-side would be slippery. It was no more likely to be so than any other fence, but because it was different his mind concentrated on it and he felt a real relief when his horse took it immaculately. He wished he could see who were next behind him, but when he tried to turn his head as he rounded the next bend he experienced such a twinge as dismissed any further hopes of a quick squint backwards.

('Mediocrity leading by eight lengths from Poisson d'Avril, The

Firefly and Cosmopolis. The following have fallen – Sporting Sam, Dhargelis and Cuneo. Man of Mystery has been pulled up.')

He led the field past the stands and began the second circuit of the three-mile ordeal. He got a momentary relief as he travelled straight down wind, but it ceased as he bent left-handed and the wind became increasingly antagonistic. He was inside the wings of one fence when a hissing gust hit them with such force that he felt his horse check perceptibly, but Mediocrity was still fresh enough to jump big and he got over with no more than a burst through the top of the packed birch.

Though it was not severe enough to unsettle his horse the pace was slowing down. Judgment of it went by the board under such conditions. Any horse that finished would be a very tired one. Worse, Ted felt that he himself was tiring. His neck was hurting more and more and, though he strove to disregard it, the pull on his arms was aggravating it. It was just bearable when he was galloping on the flat, but the change of position as he took the fences caused him to wince, and in spite of his determination he felt himself getting slacker in the saddle. It was no longer easy to help his horse. He could only concentrate on staying on top and keeping his horse balanced, and that was becoming harder as he sensed that his horse was weakening, too. Yet there was nothing he could do but sit still and try to keep a reserve for a final effort. He wondered dully what was happening behind him. He had not seen another horse since he took the lead at the start.

('It's still Mediocrity by two lengths from Poisson d'Avril and The Firefly. Only four horses still racing.')

There were three fences left now and then the run-in. He was tempted to ease his horse off a trifle to give him a short breather before the final effort that would almost certainly be required of him. But he resisted the impulse. Whatever his lead, someone behind him was trying to cut it down and it would be silly to help him. There was a saying that a good horse could give away weight but that only a world-beater could give away distance. And the next behind him was giving away both, thanks to Mediocrity's early lead before the others had warmed up. He kept his horse going and rode at the fence ahead.

('Mediocrity leads by one length from Poisson d'Avril with The Firefly ten lengths behind.')

His horse took it normally and as he was getting away he heard another one landing just behind him. It needed no more than a slight turn of the head to see that Tommy Cullen was coming up outside him, challenging. But he kept Mediocrity plugging on and Tommy seemed to make no further gain on him; and in this order they came at the last fence but one. He took it a length ahead of the other, but though Mediocrity jumped normally he slipped on landing and pecked slightly, and in that instant Tommy on Poisson d'Avril drew level.

('Mediocrity and Poisson d'Avril running together.')

Glancing sideways, Ted could see that the other horse was as tired as his own. There was a labour to his action that showed how much the effort of making up the distance under a heavy weight had told on him. Yet even as Ted noted this he saw Tommy Cullen pick up his whip and give his horse a reminder and at once they began to draw ahead. It was no more than an inch at every stride, but slowly they began to pull clear, and as they did so a blackness of mind settled on Ted. He had done his best and no man could do more, and it was not good enough. There, a length ahead of him, went his hope of a long-priced winner and with it the money that would get the TV set for his wife, and at the thought the pain in his neck and his ribs seemed to double in intensity. But he neither felt panic nor threw his hand in. He and his horse were good, he reckoned, for one last, small additional effort and it would be useless to make it too early.

('One fence to go. Poisson d'Avril leads Mediocrity by a length.')

As he saw it, his only chance was a slim one – it was to speed up his horse before the last fence and ask him for a big stand-back. A fine jump could gain a length over a normal one, and the impetus of it could carry him past his rival. But it all depended on whether the horse had the necessary 'pop' left in him. The only way he could find out if Mediocrity had it was to ask him the question, and as the last fence grew larger and clearer through the rain he began to ride him hard. He drove him up to within half a length of Poisson d'Avril, gave him a smartener and went at the jump 'with his neck for sale'. All the high endeavour and calculated recklessness in his sober mind crystallised into that moment of time and focused like a burning spot of compulsion. His horse felt it even through his weariness. He responded to the call made on him, and as he got level with the wings he put all his available energy into one tremendous jump.

Ted felt what was coming, and even as his horse over-jumped he shifted his weight back, and as Mediocrity pitched on landing he was lying back so far that he had the reins by the buckle. He felt the horse overbalancing on his landing leg, and as though in slow motion he saw him reach desperately for support with the other, fail to get it completely and begin to peck badly. All the pain and urge in Ted's body and mind combined, like a drug, to make him extra-perceptive, able to break down the flowing sequence of actions by his horse into individual movements. Slowly, it seemed to him, the horse's head went down until it momentarily touched the ground and the white snip on his nose became muddied. But even while Ted sat and suffered, expecting to feel the hindquarters rise higher and higher behind him until he was flung ahead as they curved over in a fall, the momentary support of his nose gave Mediocrity that fractional chance to save himself. With a desperate clawing motion he got a foreleg free from under him and put it out ahead, and with a stagger and a slip he kept upright and lurched forward again.

Ted knew the effort that his horse had put into saving himself and the demand that it had made on his store of energy, and he knew, too, that there would now be nothing more to give. He felt no relief or pride at having survived so bad a peck. What use was it when his plan of out-jumping his rival had been neutralised by the check and delay of the landing slither? Numb with disappointment and his body one hotbed of pain, he looked for his rival. To his amazement nothing was to be seen, and he forced his neck round for a glance back. Only then did he understand. Poisson d'Avril had fallen while he himself was striving to keep his horse up, and Tommy Cullen was slowly getting to his feet.

('Mediocrity is over the last fence thirty lengths clear of The Firefly. Poisson d'Avril has fallen.')

Ted eased his tired horse into a canter and stood up in his stirrups. Once past the post he dropped to a walk and turned back up the cinder path to the unsaddling-ring. He rode Mediocrity into the winner's pen, slid off his back and took off the saddle and weightcloth. He was near to reeling with the fatigue that is the legacy of continued pain, but his mind was full of light and radiance and colour. In his inarticulate way he felt that no one could have spent himself more unstintedly than he had and, for once, it had paid. He was too tired, too drained of emotion to take it all in fully, but he knew that he was happy. Others in the changing-room congratulated him and he answered them as best he could, but only sometimes could he hear what they said.

Two hundred miles away the Voice spoke for the last time that day.

'Starting-prices,' it said in its flat voice, 'Mediocrity – a hundred to six, The Firefly – seven to one. Only two finishers. That is all. Goodbye.'

The little crowd in Jem's room filed out into the last of the afternoon light.

Jem swept the coins out of his change-bowl into a linen bag, dropped it into his old-fashioned Gladstone, followed it up with a thick wad of notes, locked the bag and padlocked it by its chain to the metal collar round his wrist.

Ted watched, dog-tired, as the valet packed his bag for him, took it out to a waiting taxi and handed it in after him. He wanted to get home. He had done his day's work and now he wanted nothing more than to rest.

In his box, Mediocrity cleaned up his feed, walked stiffly round twice and then lay down in the golden straw.

The day's racing was over.

# THE TALE OF THE GYPSY HORSE

## *Donn Byrne*

I THOUGHT first of the old lady's face, in the candlelight of the dinner table at Destiny Bay, as some fine precious coin, a spade guinea perhaps, well and truly minted. How old she was I could not venture to guess, but I knew well that when she was young men's heads must have turned as she passed. Age had boldened the features much, the proud nose and definite chin. Her hair was grey, vitally grey, like a grey wave curling in to crash on the sands of Destiny. And I knew that in another woman that hair would be white as scutched flax. When she spoke, the thought of the spade guinea came to me again, so rich and golden was her voice.

'Lady Clontarf,' said my uncle Valentine, 'this is Kerry, Hector's boy.'

'May I call you Kerry? I am so old a woman and you are so much a boy. Also I knew your father. He was of that great line of soldiers who read their Bibles in their tents, and go into battle with a prayer in their hearts. I always seem to have known,' she said, 'that he would fondle no grey beard.'

'Madame,' I said, 'what should I be but Kerry to my father's friends!'

It seemed to me that I must know her because of her proud high face, and her eyes of a great lady, but the title of Clontarf made little impress on my brain. Our Irish titles have become so hawked and shopworn that the most hallowed names in Ireland may be borne by a porter brewer or former soap boiler. O'Conor Don and MacCarthy More mean so much more to us than the Duke of This or the Marquis of There, now the politics have so

muddled chivalry. We may resent the presentation of this title or
that to a foreigner, but what can you do? The loyalty of the
Northern Irishman to the Crown is a loyalty of head and not of
heart. Out of our Northern country came the United Men, if you
remember. But for whom should our hearts beat faster? The Stuarts
were never fond of us, and the Prince of Orange came over to us,
talked a deal about liberty, was with us at a few battles, and went
off to grow asparagus in England. It is so long since O'Neill and
O'Donnel sailed for Spain!

Who Lady Clontarf was I did not know. My uncle Valentine is
so off-hand in his presentations. Were you to come on him closeted
with a heavenly visitant he would just say: 'Kerry, the Angel
Gabriel.' Though as to what his Angelicness was doing with my
uncle Valentine, you would be left to surmise. My uncle Valentine
will tell you just as much as he feels you ought to know and no
more – a quality that stood my uncle in good stead in the days
when he raced and bred horses for racing. I did know one thing:
Lady Clontarf was not Irish. There is a feeling of kindness between
all us Irish that we recognise without speaking. One felt courtesy,
gravity, dignity in her, but not that quality that makes your
troubles another Irish person's troubles, if only for the instant. Nor
was she English. One felt her spiritual roots went too deep for
that. Nor had she that brilliant armour of the Latin. Her speech
was the ordinary speech of a gentlewoman, unaccented. Yet that
remark about knowing my father would never fondle a grey beard!

Who she was and all about her I knew I would find out later
from my dear aunt Jenepher. But about the old drawing-room of
Destiny there was a strange air of formality. My uncle Valentine
is most courteous, but to-night he was courtly. He was like some
Hungarian or Russian noble welcoming an empress. There was an
air of deference about my dear aunt Jenepher that informed me
that Lady Clontarf was very great indeed. Whom my aunt Jenepher
likes is lovable, and whom she respects is clean and great. But the
most extraordinary part of the setting was our butler James Carabine. He looked as if royalty were present, and I began to say to
myself: 'By damn, but royalty is! Lady Clontarf is only a racing
name. I know that there's a queen or princess in Germany who's
held by the Jacobites to be Queen of England. Can it be herself
that's in it? It sounds impossible, but sure there's nothing impossible where my uncle Valentine's concerned.'

★   ★   ★

At dinner the talk turned on racing, and my uncle Valentine inveighed bitterly against the late innovations on the track; the starting gate, and the new seat introduced by certain American jockeys, the crouch now recognised as orthodox in flat-racing. As to the value of the starting gate my uncle was open to conviction. He recognised how unfairly the apprentice was treated by the crack jockey with the old method of the flag, but he dilated on his favourite theme: that machinery was the curse of man. All these innovations –

'But it isn't an innovation, sir. The Romans used it.'

'You're a liar!' said my uncle Valentine.

My uncle Valentine, or any other Irishman for the matter of that, only means that he doesn't believe you. There is a wide difference.

'I think I'm right, sir. The Romans used it for their chariot races. They dropped the barrier instead of raising it.' A tag of my classics came back to me, as tags will. '*Repagula submittuntur*, Pausanias writes.'

'Pausanias, begob!' My uncle Valentine was visibly impressed.

But as to the new seat he was adamant. I told him competent judges had placed it about seven pounds' advantage to the horse.

'There is only one place on a horse's back for a saddle,' said my uncle Valentine. 'The shorter your leathers, Kerry, the less you know about your mount. You are only aware whether or not he is winning. With the ordinary seat, you know whether he is lazy, and can make proper use of your spur. You can stick to his head and help him.'

'Races are won with that seat, sir.'

'Be damned to that!' said my uncle Valentine. 'If the horse is good enough, he'll win with the rider facing his tail.'

'But we are boring you, Madame,' I said, 'with our country talk of horses.'

'There are three things that are never boring to see: a swift swimmer swimming, a young girl dancing, and a young horse running. And three things that are never tiring to speak of: God, and love, and the racing of horses.'

'A *kushto jukel* is also *rinkeno, mi pen*,' suddenly spoke our butler, James Carabine.

'*Dabla*, James Carabine, you *roker* like a *didakai*. A *jukel* to catch *kanangre!*' And Lady Clontarf laughed. 'What in all the *tem* is as *dinkeno* as a *kushti-dikin grai?*'

'A *tatsheno jukel, mi pen*, like Rory Bosville's,' James Carabine evidently stood his ground, 'that *noshered* the Waterloo Cup through *wafro bok!*'

'*Avali!* You are right, James Carabine.' And then she must have seen my astonished face, for she laughed, that small golden laughter that was like the ringing of an acolyte's bell. 'Are you surprised to hear me speak the *tawlo lshib*, the black language, Kerry? I am a gypsy woman.'

'Lady Clontarf, Mister Kerry,' said James Carabine, 'is saying there is nothing in the world like a fine horse. I told her a fine greyhound is a good thing too. Like Rory Bosville's, that should have won the Waterloo Cup in Princess Dagmar's year.'

'Lady Clontarf wants to talk to you about a horse, Kerry,' said my uncle Valentine. 'So if you would like us to go into the gunroom, Jenepher, instead of the withdrawing room while you play – '

'May I not hear about the horse, too?' asked my aunt Jenepher.

'My very, very dear,' said the gypsy lady to my blind aunt Jenepher, 'I would wish you to, for where you are sitting, there a blessing will be.'

My uncle Valentine had given up race horses for as long as I can remember. Except with Limerick Pride, he had never had any luck, and so he had quitted racing as an owner, and gone in for harness ponies, of which, it is admitted, he bred and showed the finest of their class. My own two chasers, while winning many good good Irish races, were not quite up to Aintree form, but in the last year I happened to buy, for a couple of hundred guineas, a handicap horse that had failed signally as a three-year-old in classic races, and of which a fashionable stable wanted to get rid. It was Ducks and Drakes, by Drake's Drum out of Little Duck, a beautifully shaped, dark grey horse, rather short in the neck, but the English stable was convinced he was a hack. However, as often happens, with a change of trainers and jockeys, Ducks and Drakes became a different horse and won five good races, giving me so much in hand that I was able to purchase for a matter of nine hundred guineas a colt I was optimistic about, a son of Saint Simon. Both horses were in training with Robinson at the Curragh.

And now it occurred to me that the gypsy lady wanted to buy one or the other of them. I decided beforehand that it would be across my dead body.

'Would you be surprised,' asked my uncle Valentine, 'to hear that Lady Clontarf has a horse she expects to win the Derby with?'

'I should be delighted, sir, if she did,' I answered warily. There were a hundred people who had hopes of their nominations in the greatest of races.

'Kerry,' the gypsy lady said quietly, 'I think I will win.' She had a way of clearing the air with her voice, with her eyes. What was a vague hope now became an issue.

'What is the horse, Madame?'

'It is as yet unnamed, and has never run as a two-year-old. It is a son of Irlandais, who has sired many winners on the Continent, and who broke down sixteen years ago in preparation for the Derby, and was sold to one of the Festetics. Its dam is Iseult III, who won the Prix de Diane four years ago.'

'I know so little about Continental horses,' I explained.

'The strain is great-hearted and, with the dam, strong as an oak tree. I am a gypsy woman, and I know a horse, and I am an old, studious woman,' she said, and she looked at her beautiful, un-ringed golden hands, as if she were embarrassed, speaking of something we, not Romanies, could hardly understand, 'and I think I know propitious hours and days.'

'Where is he now, Madame?'

'He is at Dax, in the Basses-Pyrénées, with Romany folk.'

'Here's the whole thing in a nutshell, Kerry: Lady Clontarf wants her colt trained in Ireland. Do you think the old stables of your grandfather are still good?'

'The best in Ireland, sir, but sure there's no horse been trained there for forty years, barring jumpers.'

'Are the gallops good?'

'Sure, you know yourself, sir, how good they are. But you couldn't train without a trainer, and stable boys – '

'We'll come to that,' said my uncle Valentine. 'Tell me, what odds will you get against an unknown, untried horse in the winter books?'

I thought for an instant. It had been an exceptionally good year for two-year-olds, the big English breeders' stakes having been bitterly contested. Lord Shere had a good horse; Mr Paris a dangerous colt. I should say there were fifteen good colts, if they wintered well, two with outstanding chances.

'I should say you could really write your own ticket. The ring will be only too glad to get money. There's so much up on Sir James and Toison d'Or.'

'To win a quarter-million pounds?' asked my uncle Valentine.

'It would have to be done very carefully, sir, here and there, in ponies and fifties and hundreds, but I think between four and five thousand pounds would do it.'

'Now if this horse of Lady Clontarf's wins the Two Thousand and the Derby, and the Saint Leger – '

Something in my face must have shown a lively distaste for the company of lunatics, for James Carabine spoke quietly from the door by which he was standing.

'Will your young Honour be easy, and listen to your uncle and my lady.'

My uncle Valentine is most grandiose, and though he has lived in epic times, a giant among giants, his schemes are too big for practical business days. And I was beginning to think that the gypsy lady, for all her beauty and dignity, was but an old woman crazed by gambling and tarot cards, but James Carabine is so wise, so beautifully sane, facing all events, spiritual and material, four-square to the wind.

' – what would he command in stud fees?' continued quietly my uncle Valentine.

'If he did this tremendous triple thing, sir, five hundred guineas would not be exorbitant.'

'I am not asking you out of idle curiosity, Kerry, or for infor-mation,' said my uncle Valentine. 'I merely wish to know if the ordinary brain arrives at these conclusions of mine; if they are, to use a word of Mr Thackeray's, apparent.'

'I quite understand, sir,' I said politely.

'And now,' said my uncle Valentine, 'whom would you suggest to come to Destiny Bay as trainer?'

'None of the big trainers will leave their stables to come here, sir. And the small ones I don't know sufficiently. If Sir Arthur Pollexfen were still training, and not so old – '

'Sir Arthur Pollexfen is not old,' said my uncle Valentine. 'He cannot be more than seventy-two or seventy-three.'

'But at that age you cannot expect a man to turn out at five in the morning and oversee gallops.'

'How little you know Mayo men,' said my uncle Valentine. 'And Sir Arthur with all his triumphs never won a Derby. He will come.'

'Even at that, sir, how are you going to get a crack jockey? Most big owners have first or second call on them. And the great free lances, you cannot engage one of those and ensure secrecy.'

'That,' said my uncle Valentine, 'is already arranged. Lady Clontarf has a Gitano, or Spanish gypsy, in whom her confidence is boundless. And now,' said my uncle Valentine, 'we come to the really diplomatic part of the proceeding. Trial horses are needed, so that I am commissioned to approach you with delicacy and ask you if you will bring up your two excellent horses Ducks and Drakes and the Saint Simon colt and help train Lady Clontarf's horse. I don't see why you should object.'

To bring up the two darlings of my heart, and put them under the care of a trainer who had won the Gold Cup at Ascot fifty years before, and hadn't run a horse for twelve years, and have them ridden by this Gitano or Spanish gypsy, as my uncle called him; to have them used as trial horses to this colt which might not be good enough for a starter's hack. Ah, no! Not damned likely. I hardened my heart against the pleading gaze of James Carabine.

'Will you or won't you?' roared my uncle diplomatically.

My aunt Jenepher laid down the lace she was making, and reaching across, her fingers caught my sleeve and ran down to my hand, and her hand caught mine.

'Kerry will,' she said.

So that was decided.

'Kerry,' said my uncle Valentine, 'will you see Lady Clontarf home?'

I was rather surprised. I had thought she was staying with us. And I was a bit bothered, for it is not hospitality to allow the visitor to Destiny to put up at the local pub. But James Carabine whispered: ''Tis on the downs she's staying, Master Kerry, in her own great van with four horses.' It was difficult to believe that the tall graceful lady in the golden and red Spanish shawl, with the quiet speech of our own people, was a roaming gypsy, with the whole world as her home.

'Good night, Jenepher. Good night, Valentine. *Boshto dok*, good luck, James Carabine!'

'*Boshto dok, mi pen*. Good luck, sister.'

We went out into the October night of the full moon – the hunter's moon – and away from the great fire of turf and bogwood in our drawing-room; the night was vital with an electric cold. One noted the film of ice in the bogs, and the drumming of snipes' wings, disturbed by some roving dog, came to our ears. So bright was the moon that each whitewashed apple tree stood out clear in the orchard, and as we took the road toward Grey River, we could see a barkentine offshore, with sails of polished silver – some boat from Bilbao probably, making for the Clyde, in the daytime a scrubby ore carrier but to-night a ship out of some old sea story, as of Magellan or our own Saint Brendan:

'*Feach air muir lionadh gealach buidhe mar ór,*' she quoted in Gaelic, 'See on the filling sea the full moon yellow as gold. . . . It is full moon and full tide, Kerry; if you make a wish, it will come true.'

'I wish you success in the Derby, Madame.'

Ahead of us down the road moved a little group to the sound of fiddle and mouth organ. It was the Romany bodyguard ready to protect their chieftainess on her way home.

'You mean that, I know, but you dislike the idea. Why?'

'Madame,' I said, 'if you can read my thoughts as easily as that, it's no more impertinent to speak than think. I have heard a lot about a great colt to-night, and of his chance for the greatest race in the world, and that warms my heart. But I have heard more about money, and that chills me.'

'I am so old, Kerry, that the glory of winning the Derby means little to me. Do you know how old I am? I am six years short of an hundred old.'

'Then the less – ' I began, and stopped short, and could have chucked myself over the cliff for my unpardonable discourtesy.

'Then the less reason for my wanting money,' the old lady said. 'Is not that so?'

'Exactly, Madame.'

'Kerry,' she said, 'does my name mean anything to you?'

'It has bothered me all the evening. Lady Clontarf, I am so sorry my father's son should appear to you so rude and ignorant a lout.'

'Mifanwy, Countess Clontarf and Kincora.'

I gaped like an idiot. 'The line of great Brian Boru. But I thought – '

'Did you really ever think of it, Kerry?'

'Not really, Madame,' I said. 'It's so long ago, so wonderful. It's like that old city they speak of in the country tales, under Ownaglass, the grey river, with its spires and great squares. It seems to me to have vanished like that, in rolling clouds of thunder.'

'The last O'Neill has vanished, and the last Plantagenet. But great Brian's strain remains. When I married my lord,' she said quietly, 'it was in a troubled time. Our ears had not forgotten the musketry of Waterloo, and England was still shaken by fear of the Emperor, and poor Ireland was hurt and wounded. As you know, Kerry, no peer of the older faith sat in College Green. It is no new thing to ennoble, and steal an ancient name. Pitt and Napoleon passed their leisure hours at it. So that of O'Briens, Kerry, sirred and lorded, there are a score, but my lord was Earl of Clontarf and Kincora since before the English came.

'If my lord was of the great blood of Kincora, myself was not lacking in blood. We Romanies are old, Kerry, so old that no man knows our beginning, but that we came from the uplands of India centuries before history. We are a strong, vital race, and we remain with our language, our own customs, our own laws until this day. And to certain families of us, the Romanies all over the world do reverence, as to our own, the old Lovells. There are three Lovells, Kerry, the *dinelo* or foolish Lovells, the *gozvero* or cunning Lovells, and the *puro* Lovells, the old Lovells. I am of the old Lovells. My father was the great Mairik Lovell. So you see I am of great stock, too.'

'Dear Madame, one has only to see you to know that.'

'My lord had a small place left him near the Village of Swords, and it was near there I met him. He wished to buy a horse from my father Mairik, a stallion my father had brought all the way from the Nejd in Arabia. My lord could not buy that horse. But when I married my lord, it was part of my dowry, that and two handfuls of uncut Russian emeralds, and a chest of gold coins, Russian and Indian and Turkish coins, all gold. So I did not come empty-handed to my lord.'

'Madame, do you wish to tell me this?'

'I wish to tell it to you, Kerry, because I want you for a friend to my little people, the sons of my son's son. You must know everything about friends to understand them.

'My lord was rich only in himself and in his ancestry. But with the great Arab stallion and the emeralds and the gold coins we were well. We did a foolish thing, Kerry; we went to London. My lord wished it, and his wishes were my wishes, although something told me we should not have gone. In London I made my lord sell the great Arab. He did not wish to, because it came with me, nor did I wish to, because my father had loved it so, but I made him sell it. All the Selim horses of to-day are descended from him, Sheykh Selim.

'My lord loved horses, Kerry. He knew horses, but he had no luck. Newmarket Heath is a bad spot for those out of luck. And my lord grew worried. When one is worried, Kerry, the heart contracts a little – is it not so? Or don't you know yet? Also another thing bothered my lord. He was with English people, and English people have their codes and ordinances. They are good people, Kerry, very honest. They go to churches, and like sad songs, but whether they believe in God, or whether they have hearts or have no hearts, I do not know. Each thing they do by rote and custom, and they are curious in this: they will make excuses for a man who has done a great crime, but no excuses for a man who neglects a trivial thing. An eccentricity of dress is not forgiven. An eccentric is an outsider. So that English are not good for Irish folk.

'My own people,' she said proudly, 'are simple people, kindly and loyal as your family know. A marriage to them is a deep thing, not the selfish love of one person for another, but involving many factors. A man will say: Mifanwy Lovell's father saved my honour once. What can I do for Mifanwy Lovell and Mifanwy Lovell's man? And the Lovells said when we were married: Brothers, the *gawjo rai*, the foreign gentleman, may not understand the gypsy way, that our sorrows are his sorrows, and our joys his, but we understand that his fights are our fights, and his interests the interests of the Lovell Clan.

'My people were always about my lord, and my lord hated it. In our London house in the morning, there were always gypsies waiting to tell my lord of a great fight coming off quietly on Epsom Downs, which it might interest him to see, or of a good horse to be bought cheaply, or some news of a dog soon to run in a coursing match for a great stake, and of the dog's excellences or his defects. They wanted no money. They only wished to do him a kindness. But my lord was embarrassed, until he began to loathe the sight of a gypsy neckerchief. Also, on the racecourses, in the betting ring where my lord would be, a gypsy would pay hard-earned entrance money to tell my lord quietly of something they had noticed that morning in the gallops, or horses to be avoided in betting, or of neglected horses which would win. All kindnesses to my lord. But my lord was with fashionable English folk, who do not understand one's having a strange friend. Their uplifted eyebrows made my lord ashamed of the poor Romanies. These things are things you might laugh at, with laughter like sunshine, but there would be clouds in your heart.

'The end came at Ascot, Kerry, where the young queen was, and the Belgian king, and the great nobles of the court. Into the paddock came one of the greatest of gypsies, Tyso Herne, who had gone before my marriage with a great draft of Norman trotting horses to Mexico, and came back with a squadron of ponies, some of the best. Tyso was a vast man, a *pawni Romany*, a fair gypsy. His hair was red, and his moustache was long and curling, like a Hungarian pandour's. He had a flaunting *diklo* of fine yellow silk about his neck, and the buttons on his coat were gold Indian mohurs, and on his bell-shaped trousers were braids of silver bells, and the spurs on his Wellingtons were fine silver, and his hands were covered with rings, Kerry, with stones in them such as even the young queen did not have. It was not vulgar ostentation. It was just that Tyso felt rich and merry, and no stone on his hand was as fine as his heart.

'When he saw me he let a roar out of him that was like the roar of the ring when the horses are coming in to the stretch.

' "Before God," he shouted, "it's Mifanwy Lovell." And, though I am not a small woman, Kerry, he tossed me in the air, and caught me in the air. And he laughed and kissed me, and I laughed and kissed him, so happy was I to see great Tyso once more, safe from over the sea.

' "Go get your *rom, mi tshai*, your husband, my lass, and we'll go to the *kitshima* and have a jeroboam of Champagne wine."

'But I saw my lord walk off with thunder in his face, and all the English folk staring and some women laughing. So I said: "I will go with you alone, Tyso." For Tyso Herne had been my father's best friend and my mother's cousin, and had held me as a baby, and no matter how he looked, or who laughed, he was well come for me.

'Of what my lord said, and of what I said in rebuttal we will not speak. One says foolish things in anger, but, foolish or not, they leave scars. For out of the mouth come things forgotten, things one thinks dead. But before the end of the meeting, I went to Tyso Herne's van. He was braiding a whip with fingers light as a woman's, and when he saw me he spoke quietly.

' "Is all well with thee, Mifanwy?"

' "Nothing is well with me, father's friend."

'And so I went back to my people, and I never saw my lord any more.'

We had gone along until in the distance I could see the gypsy fire, and turning the headland we saw the light on Farewell Point. A white flash; a second's rest; a red flash; three seconds' occultation; then white and red again. There is something heartening and brave in Farewell Light. Ireland keeps watch over her share of the Atlantic sea.

'When I left my lord, I was with child, and when I was delivered of him, and the child weaned and strong, I sent him to my lord, for every man wants his man child, and every family its heir. But when he was four and twenty he came back to me, for the roving gypsy blood and the fighting Irish blood were too much for him. He was never Earl of Clontarf. He died while my lord still lived. He married a Herne, a grandchild of Tyso, a brave golden girl. And he got killed charging in the Balkan Wars.

'Niall's wife – my son's name was Niall – understood, and when young Niall was old enough, we sent him to my lord. My lord was old at this time, older than his years, and very poor. But of my share of money he would have nothing. My lord died when Niall's Niall was at school, so the little lad became Earl of Clontarf and Kincora. I saw to it he had sufficient money, but he married no rich woman. He married a poor Irish girl, and by her had two children, Niall and Alick. He was interested in horses, and rode well, my English friends tell me. But mounted on a brute in the Punchestown races, he made a mistake at the stone wall. He did not know the horse very well. So he let it have its head at the stone wall. It threw its head up, took the jump by the roots, and so Niall's Niall was killed. His wife, the little Irish girl, turned her face away from life and died.

'The boys are fifteen and thirteen now, and soon they will go into the world. I want them to have a fair chance, and it is for this reason I wish them to have money. I have been rich and then poor, and then very rich and again poor, and rich again and now poor. But if this venture succeeds, the boys will be all right.'

'Ye-s,' I said.

'You don't seem very enthusiastic, Kerry.'

'We have a saying,' I told her, 'that money won from a book-maker is only lent.'

'If you were down on a race meeting and on the last race of the last day you won a little, what would you say?'

'I'd say I only got a little of my own back.'

'Then we only get a little of our own back over the losses of a thousand years.'

We had come now to the encampment. Around the great fire were tall swarthy men with coloured neckerchiefs, who seemed more reserved, cleaner than the English gypsy. They rose quietly as the gypsy lady came. The great spotted Dalmation dogs rose too. In the half light the picketed horses could be seen, quiet as trees.

'This is the Younger of Destiny Bay,' said the old lady, 'who is kind enough to be our friend.'

'*Sa shan, rai!*' they spoke with quiet courtesy. 'How are you, sir?'

Lady Clontarf's maid hurried forward with a wrap, scolding, and speaking English with beautiful courtesy. 'You are dreadful, sister. You go walking the roads at night like a courting girl in spring. Gentleman, you are wrong to keep the *rawnee* out, and she an old woman and not well.'

'Supplistia,' Lady Clontarf chided, 'you have no more manners than a growling dog.'

'I am the *rawnee's* watchdog,' the girl answered.

'Madame, your maid is right. I will go now.'

'Kerry,' she stopped me, 'will you be friends with my little people?'

'I will be their true friend,' I promised, and I kissed her hand.

'God bless you!' she said. And '*koshto bok, rai!*' the gypsies wished me. 'Good luck, sir!' And I left the camp for my people's house. The hunter's moon was dropping toward the edge of the world, and the light on Farewell Point flashed seaward its white and red, and as I walked along, I noticed that a wind from Ireland had sprung up, and the Bilbao boat was bowling along nor'east on the starboard tack. It seemed to me an augury.

In those days before my aunt Jenepher's marriage to Patrick Herne, the work of Destiny Bay was divided in this manner: My dear aunt Jenepher was, as was right, supreme in the house. My uncle Valentine planned and superintended the breeding of the harness ponies, and sheep, and black Dexter cattle which made Destiny Bay so feared at the Dublin Horse Show and at the Bath and West. My own work was the farms. To me fell the task of preparing the stables and training grounds for Lady Clontarf's and my own horses. It was a relief and an adventure to give up thinking of turnips, wheat, barley, and seeds, and to examine the downs for training ground. In my great-grandfather's time, in pre-Union days, many a winner at the Curragh had been bred and trained at Destiny Bay. The soil of the downs is chalky, and the matted roots of the woven herbage have a certain give in them in the driest of weather. I found out my great-grandfather's mile and a half, and two miles and a half with a turn and shorter gallops of various gradients. My grandfather had used them as a young man, but mainly for hunters, horses which he sold for the great Spanish and Austrian regiments. But to my delight the stables were as good as ever. Covered with reed thatch, they required few repairs. The floors were of chalk, and the boxes beautifully ventilated. There were also great tanks for rainwater, which is of all water the best for horses in training. There were also a few stalls for restless horses. I was worried a little about lighting, but my uncle Valentine told me that Sir Arthur Pollexfen allowed no artificial lights where he trained. Horses went to bed with the fowls and got up at cockcrow.

My own horses I got from Robinson without hurting his feelings. 'It's this way, Robinson,' I told him. 'We're trying to do a crazy thing at Destiny, and I'm not bringing them to another trainer. I'm bringing another trainer there. I can tell you no more.'

'Not another word, Mr Kerry. Bring them back when you want to. I'm sorry to say good-bye to the wee colt. But I wish you luck.'

We bought three more horses, and a horse for Ann-Dolly. So that with the six we had a rattling good little stable. When I saw Sir Arthur Pollexfen, my heart sank a little, for he seemed so much out of a former century. Small, ruddy-cheeked, with the white hair of a bishop, and a bishop's courtesy, I never thought he could run a stable. I thought, perhaps, he had grown too old and had been thinking for a long time now of the Place whither he was going, and that we had brought him back from his thoughts and he had left his vitality behind. His own servant came with him to Destiny Bay, and though we wished to have him in the house with us, yet he preferred to stay in a cottage by the stables. I don't know what there was about his clothes, but they were all of an antique though a beautiful cut. He never wore riding breeches but trousers of a bluish cloth and strapped beneath his varnished boots. A flowered waistcoat with a satin stock, a short covert coat, a grey bowler hat and gloves. Always there was a freshly-cut flower in his buttonhole, which his servant got every evening from the greenhouses at Destiny Bay, and kept overnight in a glass of water into which the least drop of whiskey had been poured. I mention this as extraordinary, as most racing men will not wear flowers. They believe flowers bring bad luck, though how the superstition arose I cannot tell. His evening trousers also buckled under his shoes, or rather half Wellingtons, such as army men wear, and though there was never a crease in them there was never a wrinkle. He would never drink port after dinner when the ladies had left, but a little whiskey punch which James Carabine would compound for him. Compared to the hard shrewd-eyed trainers I knew, this bland, soft-spoken old gentleman filled me with misgiving.

I got a different idea of the old man the first morning I went out to the gallops. The sun had hardly risen when the old gentleman appeared, as beautifully turned out as though he were entering the Show Ring at Ballsbridge. His servant held his horse, a big grey, while he swung into the saddle as light as a boy. His hack was feeling good that morning, and he and I went off toward the training ground at a swinging canter, the old gentleman half standing in his stirrups, with a light firm grip of his knees, riding as Cossacks do, his red terrier galloping behind him. When we settled down to walk he told me the pedigree of his horse, descended through Matchem and Whalebone from Oliver Cromwell's great charger The White Turk, or Place's White Turk, as it was called from the Lord Protector's stud manager. To hear him follow the intricacies of breeding was a revelation. Then I understood what a great horseman he was. On the training ground he was like a marshal commanding an army, such respect did every one accord him. The lads perched on the horses' withers, his head man, the grooms, all watched the apple-ruddy face, while he said little or nothing. He must have had eyes in the back of his head, though. For when a colt we had brought from Mr Gubbins, a son of Galtee More, started lashing out and the lad up seemed like taking a toss, the old man's voice came low and sharp: 'Don't fall off, boy.' And the boy did not fall off. The red terrier watched the trials with a keen eye, and I believe honestly that he knew as much about horses as any one of us and certainly more than any of us about his owner. When my lovely Ducks and Drakes went out at the lad's call to beat the field by two lengths over five furlongs, the dog looked up at Sir Arthur and Sir Arthur looked back at the dog, and what they thought toward each other, God knoweth.

I expected when we rode away that the old gentleman would have some word to say about my horses, but coming home, his remarks were of the country. 'Your Derry is a beautiful country, young Mister Kerry,' he said, 'though it would be treason to say that in my own country of Mayo.' Of my horses not a syllable.

He could be the most silent man I have ever known, though giving the illusion of keeping up a conversation. You could talk to him, and he would smile, and nod at the proper times, as though he were devouring every word you said. In the end you thought you had a very interesting conversation. But as to whether he had even heard you, you were never sure. On the other hand when he wished to speak, he spoke to the point and beautifully. Our bishop, on one of his pastoral visitations, if that be the term, stayed at Destiny Bay, and because my uncle Cosimo is a bishop too, and because he felt he ought to do something for our souls he remonstrated with us for starting our stable. My uncle Valentine was livid, but said nothing, for no guest must be contradicted in Destiny Bay.

'For surely, Sir Valentine, no man of breeding can mingle with the rogues, cutpurses and their womenfolk who infest racecourses, drunkards, bawds and common gamblers, without lowering himself to some extent to their level,' his Lordship purred. 'Yourself, one of the wardens of Irish chivalry, must give an example to the common people.'

'Your Lordship,' broke in old Sir Arthur Pollexfen, 'is egregiously misinformed. In all periods of the world's history, eminent personages have concerned themselves with the racing of horses. We read of Philip of Macedon, that while campaigning in Asia Minor, a courier brought him news of two events, of the birth of his son Alexander and of the winning, by his favourite horse, of the chief race at Athens, and we may reasonably infer that his joy over the winning of the race was equal to if not greater than that over the birth of Alexander. In the life of Charles the Second, the traits which do most credit to that careless monarch are his notable and gentlemanly death and his affection for his great race horse Old Rowley. Your Lordship is, I am sure,' said Sir Arthur, more blandly than any ecclesiastic could, 'too sound a Greek scholar not to remember the epigrams of Maecius and Philodemus, which show what interest these antique poets took in the racing of horses. And coming to present times, your Lordship must have heard that his Majesty (whom God preserve!) has won two Derbies, once with the leased horse Minoru, and again with his own great Persimmon. The premier peer of Scotland, the Duke of Hamilton, Duke of Chastellerault in France, Duke of Brandon in England, hereditary prince of Baden, is prouder of his fine mare Eau de Vie than of all his titles. As to the Irish families, the Persses of Galway, the Dawsons of Dublin, and my own, the Pollexfens of Mayo, have always been interested in the breeding and racing of horses. And none of these – my punch, if you please, James Carabine! – are, as your Lordship puts it, drunkards, bawds, and common gamblers. I fear your Lordship has been reading' – and he cocked his eye, bright as a wren's, at the bishop, 'religious publications of the sensational and morbid type.'

It was all I could do to keep from leaping on the table and giving three loud cheers for the County of Mayo.

Now, on those occasions, none too rare, when my uncle Valentine and I differed on questions of agricultural economy, or of national polity, or of mere faith and morals, he poured torrents of invective over my head, which mattered little. But when he was really aroused to bitterness he called me 'modern.' And by modern my uncle Valentine meant the quality inherent in brown buttoned boots, in white waistcoats worn with dinner jackets, in nasty little motor cars – in fine, those things before which the angels of God recoil in horror. While I am not modern in that sense, I am modern in this, that I like to see folk getting on with things. Of Lady Clontarf and of Irlandais colt, I heard no more. On the morning after seeing her home I called over to the caravan but it was no longer there. There was hardly a trace of it. I found a broken fern and a slip of oaktree, the gypsy patteran. But what it betokened or whither it pointed I could not tell. I had gone to no end of trouble in getting the stables and training grounds ready, and Sir Arthur Pollexfen had been brought out of his retirement in the County of Mayo. But still no word of the horse. I could see my uncle Valentine and Sir Arthur taking their disappointment bravely, if it never arrived, and murmuring some courteous platitude, out of the reign of good Queen Victoria, that it was a lady's privilege to change her mind. That might console them in their philosophy, but it would only make me hot with rage. For to me there is no sex in people of standards. They do not let one another down.

Then one evening the horse arrived.

It arrived at sundown in a large van drawn by four horses, a van belonging evidently to some circus. It was yellow and covered with paintings of nymphs being wooed by swains, in clothes hardly fitted to agricultural pursuits: of lions of terrifying aspect being put through their paces by a trainer of an aspect still more terrifying: of an Indian gentleman with a vast turban and a small loincloth playing a penny whistle to a snake that would have put the heart crosswise in Saint Patrick himself; of a most adipose lady in tights swinging from a ring while the husband and seven sons hung on to her like bees in a swarm. Floridly painted over the van was 'Arsène Bombaudiac, Prop., Bayonne.' The whole added no dignity to Destiny Bay, and if some sorceress had disclosed to Mr Bombaudiac of Bayonne that he was about to lose a van by fire at low tide on the beach of Destiny in Ireland within forty-eight hours – the driver was a burly gypsy while two of the most utter scoundrels I have ever laid eyes on sat beside him on the wide seat.

'Do you speak English?' I asked the driver.

'Yes, sir,' he answered, 'I am a Petulengro.'

'Which of these two beauties beside you is the jockey?'

'Neither, sir. These two are just gypsy fighting men. The jockey is inside with the horse.'

My uncle Valentine came down stroking his great red beard. He seemed fascinated by the pictures on the van. 'What your poor aunt Jenepher, Kerry,' he said, 'misses by being blind!'

'What she is spared, sir! Boy,' I called one of the servants, 'go get Sir Arthus Pollexfen. Where do you come from?' I asked the driver.

'From Dax, sir, in the South of France.'

'You're a liar,' I said. 'Your horses are half-bred Clydesdale. There is no team like that in the South of France.'

'We came to Dieppe with an *attelage basque*, six yoked oxen. But I was told they would not be allowed in England, so I telegraphed our chief, Piramus Petulengro, to have a team at Newhaven. So I am not a liar, sir.'

'I am sorry.'

'Sir, that is all right.'

Sir Arthur Pollexfen came down from where he had been speaking to my aunt Jenepher. I could see he was tremendously excited, because he walked more slowly than was usual, spoke with more deliberation. He winced a little as he saw the van. But he was of the old heroic school. He said nothing.

'I think, Sir Valentine,' he said, 'we might have the horse out.'

'Ay, we might as well know the worst,' said my uncle Valentine.

A man jumped from the box, and swung the crossbar up. The door opened and into the road stepped a small man in dark clothes. Never on this green earth of God have I seen such dignity. He was dressed in dark clothes with a wide dark hat, and his face was brown as soil. White starched cuffs covered half of his hands. He took off his hat and bowed first to my uncle Valentine, then to Sir Arthur, and to myself last. His hair was plastered down on his forehead, and the impression you got was of an ugly rugged face, with piercing black eyes. He seemed to say: 'Laugh, if you dare!' But laughter was the farthest thing from us, such tremendous masculinity did the small man have. He looked at us searchingly, and I had the feeling that if he didn't like us, for two pins he would have the bar across the van door again and be off with the horse. Then he spoke gutturally to some one inside.

A boy as rugged as himself, in a Basque cap and with a Basque sash, led first a small donkey round as a barrel out of the outrageous van. One of the gypsies took it, and the next moment the boy led out the Irlandais colt.

He came out confidently, quietly, approaching gentlemen as a gentleman, a beautiful brown horse, small, standing perfectly. I had just one glance at the sound strong legs and the firm ribs, before his head caught my eye. The graceful neck, the beautiful small muzzle, the gallant eyes. In every inch of him you could see breeding. While Sir Arthur was examining his hocks, and my uncle Valentine was standing weightily considering strength of lungs and heart, my own heart went out to the lovely eyes that seemed to ask: 'Are these folk friends?'

Now I think you could parade the Queen of Sheba in the show ring before me without extracting more than an off-hand compliment out of me, but there is something about a gallant thoroughbred that makes me sing. I can quite understand the trainer who, pointing to Manifesto, said that if he ever found a woman with a shape like that, he'd marry her. So out of my heart through my lips came the cry: 'Och, asthore!' which is, in our Gaelic, 'Oh, my dear!'

The Spanish jockey, whose brown face was rugged and impassive as a Pyrenee, looked at me, and broke into a wide, understanding smile.

'Si, si, Señor,' he uttered, 'si, si!'

Never did a winter pass so merrily, so advantageously at Destiny Bay. Usually there is fun enough with the hunting, but with a racing stable in winter there is always anxiety. Is there a suspicion of a cough in the stables? Is the ground too hard for gallops? Will snow come and hold the gallops up for a week? Fortunately we are right on the edge of the great Atlantic drift, and you can catch at times the mild amazing atmosphere of the Caribbean. While Scotland sleeps beneath its coverlet of snow, and England shivers in its ghastly fog, we on the north-east seaboard of Ireland go through a winter that is short as a midsummer night in Lofoden. The trees have hardly put off their gold and brown before we perceive their cheeping green. And one soft day we say: 'Soon on that bank will be the fairy gold of the primrose.' And behold, while you are looking the primrose is there!

Each morning at sun-up, the first string of horses were out. Quietly as a general officer reviewing a parade old Sir Arthur sat on his grey horse, his red dog beside him, while Geraghty, his head man, galloped about with his instructions. Hares bolted from their forms in the grass. The sun rolled away the mists from the blue mountains of Donegal. At the starting gate, which Sir Arthur had set up, the red-faced Irish boys steered their mounts from a walk toward the tapes. A pull at the lever and they were off. The old man seemed to notice everything. 'Go easy, boy, don't force that horse!' His low voice would carry across the downs. 'Don't lag there, Murphy, ride him!' And when the gallop was done, he would trot across to the horses, his red dog trotting beside him, asking how Sarsfield went. Did Ducks and Drakes seem interested? Did Rustum go up to his bit? Then they were off at a slow walk toward their sand bath, where they rolled like dogs. Then the sponging and the rubbing, and the fresh hay in the mangers kept as clean as a hospital. At eleven the second string came out. At half-past three the lads were called to their horses, and a quarter of an hour's light walking was given to them. At four, Sir Arthur made his 'stables', questioning the lads in each detail as to how the horses had fed, running his hand over their legs to feel for any heat in the joints that might betoken trouble.

Small as our stable was, I doubt if there was one in Great Britain and Ireland to compare with it in each fitting and necessity for training a race horse. Sir Arthur pinned his faith to old black tartar oats, of about forty-two pounds to the bushel, bran mashes with a little linseed, and sweet old meadow hay.

The Irlandais colt went beautifully. The Spanish jockey's small brother, Joselito, usually rode it, while the jockey's self, whose name we were told was Frasco, Frasco Moreno – usually called, he told us, Don Frasco – looked on. He constituted himself a sort of sub-trainer for the colt, allowing none else to attend to its feeding. The small donkey was its invariable stable companion, and had to be led out to exercise with it. The donkey belonged to Joselito. Don Frasco rode many trials on the other horses. He might appear small standing, but on horseback he seemed a large man, so straight did he sit in the saddle. The little boys rode with a fairly short stirrup, but the gitano scorned anything but the traditional seat. He never seemed to move on a horse. Yet he could do what he liked with it.

The Irlandais colt was at last named Romany Baw, or 'gypsy friend' in English, as James Carabine explained to us, and Lady

Clontarf's colours registered, quarter red and gold. When the winter lists came out, we saw the horse quoted at a hundred to one, and later at the call over of the Victoria Club, saw the price offered but not taken. My uncle Valentine made a journey to Dublin, to arrange for Lady Clontarf's commission being placed, putting it in the hands of a Derry man who had become big in the affairs of Tattersall's. What he himself and Sir Arthur Pollexfen and the jockey had on I do not know, but he arranged to place an hundred pounds of mine, and fifty of Ann-Dolly's. As the months went by, the odds crept down gradually to thirty-three to one, stood there for a while and went out to fifty. Meanwhile Sir James became a sensational favourite at fives, and Toison d'Or varied between tens and one hundred to eight. Some news of a great trial of Lord Shire's horse had leaked out which accounted for the ridiculously short price. But no word did or could get out about Lady Clontarf's colt. The two gypsy fighters from Dax patrolled Destiny Bay, and God help any poor tipster or wretched newspaper tout who tried to plumb the mysteries of training. I honestly believe a bar of iron and a bog hole would have been his end.

The most fascinating figure in this crazy world was the gypsy jockey. To see him talk to Sir Arthur Pollexfen was a phenomenon. Sir Arthur would speak in English and the gypsy answer in Spanish, neither knowing a word of the other's language, yet each perfectly understanding the other. I must say that this only referred to how a horse ran, or how Romany Baw was feeding and feeling. As to more complicated problems, Ann-Dolly was called in, to translate his Spanish.

'Ask him,' said Sir Arthur, 'has he ever ridden in France?'

'*Oiga, Frasco,*' and Ann-Dolly would burst into a torrent of gutturals.

'*Si, si, Doña Anna.*'

'Ask him has he got his clearance from the Jockey Club of France?'

'*Seguro, Don Arturo!*' And out of his capacious pocket he extracted the French Jockey Club's 'character'. They made a picture I will never forget, the old horseman ageing so gently, the vivid boyish beauty of Ann-Dolly, and the overpowering dignity and manliness of the jockey. Always, except when he was riding or working at his anvil – for he was our smith too – he wore the dark clothes, which evidently some village tailor of the Pyrenees made for him – the very short coat, the trousers tubed like cigarettes, his stiff shirt with the vast cuffs. He never wore a collar, nor a neckerchief. Always his back was flat as the side of a house.

When he worked at the anvil, with his young ruffian of a brother at the bellows, he sang. He had shakes and grace notes enough to make a thrush quit. Ann-Dolly translated one of his songs for us.

> *No tengo padre ni madre . . .*
> *Que desgraciado soy yo!*
> *Soy como el arbol solo*
> *Que echa frutas y no echa flor . . .*

'He sings he has no father or mother. How out of luck he is! He is like a lonely tree, which bears the fruit and not the flower.'

'God bless my soul, Kerry,' my uncle was shocked. 'The little man is homesick.'

'No, no!' Ann-Dolly protested. 'He is very happy. That is why he sings a sad song.'

One of the reasons of the little man's happiness was the discovery of our national game of handball. He strolled over to the Irish Village and discovered the court behind the Inniskillen Dragoon, that most notable of rural pubs. He was tremendously excited, and getting some gypsy to translate for him, challenged the local champion for the stake of a barrel of porter. He made the local champion look like a carthorse in the Grand National. When it was told to me I couldn't believe it. Ann-Dolly explained to me that the great game of Basque country was *pelota*.

'But don't they play *pelota* with a basket?'

'Real *pelota* is *à mains nues*, "with the hands naked." '

'You mean Irish handball,' I told her.

I regret that the population of Destiny made rather a good thing out of Don Frasco's prowess on the court, going from village to village, and betting on a certain win. The end was a match between Mick Tierney, the Portrush Jarvey and the jockey. The match was billed for the champion of Ulster, and Don Frasco was put down on the card, to explain his lack of English, as Danny Frask, the Glenties Miracle, the Glenties being a district of Donegal where Erse is the native speech. The match was poor, the Portrush Jarvey, after the first game, standing and watching the ball hiss past him with his eyes on his cheek bones. All Donegal seemed to have turned out for the fray. When the contest was over, a big Glenties man pushed his way toward the jockey.

'Dublin and London and New York are prime cities,' he chanted, 'but Glenties is truly magnificent. *Kir do lauv anshin, a railt na hooee,* "put your hand there, Star of the North".'

'*No entiendo, señor,*' said Don Frasco. And with that the fight began.

James Carabine was quick enough to get the jockey out of the court before he was lynched. But Destiny Bay men, gypsies, fishers, citizens of Derry, bookmakers and their clerks and the fighting tribes of Donegal went to it with a vengeance. Indeed, according to experts, nothing like it, for spirit or results, had been seen since or before the Prentice Boys had chased King James (whom God give his deserts!) from Derry Walls. The removal of the stunned and wounded from the courts drew the attention of the police, for the fight was continued in grim silence. But on the entrance of half a dozen peelers commanded by a huge sergeant, Joselito, the jockey's young brother, covered himself with glory. Leaping on the reserved seats, he brought his right hand over hard and true to the sergeant's jaw, and the sergeant was out for half an hour. Joselito was arrested, but the case was laughed out of court. The idea of a minuscule jockey who could ride at ninety pounds knocking out six-foot-three of Royal Irish Constabulary was too much. Nothing was found on him but his bare hands, a packet of cigarettes and thirty sovereigns he had won over the match. But I knew better. I decided to prove him with hard questions.

'Ask him in Romany, James Carabine, what he had wrapped around that horseshoe he threw away.'

'He says: "Tow, Mister Kerry." '

'Get me my riding crop,' I said; 'I'll take him behind the stables.' And the training camp lost its best lightweight jockey for ten days, the saddle suddenly becoming repulsive to him. I believe he slept on his face.

But the one who was really wild about the affair was Ann-Dolly. She came across from Spanish Men's Rest flaming with anger.

'Because a Spanish wins, there is fighting, there is anger. If an Irish wins, there is joy, there is drinking. Oh, shame of sportsmanship!'

'Oh, shut your gab, Ann-Dolly,' I told her. 'They didn't know he was a Spanish, as you call it.'

'What did they think he was if not a Spanish? Tell me. I demand it of you.'

'They thought he was Welsh.'

'Oh, in that case . . . ' said Ann-Dolly, completely mollified. *Ipsa Hibernis hiberniora!*

I wouldn't have you think that all was beer and skittles, as the English say, in training Romany Baw for the Derby. As spring came closer, the face of the old trainer showed signs of strain. The Lincoln Handicap was run and the Grand National passed, and suddenly flat-racing was on us. And now not the Kohinoor was watched more carefully than the Derby horse. We had a spanking trial on a course as nearly approaching the Two Thousand Guineas route as Destiny Downs would allow, and when Romany Baw flew past us, beating Ducks and Drakes who had picked him up at a mile for the uphill dash, and Sir Arthur clicked his watch, I saw his tense face relax.

'He ran well,' said the old man.

'He'll walk it,' said my uncle Valentine.

My uncle Valentine and Jenico and Ann-Dolly were going across to Newmarket Heath for the big race, but the spring of the year is the time that the farmer must stay by his land, and nurse it like a child. All farewells, even for a week, are sad, and I was loath to see the horses go into the races. Romany Baw had a regular summer bloom on him and his companion, the donkey, was corpulent as an alderman. Ducks and Drakes looked rough and backward, but that didn't matter.

'You've got the best-looking horse in the United Kingdom,' I told Sir Arthur.

'Thank you, Kerry,' the old man was pleased. 'And as to Ducks and Drakes, looks aren't everything.'

'Sure, I know that,' I told him.

'I wouldn't be rash,' he told me, 'but I'd have a little on both. That is, if they go to the post fit and well.'

I put in the days as well as I could, getting ready for the Spring Show at Dublin. But my heart and my thoughts were with my people and the horses at Newmarket. I could see my uncle Valentine's deep bow with his hat in his hand as they passed the Roman ditch at Newmarket, giving that squat wall the reverence that racing men have accorded it since races were run there, though why, none know. A letter from Ann-Dolly apprised me that the horses had made a good crossing and that Romany Baw was well – 'and you mustn't think, my dear, that your colt is not as much and more to us than the Derby horse, no, Kerry, not for one moment. Lady Clontarf is here, in her caravan, and oh, Kerry, she looks ill. Only her burning spirit keeps her frail body alive. Jenico and I are going down to Eastbourne to see the little Earl and his brother . . . You will get his letter, cousin, on the morning of the race. . . . '

At noon that day I could stand it no longer, so I had James Carabine put the trotter in the dogcar. 'There are some things I want in Derry,' I told myself, 'and I may as well get them to-day as to-morrow.' And we went spinning toward Derry Walls. Ducks and Drakes' race was the two-thirty. And after lunch I looked at reapers I might be wanting in July until the time of the race. I went along to the club, and had hardly entered it when I saw the boy putting up the telegram on the notice board:

1, *Ducks and Drakes*, an hundred to eight; 2, *Geneva*, four to six; 3, *Ally Sloper*, three to one.

'That's that!' I said. Another telegram gave the betting for the Two Thousand: Threes, *Sir James*; seven to two, *Toison d'Or*; eights, *Ca' Canny, Greek Singer, Germanicus*; tens, six or seven horses; twenty to one any other. No word in the betting of the gypsy horse, and I wondered had anything happened. Surely a horse looking as well as he did must have attracted backers' attention. And as I was worrying the result came in, *Romany Baw*, first; *Sir James*, second, *Toison d'Or*, third.

'Kerry,' somebody called.

'I haven't a minute,' I shouted. Neither I had, for James Carabine was outside, waiting to hear the result. When I told him he said: 'There's a lot due to you, Mister Kerry, in laying out those gallops.' 'Be damned to that!' I said, but I was pleased all the same.

I was on tenterhooks until I got the papers describing the race. Ducks and Drakes' win was dismissed, summarily, as that of an Irish outsider, and the jockey, Flory Cantillon (Frasco could not manage the weight), was credited with a clever win of two lengths. But the account of Romany Baw's race filled me with indignation.

According to it, the winner got away well, but the favourites weren't hampered at the start and either could have beaten the Irish trained horse, only that they just didn't. The race was won by half a length, a head separating second and third, and most of the account was given to how the favourites chased the lucky outsider, and in a few more strides would have caught him. There were a few dirty backhanders given at Romany's jockey, who, they said, would be more at home in a circus than on a modern race track. He sat like a rider of a century back, they described it, more like an exponent of the old manège than a modern jockey, and even while the others were thundering at his horse's hindquarters he never moved his seat or used his whip. The experts' judgment of the race was that the Irish colt was forward in a backward field, and that Romany would be lost on Epsom Downs, especially with its 'postilion rider'.

But the newspaper criticisms of the jockey and his mount did not seem to bother my uncle Valentine or the trainer or the jockey's self. They came back elated; even the round white donkey had a humorous happy look in his full Latin eye.

'Did he go well?' I asked.

'He trotted it,' said my uncle Valentine.

'But the accounts read, sir,' I protested, 'that the favourites would have caught him in another couple of strides.'

'Of course they would,' said my uncle Valentine, 'at the pace he was going,' he added.

'I see,' said I.

'You see nothing,' said my uncle Valentine. 'But if you had seen the race you might talk. The horse is a picture. It goes so sweetly that you wouldn't think it was going at all. And as for the gypsy jockey – '

'The papers say he's antiquated.'

'He's seven pounds better than Flory Cantillon,' said my uncle Valentine.

I whistled. Cantillon is our best Irish jockey, and his retaining fees are enormous, and justified. 'They said he was nearly caught napping – '

'Napping be damned!' exploded my uncle Valentine. 'This Spanish gypsy is the finest judge of pace I ever saw. He knew he had the race won, and he never bothered.'

'If the horse is as good as that, and you have as high an opinion of the rider, well, sir, I won a hatful over the Newmarket meeting, and as the price hasn't gone below twenties for the Derby, I'm going after the Ring. There's many a bookmaker will wish he'd stuck to his father's old-clothes business.'

'I wouldn't, Kerry,' said my uncle Valentine. 'I'm not sure I wouldn't hedge a bit of what I have on, if I were you.'

I was still with amazement.

'I saw Mifanwy Clontarf,' said my uncle Valentine, 'and only God and herself and myself and now you, know how ill that woman is.'

'But ill or not ill, she won't scratch the horse.'

'She won't,' said my uncle Valentine, and his emphasis on 'she' chilled me to the heart. 'You're forgetting, Kerry,' he said very quietly, 'the Derby Rule.'

Of the Derby itself on Epsom Downs, everybody knows. It is supposed to be the greatest test of a three-year-old in the world, though old William Day used to hold it was easy. The course may have been easy for Lord George Bentinck's famous and unbeaten mare Crucifix, when she won the Oaks in 1840, but most winners over the full course justify their victory in other races. The course starts up a heartbreaking hill, and swinging around the top, comes down again toward Tattenham Corner. If a horse waits to steady itself coming down it is beaten. The famous Fred Archer (whose tortured soul God rest!) used to take Tattenham Corner with one leg over the rails. The straight is uphill. A mile and a half of the trickiest, most heartbreaking ground in the world. Such is Epsom. Its turf has been consecrated by the hoofs of great horses since James I established there a race for the Silver Bell: by Cromwell's great Coffin mare; by the Arabs, Godolphin and Darby; by the great bay, Malton; by the prodigious Eclipse; by Diomed, son of Florizel, who went to America . . .

Over the Derby what sums are wagered no man knows. On it is won the Calcutta Sweepstake, a prize of which makes a man rich for life, and the Stock Exchange sweep and other sweeps innumerable. Someone has ventured the belief that on it annually are five million pounds sterling, and whether he is millions short or millions over none knows. Because betting is illegal.

There are curious customs in regard to it, as this: that when the result is sent over the ticker to clubs, in case of a dead heat, the word 'deat heat' must come first, because within recent years a trusted lawyer, wagering trust funds on a certain horse, was waiting by the tape to read the result, and seeing another horse's name come up, went away forthwith and blew his brains out. Had he been less volatile he would have seen his own fancy's name follow that, with 'dead heat' after it and been to this day rich and respected. So now, for the protection of such, 'dead heat' comes first. A dead heat in the Derby is as rare a thing as there is in the world, but still you can't be too cautious. But the quaintest rule of the Derby is this: that if the nominator of a horse for the Derby Stakes dies, his horse is automatically scratched. There is a legend to the effect that an heir-at-law purposed to kill the owner of an entry, and to run a prime favourite crookedly, and that on hearing this the Stewards of the Jockey Club made the rule. Perhaps it has a more prosaic reason. The Jockey club may have considered that when a man died, in the trouble of fixing his estates, forfeits would not be paid, and that it was best for all concerned to have the entry scratched. How it came about does not matter, it exists. Whether it is good in law is not certain. Racing folk will quarrel with His Majesty's Lord Justices of Appeal, with the Privy Council, but they will not quarrel with the Jockey Club. Whether it is good in fact is indisputable, for certain owners can tell stories of narrow escapes from racing gangs, in those old days before the Turf was cleaner than the Church, when attempts were made to nobble favourites, when jockeys had not the wings of angels under their silken jackets, when harsh words were spoken about trainers – very, very long ago. There it is, good or bad, the Derby Rule!

As to our bets on the race, they didn't matter. It was just bad luck. But to see the old lady's quarter million of pounds and more go down the pike was a tragedy. We had seen so much of shabby great names that I trembled for young Clontarf and his brother. Armenian and Greek families of doubtful antecedents were always on the lookout for a title for their daughters, and crooked businesses always needed directors of title to catch gulls, so much in the United Kingdom do the poor trust their peers. The boys would not be exactly poor, because the horse, whether or not it ran in the Derby, would be worth a good round sum. If it were as good as my uncle Valentine said, it would win the Leger and the Gold Cup at Ascot. But even with these triumphs it wouldn't be a Derby winner. And the Derby means so much. There are so many people in England who remember dates by the Derby winners' names, as 'I was married in *Bend Or's* year', or 'the *Achilles* was lost in the China seas, let me see when – that was in *Sainfoin's* year'. Also I wasn't sure that the Spanish gypsy would stay to ride him at Doncaster, or return for Ascot. I found him one day standing on the cliffs of Destiny and looking long at the sea, and I knew what that meant. And perhaps Romany Baw would not run for another jockey as he ran for him.

I could not think that Death could be so cruel as to come between us and triumph. In Destiny we have a friendliness for the Change which most folk dread. One of our songs says:

> *When Mother Death in her warm arms shall embrace me,*
> *Low lull me to sleep with sweet Erin-go-bragh –*

We look upon it as a kind friend who comes when one is tired and twisted with pain, and says: 'Listen, *avourneen*, soon the dawn will come, and the tide is on the ebb. We must be going.' And we trust him to take us, by a short road or a long road to a place of birds and bees, of which even lovely Destiny is but a clumsy seeming. He could not be such a poor sportsman as to come before the aged gallant lady had her last gamble. And poor Sir Arthur, who had come out of his old age in Mayo to win a Derby! It would break his heart. And the great horse, it would be so hard on him. Nothing will convince me that a thoroughbred does not know a great race when he runs one. The streaming competitors, the crackle of silk, the roar as they come into the straight, and the sense of the jockey calling on the great heart that the writer of Job knew so well. 'The glory of his nostril is terrible,' says the greatest of poets. 'He pauseth in the valley and rejoiceth in his strength: he goeth on to meet the armed men.' Your intellectual will claim that the thoroughbred is an artificial brainless animal evolved by men for their amusement. Your intellectual, here again, is a liar.

Spring came in blue and gold. Blue of sea and fields and trees; gold of sun and sand and buttercup. Blue of wild hyacinth and blue bell; gold of primrose and laburnum tree. The old gypsy lady was with her caravan near Bordeaux, and from the occasional letter my uncle Valentine got, and from the few words he dropped to me, she was just holding her own. May drowsed by with the cheeping of the little life in the hedgerows. The laburnum floated in a cloud of gold and each day Romany Baw grew stronger.

When his blankets were stripped from him he looked a mass of fighting muscle under a covering of satin, and his eye showed that his heart was fighting too. Old Sir Arthur looked at him a few days before we were to go to England, and he turned to me.

'Kerry,' he said, very quietly.

'Yes, Sir Arthur.'

'All my life I have been breeding and training horses, and it just goes to show,' he told me, 'the goodness of God that he let me handle this great horse before I died.'

The morning before we left my uncle Valentine received a letter which I could see moved him. He swore a little as he does when moved and stroked his vast red beard and looked fiercely at nothing at all.

'Is it bad news, sir?' I asked.

He didn't answer me directly. 'Lady Clontarf is coming to the Derby,' he told me.

Then it was my turn to swear a little. It seemed to me to be but little short of maniacal to risk a Channel crossing and the treacherous English climate in her stage of health. If she should die on the way or on the Downs, then all her planning and our work was for nothing. Why could she not have remained in the soft French air, husbanding her share of life until the event was past!

'She comes of ancient, violent blood,' thundered my uncle Valentine, 'and where should she be but present when her people or her horses go forth to battle?'

'You are right, sir,' I said.

The epithet of 'flaming' which the English apply to their June was in this year of grace well deserved. The rhododendrons were bursting into great fountains of scarlet, and near the swans the cygnets paddled, unbelievably small. The larks fluttered in the air above the Downs, singing so gallantly that when you heard the trill of the nightingale in the thicket giving his noontime song, you felt inclined to say: 'Be damned to that Italian bird; my money's on the wee fellow!' All through Surrey the green walls of spring rose high and thick, and then suddenly coming, as we came, through Leatherhead and topping the hill, in the distance the black colony of the downs showed like a thundercloud. At a quarter mile away, the clamour came to you, like the vibration when great bells have been struck.

The stands and enclosure were packed so thickly that one wondered how movement was possible, how people could enjoy themselves, close as herrings. My uncle Valentine had brought his beautiful harness ponies across from Ireland, 'to encourage English interest in the Irish horse' he explained it, but with his beautifully-cut clothes, his grey high hat, it seemed to me that more people looked at him as we spun along the road than looked at the horses. Behind us sat James Carabine, with his face brown as autumn and the gold rings in his thickened ears. We got out near the paddock and Carabine took the ribbons. My uncle Valentine said quietly to him: 'Find out how things are, James Carabine.' And I knew he was referring to the gypsy lady. Her caravan was somewhere on the Downs guarded by her gypsies, but my uncle had been there the first day of the meeting, and on Monday night, at the National Sporting, some of the gypsies had waited for him coming out and given him news. I asked him how she was, but all his answer was: 'It's in the hands of God.'

Along the track toward the grandstand we made our way. On the railings across the track the bookmakers were proclaiming their market: 'I'll give fives the field. I'll give nine to one bar two. I'll give twenty to one bar five. Outsiders! Fives *Sir James*. Seven to one *Toison d'Or*. Nines *Honey Bee*. Nines *Welsh Melody*. Ten to one the gypsy horse.'

'It runs all right,' said my uncle Valentine, 'up to now.'

'Twenty to one *Maureen Roe*: Twenties *Asclepiades*: Twenty-five *Rifle Ranger*. Here thirty-three to one *Rifle Ranger, Monk of Sussex,* or *Presumptuous* – '

'Gentlemen, I am here to plead with you not to back the favourite. In this small envelope you will find the number of the winner. For the contemptible sum of two shillings or half a dollar, you may amass a fortune. Who gave the winner of last year's Derby?' a tipster was calling. 'Who gave the winner of the Oaks? Who gave the winner of the Stewards' Cup?'

'All right, guv'nor, I'll bite. 'Oo the 'ell did?'

Opposite the grandstand the band of the Salvation Army was blaring the music of 'Work, for the Night is Coming'. Gypsy girls were going around *dukkering* or telling fortunes. 'Ah, gentleman, you've a lucky face. Cross the poor gypsy's hand with silver – '

'You better cut along and see your horse saddle,' said my uncle Valentine. Ducks and Drakes was in the Ranmore Plate and with the penalty he received after Newmarket, Frasco could ride him. As I went toward the paddock I saw the numbers go up, and I saw we were drawn third, which I think is best of all on the tricky Epsom five-furlong dash. I got there in time to see the gypsy swing into the saddle in the green silk jacket and orange cap, and Sir Arthur giving him his orders. 'Keep back of the Fusilier,' he pointed to the horse, 'and then come out. Hit him once if you have to, and no more.'

'*Sí, sí, Don Arturo!*' And he grinned at me.

'Kerry, read this,' said the old trainer, and he gave me a newspaper, 'and tell me before the race,' his voice was trembling a little, 'if there's truth in it.'

I pushed the paper into my pocket and went back to the box where my uncle Valentine and Jenico and Ann-Dolly were. 'What price my horse?' I asked in Tattersall's.

'Sixes, Mister MacFarlane.'

'I'll take six hundred to an hundred twice.' As I moved away there was a rush to back it. It tumbled in five minutes to five to two.

'And I thought I'd get tens,' I said to my uncle Valentine, 'with the Fusilier and Bonny Hortense in the race. I wonder who's been backing it.'

'I have,' said Ann-Dolly. 'I got twelves.'

'You might have the decency to wait until the owner gets on,' I said bitterly. And as I watched the tapes went up. It was a beautiful start. Everything except those on the outside seemed to have a chance as they raced for the rails. I could distinguish the green jacket but vaguely until they came to Tattenham Corner, when I could see Fusilier pull out, and Bonny Hortense follow. But behind Fusilier, racing quietly beside the filly, was the jacket green.

'I wish he'd go up,' I said.

'The favourite wins,' they were shouting. And a woman in the box next us began to clap her hands calling: 'Fusilier's won. Fusilier wins it!'

'You're a damn fool, woman,' said Ann-Dolly, 'Ducks and Drakes has it.' And as she spoke, I could see Frasco hunch forward slightly and dust his mount's neck with his whip. He crept past the hard-pressed Fusilier to win by half a length.

In my joy I nearly forgot the newspaper, and I glanced at it rapidly. My heart sank. 'Gypsy Owner Dying as Horse Runs in Derby,' I read, and reading down it I felt furious. Where the man got his information from I don't know, but he drew a picturesque account of the old gypsy lady on her death bed on the Downs as Romany Baw was waiting in his stall. The account was written the evening before, and 'it is improbable she will last the night', it ended. I gave it to my uncle Valentine, who had been strangely silent over my win.

'What shall I say to Sir Arthur Pollexfen?'

'Say she's ill, but it's all rot she's dying.'

I noticed as I went to the paddock a murmur among the race-goers. The attention of all had been drawn to the gypsy horse by its jockey having won the Ranmore Plate. Everywhere I heard questions being asked as to whether she were dead. Sir James had hardened to fours. And on the heath I heard a woman proffer a sovereign to a bookmaker on Romany Baw, and he said, 'That horse don't run, lady.' I forgot my own little triumph in the tragedy of the scratching of the great horse.

In the paddock Sir Arthur was standing watching the lads leading the horses around. Twenty-seven entries, glossy as silk, muscled like athletes of old Greece, ready to run for the Derby Stakes. The jockeys, with their hard wizened faces, stood talking to trainers and owners, saying nothing about the race, all already having been said, but just putting in the time until the order came to go to the gate. I moved across to the old Irish trainer and the gypsy jockey. Sir Arthur was saying nothing, but his hand trembled as he took a pinch of snuff from his old-fashioned silver horn. The gypsy jockey stood erect, with his overcoat over his silk. It was a heart-rending five minutes standing there beside them, waiting for the message that they were not to go.

My uncle Valentine was standing with a couple of the Stewards. A small race official was explaining something to them. They nodded him away. There was another minute's conversation and my uncle came toward us. The old trainer was fumbling pitifully with his silver snuff horn, trying to find the pocket in which to put it.

'It's queer,' said my uncle Valentine, 'but nobody seems to know where Lady Clontarf is. She's not in her caravan.'

'So – ' questioned the old trainer.

'So you run,' said my uncle Valentine. 'The horse comes under starter's orders. You may have an objection, Arthur, but you run.'

The old man put on youth and grandeur before my eyes. He stood erect. With an eye like an eagle's he looked around the paddock.

'Leg up, boy!' he snapped at Frasco.

'Here, give me your coat.' I helped throw the golden-and-red shirted figure into the saddle. Then the head lad led the horse out.

We moved down the track and into the stand, and the parade began. Lord Shire's great horse, and the French hope Toison d'Or; the brown colt owned by the richest merchant in the world, and the little horse owned by the Leicester butcher, who served in his own shop; the horse owned by the peer of last year's making; and the bay filly owned by the first baroness in England. They went down past the stand, and turning breezed off at a gallop back, to cross the Downs toward the starting gate, and as they went with each went someone's heart. All eyes seemed turned on the gypsy horse, with his rider erect as a Life Guardsman. As Frasco raised his whip to his cap in the direction of our box, I heard in one of the neighbouring boxes a man say: 'but that horse's owner is dead!'

'Is that so, uncle Valentine?' asked Ann-Dolly. There were tears in her eyes. 'Is that true?'

'Nothing is true until you see it yourself,' parried my uncle Valentine. And as she seemed to be about to cry openly – 'Don't you see the horse running?' he said. 'Don't you know the rule?' But his eyes were riveted through his glasses on the starting gate. I could see deep furrows of anxiety on his bronze brow. In the distance, over the crowd's heads, over the bookmakers' banners, over the tents, we could see the dancing horses at the tape, the gay colours of the riders moving here and there in an intricate pattern, the massed hundreds of black figures at the start. Near us, across the rails, some religious zealots let fly little balloons carrying banners reminding us that doom was waiting. Their band broke into a lugubrious hymn, while nasal voices took it up. In the silence of the crowded downs, breathless for the start, the religious demonstration seemed startlingly trivial. The line of horses, formed for the gate, broke, and wheeled. My uncle snapped his fingers in vexation.

'Why can't the fool get them away?'

Then out of a seeming inextricable maze, the line formed suddenly and advanced on the tapes. And the heavy silence exploded into a low roar like growling thunder. Each man shouted: 'They're off – ' The Derby had started.

It seemed like a river of satin, with iridescent foam, pouring, against all nature, uphill. And for one instant you could distinguish nothing. You looked to see if your horse had got away well, had not been kicked or cut into at the start, and as you were disentangling them, the banks of gorse shut them from your view, and when you saw them again they were racing for the turn of the hill. The erect figure of the jockey caught my eye before his colours did.

'He's lying fifth,' I told my uncle Valentine.

'He's running well,' my uncle remarked quietly.

They swung around the top of the hill, appearing above the rails and gorse, like something tremendously artificial, like some theatrical illusion, as of a boat going across the stage. There were three horses grouped together, then a black horse – Esterhazy's fine colt – then Romany Baw, then after that a stretching line of horses. Something came out of the pack at the top of the hill, and passed the gypsy horse and the fourth.

'Toison d'Or is going up,' Jenico told me.

But the gallant French colt's bolt was flown. He fell back, and now one of the leaders dropped back. And Romany was fourth as they started downhill for Tattenham Corner. 'How slow they go!' I thought.

'What a pace!' said Jenico, who had his watch in his hand.

At Tattenham Corner the butcher's lovely little horse was beaten, and a sort of moan came from the rails where the poor people stood. Above the religious band's outrageous nasal tones, the ring began roaring: 'Sir James! Sir James has it. Twenty to one bar Sir James!'

As they came flying up the stretch I could see the favourite going along, like some bird flying low, his jockey hunched like an ape on his withers. Beside him raced an outsider, a French-bred horse owned by Kazoutlian, an Armenian banker. Close to his heels came the gypsy horse on the inside, Frasco sitting as though the horse were standing still. Before him raced the favourite and the rank outsider.

'It's all over,' I said. 'He can't get through. And he can't pull round. Luck of the game!'

And then the rider on the Armenian's horse tried his last effort. He brought his whip high in the air. My uncle Valentine thundered a great oath.

'Look, Kerry!' His fingers gripped my shoulder.

I knew, when I saw the French horse throw his head up, that he was going to swerve at the whip, but I never expected Frasco's mad rush. He seemed to jump the opening, and land the horse past Sir James.

'The favourite's beat!' went up the cry of dismay.

Romany Baw, with Frasco forward on his neck, passed the winning post first by a clear length.

Then a sort of stunned silence fell on the Derby crowd. Nobody knew what would happen. If, as the rumour went around, the owner was dead, then the second automatically won. All eyes were on the horse as the trainer led him into the paddock, followed by second and third. All eyes turned from the horse toward the notice board as the numbers went up: 17, 1, 26. All folk were waiting for the red objection signal. The owner of the second led his horse in, the burly Yorkshire peer. An old gnarled man, with a face like a walnut, Kazoutlian's self, led in the third.

'I say, Kerry,' Jenico called quietly, 'something's up near the paddock.'

I turned and noticed a milling mob down the course on our right. The mounted policeman set off at a trot toward the commotion. Then cheering went into the air like a peal of bells.

Down the course came all the gypsies, all the gypsies in the world, it seemed to me. Big-striding, black men with gold earrings and coloured neckerchiefs, and staves in their hands. And gypsy women, a-jingle with coins, dancing. Their tambourines jangled, as they danced forward in a strange East Indian rhythm. There was a loud order barked by the police officer, and the men stood by to let them pass. And the stolid English police began cheering too. It seemed to me that even the little trees of the Downs were cheering, and in an instant I cheered too.

For behind an escort of mounted gypsies, big foreign men with moustaches, saddleless on their shaggy mounts, came a gypsy cart with its cover down, drawn by four prancing horses. A wild-looking gypsy man was holding the reins. On the cart, for all to see, seated in a great armchair, propped up by cushions, was Lady Clontarf. Her head was laid back on a pillow, and her eyes were closed, as if the strain of appearing had been too much for her. Her little maid was crouched at her feet.

For an instant we saw her, and noticed the aged beauty of her face, noticed the peace like twilight on it. There was an order from a big Roumanian gypsy and the Romany people made a lane. The driver stood up on his perch and manoeuvring his long snakelike whip in the air, made it crack like a musket. The horses broke into a gallop, and the gypsy cart went over the turfed course toward Tattenham Corner, passed it, and went up the hill and disappeared over the Surrey downs. All the world was cheering.

'Come in here,' said my uncle Valentine, and he took me into the cool beauty of our little church of Saint Columba's in Paganry. 'Now what do you think of that?' And he pointed out a brass tablet on the wall.

'In Memory of Mifanwy, Countess of Clontarf and Kincora,' I read. Then came the dates of her birth and death, 'and who is buried after the Romany manner, no man knows where.' And then came the strange text, 'In death she was not divided.'

'But surely,' I objected, 'the quotation is: "In death they were not divided." '

'It may be,' said my uncle Valentine, 'or it may not be. But as the living of Saint Columba's in Paganry is in my gift, surely to God!' he broke out, 'a man can have a text the way he wants it in his own Church.'

This was arguable, but something more serious caught my eye.

'See, sir,' I said, 'the date of her death is wrong. She died on the evening of Derby Day, June the second. And here it is given as June the first.'

'She did not die on the evening of Derby Day. She died on the First.'

'Then,' I said, 'when she rode down the course on her gypsy cart,' and a little chill came over me, 'she was – '

'As a herring, Kerry, as a gutted herring,' my uncle Valentine said.

'Then the rule was really infringed, and the horse should not have won.'

'Wasn't he the best horse there?'

'Undoubtedly, sir, but as to the betting?'

'The bookmakers lost less than they would have lost on the favourite.'

'But the backers of the favourite.'

'The small backer in the silver ring is paid on the first past the post, so they'd have lost, anyway. At any rate, they all should have lost. They backed their opinion as to which was the best horse, and it wasn't.'

'But damn it all, sir! and God forgive me for swearing in this holy place – there's the Derby Rule.'

' "The letter killeth," Kerry,' quoted my uncle gravely, even piously. ' "The letter killeth." '

# PULLINSTOWN

## *Molly Keane*

I T was Sir Richard who asked me to stay at Pullinstown for the
Springwell Harriers' point-to-point meeting. That his children
had nothing to do with the invitation was evident from the
very politeness of their greetings – greetings which they concluded
as swiftly as the conventions permitted, leaving me to the conver-
sational mercies of their father. But he, after a question as to how
my journey had prospered with me, and a comment on the rival
unpunctuality of trains and boats, sank his haggard (and once
splendid) shoulders into the back of his chair, and, setting his old-
fashioned steel pince-nez all askew on his nose, devoted himself to
the day's paper in a manner that brooked of no interruptions on
less trivial matters. Since my cousins (in a second and third degree)
made no demands on my attention, I looked about me and main-
tained what I hoped was a becoming silence.

The hall where we were sitting was lovely. Whoever designed
this old Irish house had certainly a peculiar sense of the satisfying
fitness of curving walls, of ceiling mouldings continuously beautiful, while the graceful proportioning of a distant stairway drew
the eyes down the length of the oval room and upwards to the
light coming in kindly dusty radiance through a great window on
the stairs. Sheraton had made the hooped table on which lay a
medley of hunting-whips, ash-plant switches, gloves, two silver
hunting-horns, and a vast number of dusty letters and unopened
papers. Through the doors of a glass-fronted cupboard (his work
too), I could see reels and lines, glimpses of wool and bright
feathers for fly-tying, with bottles of pink prawns, silver eels' tails
and golden sprats, all lures for the kingly salmon. There were
pictures on the walls, not many, but Raeburn must have painted
that lady in the dress like a luminous white cloud. She looked out

of her picture with foxy eyes very like those of the silent little cousin who was now reading a discarded sheet of her father's newspaper with inherited concentration. The gentleman in the bright blue coat might have been Sir Richard in fancy dress, but he was a Sir Richard who had died fighting for King James at the battle of the Boyne. This they told me afterwards.

Still my cousins, Willow and Dick, sat saying never a word. Sir Richard sniffed a little, deprecatingly, as he read the paper, and Willow, the light slanting over her, appeared absorbed in her sheet. She was like her own name to look at, Willow, pale as a peeled sally wand, hair and all, and green flickering eyes. Her brother Dick was an arrogant and beautiful sixteen. I disliked the pair of them heartily.

A door opened, breaking the spell of quiet, and a wheezing and decrepit old butler came in to arrange a tea-table in the window.

'Is that the evening paper you have, Miss Willow? Excuse me, Did Silver-Tip win in Mallow?'

'He did not. The weight beat him.' Miss Willow did not lift her eyes during her brief reply, nor when she added, 'Run up to the Post Office, James, after your tea, and buy me fifty Gold Flake. Only I have a little job to do for the Sir, I'd go myself.'

'And what about James?' inquired the old butler with restrained acerbity. 'Haven't he one hundred and one little jobs to do for the Sir? God is my witness, Miss Willow, the feet is bet up under me this living minyute, and how I'll last out the length o' dinner in the boots is unknown to me, leave alone to travel the roads after thim nasty trash o' cigarettes. Thim's only poison to you, child, believe you me.'

'It's a pity about poor James.' Willow addressed her brother. 'I suppose the boots wouldn't carry him as far as the river to catch a salmon in the Tinker's stream to-night. Who stole my claret hackles, I wonder?' This last with sudden vicious intensity.

'An' who whipped six pullets' eggs out o' me pantry to go feed her ould racehorse,' James countered nimbly, 'that poor Molly Byrne had gothered for the Sir – '

'If Molly Byrne had as much as six eggs in the day from those hens, she'd run mad from this to Ballybui telling it out the two sides of the road.

'Are you ready for your tea, Sir Richard?' She whirled round suddenly on her father, 'James, show Mr Oliver his room.'

So I was sufficiently one of the family, I reflected, as I followed James's shuffling footsteps up the stairs, to be Mr Oliver – it was rather pleasing. James peered at me, blinking in the afternoon sun that flooded the bedroom to which he led me.

'The maker's name is on the blade,' he announced with dramatic suddenness. 'Ye'r the dead spit and image of the father. God, why wouldn't I know ye out of him? Wasn't he rared on the place along with the Sir? He was, 'faith. Sure meself was hall-boy under ould Dinny Mahon those times. Your poor Da could remember me well – many a good fish I struck the gaff in for him the days I'd cod ould Dinny and slip away down to him on the river. Didn't he send me a silk out of India and red feathers ye couldn't beat to tie in a fiery fly – may Almighty God grant him to see the light o' the glory of heaven – he was a good sort.'

I was glad some one remembered my father. He had told me so much and so often of his early days there with those Irish cousins that I had come to Pullinstown with a feeling of intimacy for the place and for my cousins which the very politeness of their first greeting to me had dispelled as strangely as the silence that followed it. James left me with a restored right to my pleasant intimacies.

My room was a large one. A vast bed with twisted fluted bedposts, ruthlessly cut down, took up most of one wall – the furnishing otherwise was sparse. A cupboard was full of my cousin Willow's summer clothes, while a large, coffin-like receptacle contained what looked like her mother's or grandmother's. There remained a yellow-painted chest of drawers. I opened the top drawer, which was empty, but as it obstinately refused to close again, I could only hope that the other three were empty too.

The view from the two tall windows held me longer even than my struggle with the chest of drawers. I looked down across garden beds, their disorder saved from depression by the army of daffodils that flung gold regiments alike over the beds and through the grass that divided them, out across a park-like field where five young horses and a donkey moved soberly, and a grey shield of water held the quiet evening light, over the best of a fair hunting country to the far secrecy of the mountains. And looking, I envied my father those wild young days of his fox-hunting and fishing, shooting snipe, and skylarking with those Irish cousins here in Westcommon.

They had waited tea for me, I found to my embarrassment, and with an incoherent apology for my delay, I sat down beside Willow. She bestirred herself to be polite.

'The Sir – er – father was telling us you are an artist,' she said, with less interest if with more dislike than she might have displayed had father told her I was a Mormon. 'Well, I would like to be able to paint pictures,' she continued, studiously avoiding the eye of her brother directed meaningly at her from across the table, a jeer in his silence.

'You would, I'm sure,' said he suddenly.

'I would,' his sister flashed round on him. 'I'd paint a picture of you falling off Good-Day over the last fence in Cooladine last week.'

'I did not fall off her – the mare stood on her head and well you know it.'

'And small wonder for her – the way you had the head pulled off her going into every fence. Dick's an awful coward – isn't that right, Sir Richard?'

'I wouldn't mind him being a coward if he wasn't a fool as well.' Sir Richard eyed his heir sternly. 'When did I give you permission to enter the mare in the open race to-morrow?' he demanded.

Dick blushed. 'I was waiting to ask you. May I?'

'You may not. The mare will go in the Ladies' Race, and Willow can ride her.'

'Oh, father – ' Young Dick's blush sank deeper in his skin. 'I did *not* fall off her.' On the point of tears he was.

'I'll ride my own horse in the Ladies' Race or I'll not ride at all.' Willow's small silvery face expressed more acute determinaton than I have often seen. 'If I can't beat those Leinster girls on Romance, I'll not beat them on that rotten brute Good-Day. You know right well she'll run out with me. Dick's the only one can get any good of her, and well you know it, Sir Richard.'

'I'd sooner put an old woman up to ride the mare than that nasty little officer.' Sir Richard tapped the table forbiddingly with a lump of sugar before dropping it into his teacup.

'Well, *I'll* not ride her,' said Willow. She pushed back her chair, lit a cigarette, and walked out into the bright tangled garden. After a minute Dick followed her, and two sour-looking little terriers of indeterminate breed followed him without fuss. He would show them sport, I thought, watching the light swing of his shoulders in the seedy old tweed coat. It was as stern a business to him as to them.

Sir Richard looked out after his retreating family. 'That's a right good boy,' he said, with sudden almost impersonal approval, 'and b'Gad – a terror to ride. Why wouldn't he? He's bred the right way, though I say it myself. But he'll never be as good as Willow. She's a divil.'

Compared to the terror and the devil of his begetting, I felt that I must appear but a poor specimen to my cousin. However, he suffered my interest in an incomplete series of old coaching prints with kindly tolerance, and showed me a Queen Anne chair, a Sèvres cup, and some blue glass bottles with quickening interest. 'I forget about these things,' he complained; 'the children don't care for them, you see; it's all the horses with them. Come out and have a look at the skins – would you care to?'

We followed a greened path round one of the long, grey wings that flanked on each side the square block of the house, and turning the corner came to the high stone archway leading into the stable-yard. In the dusk of the archway young Dick and Willow stood, fair, like two slight swords in that dark place.

'Father,' said they, 'Tom Kenny is here with a horse.'

'Well, I have no time to waste looking at the horses Tom Kenny peddles around the country. What sort is it?'

'Oh, a common brute,' said Willow, with indifferent decision. 'The man only came over to see you about the fox covert in Lyran.'

'Well, if you say it's a common brute, there's some hope of seeing a bit of bone and substance about the horse. If *you* don't like him, he may be worth looking at.' Sir Richard advanced into the yard, and I, following him, caught just the edge of the perfectly colourless wink that passed between his son and daughter. The match of their guile being now well and truly laid to the desired train, they proceeded carelessly on their way. A minute later the two terriers, a guilty pig-bucket look about them, hurried out of the yard in pursuit.

Inside the archway I paused. I love stables and horses and grooms, the cheerful sound of buckets, the heady smell of straw, the orderly fussiness of a saddle-room; always the same and ever different. The mind halts, feeling its way into gear with a new brave set of values at the moment when one sets foot within a stable-yard.

The stables at Pullinstown had been built for a larger stud than lodged there now. More than a few doors were fastened up, but there was still a stir and movement about some of the boxes. A lean old hunter's head looked quietly out across the half-door of his box, hollows of age above his eyes, the stamp of quality and bravery on him unmistakably. Next door the shrill voice of the very young complained against this new unknown discipline – the sweat of the breaking tackle still black on an untrimmed neck. A bright bay three-year-old this was, full of quality, and would be up to fourteen stone before he was done with. Such a set of limbs on him too. Bone there you'd be hard to span. 'That's the sort,' said Sir Richard, nodding at him. 'Ah, if I was twenty years younger I'd give myself a present of that horse. Go back to your stable, I'd say; I'll never sell you. Good-Day and Romance are over there. I sold a couple of horses last week. Now listen – I *hate* to sell a horse that suits the children; but they must go – make room for more – this place is rotten with horses. Well, Tom' – he craned round to a small dark man who appeared quietly from the black mouth of the saddle-room door – 'did you get that furze stubbed out of the hill yet?'

'B'God I did, sir. Now look-at, the torment I got on the hill of Lyran there's no man will believe. I'm destroyed workin' in it. A pairson wouldn't get their health with them old furzy pricks in their body as thick as pins in a bottle. And then to say five pounds is all the hunt should give me for me trouble! I'm a poor man, Sir Richard, and a long backwards family to rare, and a delicate dying brother on the place.'

'Did Doctor Murphy give you a bottle for him?' Sir Richard interrupted the recital. 'I told him he should go see poor Dan last week.'

'Ah, he did, he did, sir. Sure, then the bottle the doctor left played puck with him altogether, though indeed the doctor is a nice quiet man, and he had to busht out crying when he clapped an eye on poor Dan. He was near an hour there with him, going hither and over on his body with a yoke he had stuck in his two ears. Indeed he was very nice, and Dan was greatly improved in himself after he going. Faith, he slapped into the bottle o' medicine, and he'd take a sup now and a sup again till – be the holy, I'll not lie to ye, sir – whatever was in the bottle was going through him in standing leps. I thought he'd die,' Tom Kenny concluded with a pleasant laugh.

'Did he take the dose the doctor ordered?' Sir Richard's long knotted fingers were crossed before him on the handle of his walking stick. His head was bent in grave attention to the tale. What, I wondered, of Tom Kenny's horse? And what, again, of his brother?

'Is it what poor Doctor Murphy told him?' A pitying smile appeared for a moment on Tom Kenny's face. 'Well, I'll always give it in to the doctor, he's dam nice, but sure a child itself'd nearly know what good would one two teaspoons do wandering the inside through of a great big wilderness of a man the like o' poor Danny. Sure he drank down what was in the bottle, o' course, and that was little enough for the money, God knows.'

'Ah, psha!' Impossible to describe the mixture of anger and hopeless tolerance in Sir Richard's exclamation. 'Well' – he lifted his head, stabbing at the ground with the point of his walking-stick – 'I suppose it's to pay funeral expenses you're trying to sell the horse.'

'Now God is my witness, Sir Richard, if I was to get the half o' what this young horse is worth, it'd be more money than poor Danny'll ever see at his funeral or any other time in his life.'

'Ah, have done chatting and pull out the horse till I see what sort he is.' Sir Richard bent to the match in his cupped hands.

Following on this, Tom Kenny retired into a distant loose-box, from which there issued presently sounds of an encouraging nature, in voices so varied as to suggest that a large proportion of the male staff of Pullinstown had assembled in the box.

'Stand over, Willy. Mind out would he split ye!'

'Go on out you, Tom, before him.'

'Sure every horse ye'll see rared a pet is wayward always.'

'Well, now isn't he the make and shape of a horse should have a dash o' speed?'

'Is it them Grefelda horses? Did ye ever see one yet wasn't as slow as a man?'

'Well, he's very pettish, Tom. What way will we entice him?'

'*Hit him a belt o' the stick!*' came with sudden thunder from across the yard where Sir Richard still stood. Whether or not his advice was acted upon, a moment later the Grefelda horse shot like a rocket out of the stable door, his owner hazardously attached to his head by a single rein of a snaffle bridle.

'Woa – boy – woa the little horse.' Tom Kenny led him forward, nagging him to a becoming stance with every circumstance of pompous ownership.

I am a poor enough judge of a horse in the rough, but this one seemed to me to have the right outline. There was here a valuable alliance of quality and substance, and as he was walked away and back to us, a length of stride promising that he should gallop.

'That'll do,' said Sir Richard, after a prolonged, sphinx-like inspection. 'I'm sorry to see he plucks that hock, Tom; only for that he's not a bad sort at all. Turn him around again. Ah, a pity!'

'May God forgive yer honour,' was Tom Kenny's pious retort; 'ye might make a peg-top o' this horse before ye'd see the sign of a string-halt on him. Isn't that right, Pheelan?' He appealed to a small man with a wry neck and a surprising jackdaw blue eye, who had stood by throughout the affair in a deprecating silence, unshaken even by this appeal.

'What height is he? Sixteen hands?' Sir Richard stood in to the horse.

'Sixteen one, as God is my judge,' corrected the owner. 'Well, now,' he compromised, as Sir Richard remained unshaken, 'look – he's within the black o' yer nail of it.'

Even this distance I judged, after a glance at Tom Kenny's outstretched thumb, would leave him no more than a strong sixteen. However that might be, I more than liked the horse, and so I rather suspected did Sir Richard, the more when I saw him shake his head and turn a regretful back to the affair.

'Sir Richard' – Tom Kenny's head shot forward tortoise-like from his coat collar – 'look-at – eighty pounds is my price – eighty pounds in two nutshells.'

'Well, Tom,' Sir Richard smiled benignantly, 'I'm always ready to help a friend, as you know.' He paused, his head bent again in thought. 'Now if I was to ride the horse, and that is to say if I *like* the horse, I wouldn't say I mightn't give you sixty-five pounds for him,' came with sudden generous resolve.

'May God forgive you, sir.' Tom Kenny turned from the impious suggestion with scarcely concealed horror. Tears loomed in his voice as he continued in rapt encomium, 'Don't ye know yerself ye might do the rounds o' the world before ye'd meet a horse the like o' that! This horse'll sow and he'll plough and he'll sweep the harvest in off o' the fields for ye. Look at!' (with sudden drama). 'If ye were to bring this horse home with ye to-day, ye mightn't have a stick o' harvest left standing to-morra night. And he'll be a divil below a binder.'

'Faith, true for you, Tom Kenny. That one's very lonely for the plough,' Pheelan of the jackdaw eyes struck in with irresistible sarcasm. 'Sure, it's for Master Dick to hunt him the Sir'll buy him.'

Without a change of expression, Tom Kenny tacked into the wind again. 'Well, ye'd tire three men galloping this horse, and there's not a ditch in the globe of Ireland where ye'd fall him,' said he with entire and beautiful conviction.

'Ah, have done. Get up on him, you, Pheelan, and see would you like him.' Sir Richard spoke with brief decision.

Following on this the prospective purchase was ridden and galloped into a white lather by Pheelan, whose hissed 'Buy him, sir he's a *topper!*' I overheard as Sir Richard prepared to mount, and having done so, whacked the now most meek and biddable horse solemnly round the yard with his walking-stick, before he changed hands for the sum of sixty-eight pounds, a yearling heifer, and thirty shillings back for 'luck.'

'And damned expensive, too,' said my cousin as, the deal concluded, we pursued our way onwards to look at the young horses; 'only I *hate* bargaining and talking I'd have bought him twice as cheap. . . . Isn't that a great view? You should paint that. I would if I was an artist.'

We had walked up a hilly lane-way, splitting a flock of sheep driven by a young lad as we went. The river lay low on our right hand now. Everywhere the gorse shone like sweet gold money, and primroses spread pale lavish flames. The whole air was full of a smoky gold light. It lay low against the rose of the ploughed fields. It was weighted with the scent of the gorse. The young horses were splendidly bathed in light. They grouped themselves nobly against the hillside before they swung away from us, with streaming manes and tails, to crest the hill like a wave, and thunder away into the evening. Nor, though we stayed there an hour, could we get near them again. My cousin, at last exasperated, led me back to the house and dinner.

'Don't change,' he said as we parted; so only his own round

skull-cap of bruised purple velvet lent ceremony to the occasion of my first dinner at Pullinstown. Willow had not changed, and Dick came up from the river just as we sat down, Willow's hair was as pale as wood ashes in the candle-light, and her infrequent, shadowy voice oddly pleasing. Still she did not talk to me, but held stubborn argument with James as to the date on which the salmon we were eating had last swum in the river. Dick talked to her. He had risen a fish twice on a strange local fly called a 'goat's claret.' They both addressed their father as 'Sir Richard' in ceremonious voices, and he talked to me about my father and the fun they had together, James, as he ministered punctiliously to our needs, occasionally supplying the vital point of a half-remembered anecdote or forgotten name.

After dinner we played bridge, the army of cards falling and whispering quietly between us of our black and red skirmishes, adventures and defeats. Sir Richard and I were three shillings down on the rubber when Willow put the old painted packs of cards back in their pale ivory fort and went out with Dick to plait her mare's mane for the race to-morrow.

'Why in God's name did you not do it by daylight, child?' her father complained.

'Because Pheelan locked the stable door on me. He thinks no one but himself can plait up a mane.'

'And he's right too, I dare say.' Sir Richard contemplated his daughter with serene approval.

'I was ashamed of my life the way he had her mane in Coolad-ine.' Willow was sorting reels of thick, linen thread. 'Will you come, Dick?' she said.

'And the reason why I play cards so well' – Dick rose to his feet, sliding my three shillings up and down his trouser pocket – 'is because I can use my brains to think out problems.' He was not boasting, merely voicing his private ruminations.

'Good-night, Sir Richard,' they both said. '*Good*-night,' they said to me with extreme politeness, and went out together.

Soon after this we went up to bed, Sir Richard and I, armed each with shining silver candlestick like an evening star, and I sat for a while smoking a cigarette, leaning out of my window to the hushed bosom of the night. I saw a star caught in the flat water more silver than the moon. A white owl slanted by and was gone, low among the trees, and the sound of a fiddle jigging out some hesitant tune picked sweetly at the stillness.

'Play "The wind that shakes the barley," ' a voice prompted the fiddler. 'That's not it – it's the "Snowy-breasted Pearl" yer in on now.'

'Jig it for me, you.'

'God, I wouldn't be able to jig it. There's the one turn on the whole o' them tunes – 'twouldn't be easy to know them – '

I was sorry when the fiddling ceased, but when there drifted on the air a tale astir with every principle of drama, I forgot even that I was eavesdropping, and strained against the night to hear. . . . 'Well, it was a long, lonely lane and two gates on it; that'll give ye an idea how long it was – ' Followed a period of sibilant murmuring, and then a sudden protest: 'Ah, go on! It's all very well to be talkin' how ye's box this one and box that one – if a fella lepped out on ye, what'd ye do?'

It was at this interesting moment that a window above my own shot open, and the irate voice of James ordered Lizzie Doyle and Mary Josey to their respective beds.

'Begone now!' he commanded, and with Biblical directions told the garden what he thought of a domestic staff that sat all day with their elbows up on the kitchen table drinking tea, and spent the nights trapseing the countryside.

'Oh, Jesus, Mary and Joseph! Isn't that frightful?' I heard amid the scuffle of retreat, and then, as though in submission to the moods of fate: 'Well, the ways o' God are something fierce.' In the succeeding silence I too betook myself to bed.

The morning was unbelievably young when I woke to the faint squawk and flapping of birds on the water below. A heron in a Scotch fir-tree was pencil-etched against the grey sky. In the very early mornings churches and bridges too have the air of nearly forgotten stories; but never did romance so hinge itself to possibility for me as now when, like two sentinels of the morning's quietness, I saw Willow and Dick ride out of the stable arch and walk their horses away from sight into the slowly silvering morning. The breathless picture they made is with me still – both sitting a little carefully, perhaps, with saddles still cold on their horses' backs. And you could hardly have told, but for the square-cut pale hair of one, which of them was Willow and which was Dick.

Bright and unkind the two blood-horses looked in the grey light, and their riders forlorn in the gallantry of the very young passed on to face who knows what horrors of schooling in cold blood at that deathly hour.

At breakfast they were touched with the unimpeachable import-ance of those who rise up early to accomplish dangerous matters while others are still in bed. I found them less romantic. Willow ate some strange cereal with lavish cream. 'Good for the body,' she said in reply to her father's comment. 'Have some yourself. Will you have some?' she added to me.

There was a patch of mud on the shoulder of Dick's tweed coat, and Sir Richard scolded and grumbled all through the meal at the rottenness of those who face young horses into impossible fences. Dick made neither defence nor answer. Occasionally he stuck a finger between his neck and the spotted handkerchief he wore round it, loosening its folds abstractedly. He ate an apple and one piece of dry toast very slowly, and just before he lit a cigarette he said, 'There's no one can ride that mare, only myself. She's a queer-tempered divil, but when Cherry'd be good' – there was almost a croon in his voice – '*then* I'd give her an apple.' Where-upon he went out of the room, shutting the door behind him, and Willow, who was feeding the dogs, said:

'That was an awful toss he took. I thought he was quinched. Ah – he was only winded. What time do you want to start for the races, father? You should bring the lunch in your car. Dick and I have to go on early to walk the course.'

Clearly I perceived that I was included under the heading lunch as their father's passenger. I saw them leave the house at about eleven, James following them to pack a suitcase, a medly of saddles, a weight cloth, a handful of boot pulleys and jockeys, a mackintosh coat, a cutting-whip and a spare horse-sheet into the crazy brass-bound Ford car which waited pompously beneath the great, granite-pillared porch.

'Good-bye, now.' He fastened the last button of the side curtains as the Ford started on its way with that unearthly hiccup common to its species.

'Mind!' – Willow put her head out of the car – 'see and squeeze the cherry brandy out of the Sir for lunch.'

James returned to the hall at a busy if rather dickey trot. 'Merci-ful God!' – he halted in horror – 'if they didn't leave the little safety-hat after them.' He surveyed a black silk-covered crash-helmet with dismay. 'Ah, well, it'll only have to follow on with ourselves and the lunch.'

This was my first intimation that James was to be of the party. Had I known the ways of Pullinstown more intimately it would never have occurred to me that any expedition could be undertaken without his presence. But never can I forget my first sight of him an hour later in his race-going attire. He wore a rather steeple-crowned bowler hat, green with age, and a very long box-cloth overcoat with strongly stitched shoulder patches and smartly cut pocket flaps. It was a coat, indeed, that could only have been worn with complete success by the most famous of England's sporting peers. From his breast pocket peeped a pair of minute mother-of-pearl opera glasses (no doubt removed from one of the glass-topped tables in the drawing-room), and round his neck, tied with perfect symmetry, was a white flannel stock, polka dotted with red.

'James has to sit in front with me.' Sir Richard, more than usually haggard and untidy, slid himself crabbedly behind the wheel of the big Bentley, cursing his sciatica in a brief aside. 'He always remembers where the self-starter is. I never can find it. It's a cursed nuisance to me in race traffic. What's that, James?' He pointed to a small fish-basket which James was stowing away in the back.

'There's a change o' feet for Miss Willow, Sir Richard. There's no way ye'll soak the cold only out o' wet boots, and ye couldn't tell but they'd slip the child into a river or a wet ditch, or maybe she'd be lying quinched under the mare in a boggy place. Sure – '

'Ah, get into the car, ye old fool, and stop talking. Maybe it's a coffin you should have brought with you, let alone the boots. Have we all now?'

'We have, Sir Richard.' James laid the crash-helmet on top of the lunch basket and stepped in beside his master.

By what seemed only a series of surprising accidents, Sir Richard fought his noisy way into top gear, and determined to stay in at all costs, took risks with ass carts and other hazards of the twisty roads which appalled me. What, I wondered, would be our progress though the race traffic, if indeed we ever came so near the course? We had left the wide demesne fields of Pullinstown behind us now, and the country on either hand was more enclosed. Banks

I saw, tall single ones, and wondered if they raced over these in Ireland; big stone facers too, solid and kind, plenty of room on them; and an occasional loose-built stone wall – no two consecutive fences quite alike and not a strand of wire to be seen. The going was mostly grass, though here and there a field of plough showed up rawly, white gulls stooping and wheeling above it, dim like sawn-out pearl in the grey soft air; and always the mountains, ringing the country like a precious cup.

'That's a great bog for snipe,' Sir Richard would say. 'That's a right snug bit of covert.' or 'That's the best pool on the river,' pointing to a secret turn of water low under distant woods. 'I killed a thirty-pound salmon there – on a "Mystery," it was. Two hours I had him on before James got a chance to gaff him. Ah, he was a tiger! God! I took a right fall over that fence one time. No, but the high devil with the stones in it. Wasn't his father out that day, James? He was, of course. Tell him I showed you the place King Spider nearly killed me. He'll remember – dear me, I'm forgetting he's dead – poor Harry! Is this the turn now, James? To the right?'

'Wheel left, Sir Richard, wheel left,' James corrected easily; and wheel left we did, but with such surprising velocity that the heavy car skidded and spun about in the road, pointing at last in the direction from which he had come.

'Oh, fie, Sir Richard!' James, quite unmoved, reached out a respectable black-trousered leg towards the self-starter. 'Do you not know the smallest puck in the world is able to do the hell of a job on that steering? If the like o' that should happen us in strong race traffic, we were three dead men.'

The race traffic, of which I had heard a good deal, did not become apparent till we were within the last couple of miles from our destination, when indeed the narrow lane that led up to the car park was congested enough. Old and young, the countryside attended the races. Mothers of infants who could not by any stretching of possibilities be left a day long without sustenance, avoided the difficulty by taking their progeny along with them; and the same held good, I imagined, in the case of those old men who, had they remained at home, would certainly have fallen into the fire or otherwise injured themselves during the absence of the race-goers. Ford cars conveyed parties of eight or more. Pony carts, ass carts, and bicycles did their share, while a fair sprinkling

of expensive cars had to regulate their pace by that of the slowest
ass cart that preceded them in the queue. A shawled and handsome
fury, selling race-cards, jumped on the step of our car during a
momentary stoppage of the traffic; her tawny head blazed raggedly
in the sunlight.

'Race-card – a shillin' the race-card,' she bawled hideously. She
carried a baby on her arm. I saw the outline of its round head
beneath the heavy shawl, but, quite unimpeded by its burden, she
leaped like a young goat from the step of our car to attack the
next in the line.

'Easy, Sir Richard! Mind the cycle now! Stop, sir! They want
the five bob for the car now. Wheel west for the gate. Cross out
over the furzy bushes. Slip in there now; that's Miss Willow's car.'
So piloted by James we came at last to a standstill.

From the top of the little hill where the cars were parked, we
could see below us the weighing tent and paddock (a few horses
already stood there in their sheets), the bookies establishing themselves in their stand (we were in good time; they had not begun
to bet on the first race yet), and at the foot of the hill the railing
run in to the finish; while out in the country here and there the
eye picked up the lonely flutter of a little white flag.

'Leave Red Flags on the Right and White Flags on the Left,' I
read on my race-card below 'Conditions of the Meeting.' And
then:

'First Race, 1.30.
Hunt Race: A sweepstake for horses, the property of members
of the Springwell Hunt.'

Then the Sporting Farmers' Open Race, and

'Third Race: Open Race – of £30, of which the second receives
£5.
1. Major O'Donnel's Wayward Gipsy (black, yellow cap).
2. Mr Devereux's ch. geld, Bright Love.
3. Sir Richard Pulleyn's br. mare Good-Day, aged (blue, black
cap).'

Six more runners were down to go for that race, but I turned
the card over and read: 'Ladies' Race. Open. For a cup.' And Miss
Pulleyn's Romance heading the list.

'Romance'll win it,' Sir Richard prophesied bleakly, 'But there's a lot of good horses against the boy. Have you me glasses, James? Have you me stick? Right. Come on now till we see the horses saddled for this first race. We'll have lunch then, James.'

Down the hill towards the saddling enclosure we went, almost fighting our way between groups of gossiping country women, stalls of oranges and bananas, roulette boards, and exponents of the three-card trick.

'Clancy's horse'll win it, you'll see,' I heard.

'See now – he's like nothin' only a horse ye'd see on paper; he's like a horse was painted.'

'What about Amber Girl?' interpolated a rival's supporter.

'Well, what about her? Now look-at, I seen this horse win a race in Ballyowen. Well, he was four length from the post and four horses in front of him, and the minute Clancy stirred on him he come through the lot to win be two lengths. Clancy made a matter o' ninety pound about it. Ah! he never let him run idle.'

'Well, what about Amber Girl?' reiterated Amber Girl's supporter.

What indeed, I wondered; how would she run against a horse that could accomplish so spectacular a finish after three miles over a country? But I was never to hear. A section of the crowd melting at that moment, we pushed on towards the paddock, and here, lost in joint disapproving contemplation of the six starters waiting to be saddled for their race, we found Willow and Dick. They were as quiet as two fish in a pool, but I felt all the same that very little in that busy ring escaped their devastating attention.

'Is Pheelan here with the horses yet?' Sir Richard asked them.

'He wasn't here five minutes ago. Did you not pass him on the road?' Willow looked worried. 'I hope he didn't go round by Mary Pheelan's pub,' she said to Dick, as they went out of the ring to look for him. And really, for Pheelan's sake, I found myself hoping that he had not. Nor had he. But his subsequent discovery, blamelessly sheltering with the horses behind a gorse-crowned bank of primroses, wrung from Willow a sufficiently stinging reprimand.

Because of the search for Pheelan we missed most of the first race, and I failed to accomplish my nearest ambition, which was to see a bank jumped at really close quarters. Through my glasses I could see the distant horses flip on and off their fences with the deceptive ease that distance lends to the most strenuous effort, and the last fences before the finish were two that did not take a lot of doing. A disappointing race from the spectator's point of view: won in a distance. Three finished.

We ate our lunch after this. That is, Sir Richard and I ate sandwiches, and Willow and Dick watched us with the avid importance of jockeys.

Dick studied the field for his race: 'The only horse I'm afraid of is that Bright Love – that's a Punchestown horse.'

'Ah, it'll fall,' from Willow, easily.

She read bits from the race-card. 'Patrick Byrne's Sissy – that's a great pattern of a cob. Purplish waistcoat and white shirt sleeves. Could he not say he was wearing the top half of his Sunday suit?'

'Doris is going to ride her own mare in the Ladies' Race. You'll have to mind yourself, Willow.'

'I rode against Doris in Duffcarry, father. I had right sport with her. Sure she was nearly crying with fright down at the start. "Go slow into the last fence, girls," I said, "*whatever* you do – that's a murderous brute of a place." I was only teasing them about it, but didn't Doris and Susan pull into a trot very nearly. Ah, that was where I slipped on a bit and they never caught me. A bad fence? – not it – the sort you'd get up in the night to jump.'

'You know, Dick,' she said, 'I hate the way they jump that narrow one – right on the turn.'

'Oh, there's nothing in it.'

We were watching the second race. They did not eat, but sat on their shooting-sticks and drank a thimbleful of black coffee each.

'I'll have a good drink with you after my race, Dick,' Willow said. They dived into their Ford car, throwing out a suitcase and a weight cloth. James followed them down the hillside.

In the ring Willow held Good-Day, while Pheelan fussed and chided about her saddling. She was a little bit of a mare, Good-Day – a bright blood bay, all quality. The single rein of her plain snaffle was turned over her head. She looked to be fairly fit, and I guessed would take some beating. I said so to Sir Richard.

'Ah, a right mare if she was half ridden.' Dick just caught the answer. I saw the tips of his ears go scarlet against the black cap that Willow was tying on his head. The wind blew cold through his jersey. It looked as though it must whistle through his body too, so fine drawn he was and so desperately keen. Pheelan gave him a leg up. As he sat, feeling the length of his stirrups, Good-Day turned her head round, nipping the air funnily.

'She'll be good to-day,' Dick said, 'you'll see,' picking up his rubber-laced rein.

James came sidling up to say behind his hand, 'Master Dick, keep east the fence before the wood – there's a paling gone out of it. Ye may gallop through. Mickey Doyle bid me tell you.'

Dick smiled a little wintry smile and nodded.

They were out of the ring now, Pheelan leading the mare down through the crowd.

'Stop on the hill, father,' said Willow; 'James and I are going down out in the country.'

'Go down, you,' Sir Richard said to me; 'you'd be more use than old James.' I thought he looked distinctly shaky and just a thought grim as he walked slowly back to the car.

James and Willow and I took a short-cut down to the start. We jumped three formidable banks, pulling James after us, before we reached the place of vantage Willow had in her mind's eye.

Now we could see the field lined up for a start below us – eight horses in it – Dick and the little mare seemed so far away from any hope but each other. Willow was straining her eyes on them. A false start, and all to do over again. They were off. Hardly room to steady a horse before the first fence, and Dick did not even try to do so. They were up – they were over. Certainly Good-day wasted no time over her fences. A rough piece of moorland and every one taking a pull. The horses turned away from us to drop into a laneway. Then we saw them over two more fences. Good-Day leading still – a raking chestnut striding along second; then the bay mare Wayward Gipsy and six more all in a bunch. Two horses fell at the fourth fence, a little puff of dust rising from the bank as they hit it. One jockey remounted, and the other lay where he had fallen, his horse galloping on. Willow did not even put her glasses on him. She was aware of nothing but Dick and Good-Day.

'The mare beat Bright Love over her fences,' she said, 'but he'll gallop away from her, James, if he stands up. He jumped that badly. Steady now, Dick, take a pull on her, this is a divil. He's over. Now we lose them. Come on, boys; we'll slip across to this big fence and see them come home.'

Over a field we ran, Willow just beating me, James a very bad third, to take up our stand beside a high, narrow bank with a ditch on the landing side. Not a choice obstacle for a tired horse. And three fences from home they'd be racing too. 'Oh, a filthy spot,' said Willow.

A little knot of country boys gathered round her. 'Eh, Miss Pulleyns, can ye see the horses? Eh, Miss Pulleyns, did they cross out the big ditch yet? Look-at, look-at! Mr Pulleyns is down.'

'Almighty Lord God! Should the horse have fallen with him?' queried an emotional lady friend.

'No, but he fell from the horse beyond the wood.'

'Oh! Oh! Is he hurted?'

'Hurt! He's killed surely. Isn't the head burst!'

Knowing that my glasses could not hope to equal the hawk-like vision of my informants, I said nothing, but focused them on a point beyond the plantation and waited for the horses to appear. When they did, Dick and Good-day were, as I had indeed supposed, still among them – lying third now, with the big chestnut Bright Love in the lead and Wayward Gipsy second, but I thought she was pretty well done with.

'He'll not catch the chestnut now,' Willow said. 'He's let him get too far in front of him. Wait now – this fence takes some doing. THEY'RE DOWN!' she said. 'Ah, Dick wins now. Wayward Gipsy's beat.'

'Come on, Master Dick,' James piped, hopping from foot to foot in his excitement, his opera glasses clapped on the horses. 'More power, Master Dick – he have the mare cot! 'Tis only a ride home now.'

Two more fences and Good-Day was galloping down to the bank where we stood, Wayward Gipsy half a field behind her; Bright Love, remounted, a bad third; and the rest nowhere.

'Steady, Dick, now.' The boy was burning with the effort of his race. The sour little mare had jumped everything right; nothing could go wrong with them now. He may have let her go on at it a bit faster than he need have done (I am no judge of pace in riding over banks). I only know she failed to get right on top, and came off that tall fence end over end in as unpleasant a looking crash as I hope I may never see again. It shakes one.

Young Dick lay hunched quietly where he had fallen, but the mare was up in a flash. It was I who caught her, and James who threw me into the saddle just as Wayward Gipsy jumped the fence beside us.

Never shall I forget the horror of that ride in. How I sat in Dick's five-pound saddle, the flaps wrinkling back from under my knees and the off stirrup gone in the fall, I shall never know – for one who fancies himself not a little over fences I must, across the two first very moderate banks I jumped in Ireland, have presented a sorry enough spectacle. Had there been an inch more left in Wayward Gipsy we were beaten. As it was, the judge just gave it to Good-Day – a short head on the post.

I weighed in all right. I knew I must ride nearly a stone above Dick's weight (a bit of a penalty for the little mare to carry home after such a shattering fall), and as I walked out of the tent I met Willow coming in to weigh out for her race.

'That was pretty quick of you,' she said to me. 'I'd never have got the weight. Oh, Dick's all right – only shaken and badly winded. The Sir's running mad round the place looking for you.'

Dick was saddling Willow's horse when I next saw him, and too busy to spare any time for me. She was late: three other horses had gone down to the start.

'Now, Doris,' Willow called to a pretty girl who looked excited and nervous as a cat as she was put up by a firmly adoring young man, 'all fences on this course to be jumped at a slow pace. I'm very shook indeed, with my only brother nearly quinched before my eyes.'

The girl laughed; she was all nerves, though I dare say a tigress when she got going. 'Stay with me down to the post, Willow. I'll be kicked off for certain.'

'Very dangerous work this, girls!' Willow laughed, pulling up her leathers. 'Now, Dick, I'm right.' She caught my eye as she rode out of the ring and gave me a small friendly nod as I wished her good luck.

'Go down to the old spot,' she said, 'and I *hope* I won't need you as much as Dick did.'

Nor did she. From the same view-point as before, Dick and James and myself watched the flash of Willow's blue shirt as she led round that course at a wicked pace. . . .

'Wait till Sir Richard sees her,' Dick murmured; 'he'll not leave a feather on her body, and the reason is she's making every post a winning post.'

A hot class of horses and the fastest run race of the day. Romance jumped the fence where we stood in perfect style – on and off – clever as a dog, never dwelling an instant, and galloped home to win in a distance.

Dick saw the last lady over without mishap before we turned to follow James back to the hill.

'Look!' said he suddenly, stooping to the ditch to pick up a half-buried stirrup-iron and leather. He turned it over. 'It's me own.' He looked at me, an expression almost of friendliness dawning in his face. 'And you in trousers,' he murmured.

We found Willow at the car, where her father was measuring her out a niggardly drink and expressing his unstinted disapproval of her method of winning a race, while James alternately begged her to put on her coat and eat a sandwich. Failing in both objects, he presented her with a small comb and glass, and bade her tease out her hair, for it was greatly tossed with the race.

'Ah, don't annoy me, James,' Willow finished her drink, stuck her arms into the leather coat he held out for her, clapped a beret on her surprising hair, and said to her father, 'I'll drive Dick and Oliver home. Major Barry wants you to take him. Come on, boys, till we gather up our winnings.'

Later, as the Ford rocked and bumped its way out of the field, and I sat, shaken to the core, in the back seat with a horse-sheet over my knees and one of Willow's gold-flake cigarettes in my mouth, Dick turned round to say –

'And the reason why I think you should stop on for Punchestown is because that's a meeting you should really enjoy.'

'That's right,' Willow agreed.

And, strange as it may seem, I gloried to know the accolade of their acceptance mine.

# OCCASIONAL LICENCES

## *E. Œ. Somerville & Martin Ross*

'I T's out of the question,' I said, looking forbiddingly at Mrs Moloney through the spokes of the bicycle that I was pumping up outside the grocer's in Skebawn.

'Well, indeed, Major Yeates,' said Mrs Moloney, advancing excitedly, and placing on the nickel plating a hand that I had good and recent cause to know was warm, 'sure I know well that if th' angel Gabriel came down from heaven for a licence for the races, your honour wouldn't give it to him without a charackther, but as for Michael! Sure, the world knows what Michael is!'

I had been waiting for Philippa for already nearly half-an-hour, and my temper was not at its best.

'Character or no character, Mrs Moloney,' said I with asperity, 'the magistrates have settled to give no occasional licences, and if Michael were as sober as – '

'Is it sober! God help us!' exclaimed Mrs Moloney with an upward rolling of her eye to the Recording Angel; 'I'll tell your honour the truth. I'm his wife, now, fifteen years, and I never seen the sign of dhrink on Michael only once, and that was when he went out o' good-nature helping Timsy Ryan to whitewash his house, and Timsy and himself had a couple o' pots o' porther, and look, he was as little used to it that his head go light, and he walked away out to dhrive in the cows and it no more than eleven o'clock in the day! And the cows, the craytures, as much surprised, goin' hither and over the four corners of the road from him! Faith, ye'd have to laugh. "Michael," says I to him, "ye're dhrunk!" "I am," says he, and the tears rained from his eyes. I turned the cows from him. "Go home" I says, "and lie down on Willy Tom's bed – " '

At this affecting point my wife came out of the grocer's with a

large parcel to be strapped to my handlebar, and the history of Mr
Moloney's solitary lapse from sobriety got no further than Willy
Tom's bed.

'You see,' I said to Philippa, as we bicycled quietly home
through the hot June afternoon, 'we've settled we'll give no licences
for the sports. Why even young Sheehy, who owns three pubs in
Skebawn, came to me and said he hoped the magistrates would
be firm about it, as these one-day licences were quite unnecessary,
and only led to drunkenness and fighting, and every man on the
Bench has joined in promising not to grant any.'

'How nice, dear!' said Philippa absently. 'Do you know Mrs
McDonnell can only let me have three dozen cups and saucers; I
wonder if that will be enough?'

'Do you mean to say you expect three dozen people?' said I.

'Oh, it's always well to be prepared,' replied my wife evasively.

During the next few days I realised the true inwardness of what
it was to be prepared for an entertainment of this kind. Games
were not at a high level in my district. Football of a wild, guerilla
species, was waged intermittently, blended in some inextricable
way with Home Rule and a brass band, and on Sundays gatherings
of young men rolled a heavy round stone along the roads, a
rudimentary form of sport, whose fascination lay primarily in the
fact that it was illegal, and, in lesser degree, in betting on the
length of each roll. I had had a period of enthusiasm, during
which I thought I was going to be the apostle of cricket in the
neighbourhood, but my mission dwindled to single wicket with
Peter Cadogan, who was indulgent but bored, and I swiped the
ball through the dining-room window, and someone took one of
the stumps to poke the laundry fire. Once a year, however, on
that festival of the Roman Catholic Church which is familiarly
known as 'Pether and Paul's day,' the district was wont to make
a spasmodic effort at athletic sports, which were duly patronised
by the gentry and promoted by the publicans, and this year the
honour of a steward's green rosette was conferred upon me. Philippa's genuis for hospitality here saw its chance, and broke forth
into unbridled tea-party in connection with the sports, even involving me in the hire of a tent, the conveyance of chairs and tables,
and other large operations.

It chanced that Flurry Knox had on this occasion lent the fields
for the sports, with the proviso that horse-races and a tug-of-war

were to be added to the usual programme; Flurry's participation in events of this kind seldom failed to be of an inflaming character. As he and I planted larch spars for the high jump, and stuck furze-bushes into hurdles (locally known as 'hurrls'), and skirmished hourly with people who wanted to sell drink on the course, I thought that my next summer leave would singularly coincide with the festival consecrated to St Peter and St Paul. We made a grandstand of quite four feet high, out of old fish-boxes, which smelt worse and worse as the day wore on, but was, none the less, as sought after by those for whom it was not intended, as is the Royal enclosure at Ascot; we broke gaps in all the fences to allow carriages on to the ground, we armed a gang of the worst black-guards in Skebawn with cart-whips, to keep the course, and felt the organisation could go no farther.

The momentous day of Pether and Paul opened badly, with heavy clouds and every indication of rain, but after a few thunder showers things brightened, and it seemed within the bounds of possibility that the weather might hold up. When I got down to the course on the day of the sports the first thing I saw was a tent of that peculiar filthy grey that usually enshrines the sale of porter, with an array of barrels in a crate beside it; I bore down upon it in all the indignant majesty of the law, and in so doing came upon Flurry Knox, who was engaged in flogging boys off the Grand Stand.

'Sheehy's gone one better than you!' he said, without taking any trouble to conceal the fact that he was amused.

'Sheehy!' I said; 'why, Sheehy was the man who went to every magistrate in the country to ask them to refuse a licence for the sports.'

'Yes, he took some trouble to prevent anyone else having a look in,' replied Flurry; 'he asked every magistrate but one, and that was the one that gave him the licence.'

'You don't mean to say that it was you?' I demanded in high wrath and suspicion, remembering that Sheehy bred horses, and that my friend Mr Knox was a person of infinite resource in the matter of a deal.

'Well, well,' said Flurry, rearranging a disordered fish-box, 'and me that's a churchwarden, and sprained my ankle a month ago with running downstairs at my grandmother's to be in time for prayers! Where's the use of a good character in this country?'

'Not much when you keep it eating its head off for want of exercise,' I retorted; 'but if it wasn't you, who was it?'

'Do you remember old Moriarty out at Castle Ire?'

I remembered him extremely well as one of those representatives of the people with whom a paternal Government had leavened the effete ranks of the Irish magistracy.

'Well,' resumed Flurry, 'that licence was as good as a five-pound note in his pocket.'

I permitted myself a comment on Mr Moriarty suitable to the occasion.

'Oh, that's nothing,' said Flurry easily; 'he told me one day when he was half screwed that his Commission of the Peace was worth a hundred and fifty a year to him in turkeys and whisky, and he was telling the truth for once.'

At this point Flurry's eye wandered, and following its direction I saw Lady Knox's smart 'bus cleaving its way through the throng of country people, lurching over the ups and downs of the field like a ship in a sea. I was too blind to make out the component parts of the white froth that crowned it on top, and seethed forth from it when it had taken up a position near the tent in which Philippa was even now propping the legs of the tea-table, but from the fact that Flurry addressed himself to the door, I argued that Miss Sally had gone inside.

Lady Knox's manner had something more than its usual bleakness. She had brought, as she promised, a large contingent, but from the way that the strangers within her gates melted impalpably and left me to deal with her single-handed, I drew the further deduction that all was not well.

'Did you ever in your life see such a gang of women as I have brought with me?' she began with her wonted directness, as I piloted her to the Grand Stand, and placed her on the stoutest looking of the fish-boxes. 'I have no patience with men who yacht! Bernard Shute has gone off to the Clyde, and I had counted on his being a man at my dance next week. I suppose you'll tell me you're going away too.'

I assured Lady Knox that I would be a man to the best of my ability.

'This is the last dance I shall give,' went on her ladyship, unappeased; 'the men in this country consist of children and cads.'

I admitted that we were a poor lot, 'but,' I said, 'Miss Sally told me – '

'Sally's a fool!' said Lady Knox, with a falcon eye at her daughter, who happened to be talking to her distant kinsman, Mr Flurry of that ilk.

The races had by this time begun with a competition known as the 'Hop, Step, and Lep'; this, judging by the yells, was a highly interesting display, but as it was conducted between two impervious rows of onlookers, the aristocracy on the fish-boxes saw nothing save the occasional purple face of a competitor, starting into view above the wall of backs like a jack-in-the-box. For me, however, the odorous sanctuary of the fish-boxes was not to be. I left it guarded by Slipper with a cart-whip of flail-like dimensions, as disreputable an object as could be seen out of low comedy, with someone's old white cords on his bandy legs, butcher-boots three sizes too big for him, and a black eye. The small boys fled before him; in the glory of his office he would have flailed his own mother off the fish-boxes had occasion served.

I had an afternoon of decidedly mixed enjoyment. My stewardship blossomed forth like Aaron's rod, and added to itself the duties of starter, handicapper, general referee, and chucker-out, besides which I from time to time strove with emissaries who came from Philippa with messages about water and kettles. Flurry and I had to deal single-handed with the foot-races (our brothers in office being otherwise engaged at Mr Sheehy's), a task of many difficulties, chiefest being that the spectators all swept forward at the word 'Go!' and ran the race with the competitors, yelling curses, blessings, and advice upon them, taking short cuts over anything and everybody, and mingling inextricably with the finish. By fervent applications of the whips, the course was to some extent purged for the quarter-mile, and it would, I believe, have been a triumph of handicapping had not an unforeseen disaster overtaken the favourite – old Mrs Knox's bath-chair boy. Whether, as was alleged, his braces had or had not been tampered with by a rival was a matter that the referee had subsequently to deal with in the thick of a free fight; but the painful fact remained that in the course of the first lap what were described as 'his galluses' abruptly severed their connection with the garments for whose safety they were responsible, and the favourite was obliged to seek seclusion in the crowd.

The tug-of-war followed close on the *contretemps*, and had the excellent effect of drawing away, like a blister, the inflammation set up by the grievances of the bath-chair boy. I cannot at this moment remember of how many men each team consisted; my sole aim was to keep the numbers even, and to baffle the volunteers who, in an ecstasy of sympathy, attached themselves to the tail of the rope at moments when their champions weakened. The rival forces dug their heels in and tugged, in an uproar that drew forth the innermost line of customers from Mr Sheehy's porter tent, and even attracted 'the quality' from the haven of the fish-boxes, Slipper, in the capacity of Squire of Dames, pioneering Lady Knox through the crowd with the cart-whip, and with language whose nature was providentially veiled, for the most part, by the din. The tug-of-war continued unabated. One team was getting the worst of it, but hung doggedly on, sinking lower and lower till they gradually sat down; nothing short of the trump of judgment could have conveyed to them that they were breaking rules, and both teams settled down by slow degrees on to their sides, with the rope under them, and their heels still planted in the ground, bringing about complete deadlock. I do not know the record duration for a tug-of-war, but I can certify that the Cullinagh and Knockranny teams lay on the ground at full tension for half-an-hour, like men in apoplectic fits, each man with his respective adherents howling over him, blessing him, and adjuring him to continue.

With my own nauseated eyes I saw a bearded countryman, obviously one of Mr Sheehy's best customers, fling himself on his knees beside one of the combatants, and kiss his crimson and streaming face in a rapture of encouragement. As he shoved unsteadily past me on his return journey to Mr Sheehy's, I heard him informing a friend that 'he cried a handful over Danny Mulloy, when he seen the poor brave boy so shtubborn, and, indeed, he couldn't say why he cried.'

'For good-nature ye'd cry,' suggested the friend.

'Well, just that, I suppose,' returned Danny Mulloy's admirer resignedly; 'indeed, if it was only two cocks ye seen fightin' on the road, yer heart'd take part with one o' them!'

I had begun to realise that I might as well abandon the tug-of-war and occupy myself elsewhere, when my wife's much harassed messenger brought me the portentous tidings that Mrs Yeates wanted me at the tent at once. When I arrived I found the tent literally bulging with Philippa's guests; Lady Knox, seated on a hamper, was taking off her gloves, and loudly announcing her desire for tea, and Philippa, with a flushed face and a crooked hat, breathed into my ear the awful news that both the cream and the milk had been forgotten.

'But Flurry Knox says he can get me some,' she went on; 'he's gone to send people to milk a cow that lives near here. Go out and see if he's coming.'

I went out and found, in the first instance, Mrs Cadogan, who greeted me with the prayer that the divil might roast Julia McCarthy, that legged it away to the races like a wild goose, and left the cream afther her on the servants' hall table. 'Sure, Misther Flurry's gone looking for a cow, and what cow would there be in a backwards place like this? And look at me shtriving to keep the kettle simpering on the fire, and not as much coals undher it as'd redden a pipe!'

'Where's Mr Knox?' I asked.

'Himself and Slipper's galloping the counthry like the deer. I believe it's to the house above they went, sir.'

I followed up a rocky hill to the house above, and there found Flurry and Slipper engaged in the patriarchal task of driving two brace of coupled and spancelled goats into a shed.

'It's the best we can do,' said Flurry briefly; 'there isn't a cow to be found, and the people are all down at the sports. Be d – d to you, Slipper, don't let them go from you!' as the goats charged and doubled like football players.

'But goats' milk!' I said, paralysed by horrible memories of what tea used to taste like at Gib.

'They'll never know it!' said Flurry, cornering a venerable nanny; 'here, hold this divil, and hold her tight!'

I have no time to dwell upon the pastoral scene that followed. Suffice it to say, that at the end of ten minutes of scorching profanity from Slipper, and incessant warfare with the goats, the latter had reluctantly yielded two small jugfulls, and the dairymaids had exhibited a nerve and skill in their trade that won my lasting respect.

'I knew I could trust *you*, Mr Knox!' said Philippa, with shining eyes, as we presented her with the two foaming beakers. I suppose a man is never a hero to his wife, but if she could have realised the bruises on my legs, I think she would have reserved a blessing for me also.

What was thought of the goats' milk I gathered symptomatically from a certain fixity of expression that accompanied the first sip of the tea, and from observing that comparatively few ventured on second cups. I also noted that after a brief conversation with Flurry, Miss Sally poured hers secretly on to the grass. Lady Knox had throughout the day preserved an aspect so threatening that no change was perceptible in her demeanour. In the throng of hungry guests I did not for some time notice that Mr Knox had withdrawn until something in Miss Sally's eye summoned me to her, and she told me she had a message from him for me.

'Couldn't we come outside?' she said.

Outside the tent, within less than six yards of her mother, Miss Sally confided to me a scheme that made my hair stand on end. Summarised, it amounted to this: That, first, she was in the primary stage of a deal with Sheehy for a four-year-old chestnut colt, for which Sheehy was asking double its value on the assumption that it had no rival in the country; that, secondly, they had just heard it was going to run in the first race; and, thirdly and lastly, that as there was no other horse available, Flurry was going to take old Sultan out of the 'bus and ride him in the race; and that Mrs Yeates had promised to keep mamma safe in the tent, while the race was going on, and 'you know, Major Yeates, it would be delightful to beat Sheehy after his getting the better of you all about the licence!'

With this base appeal to my professional feelings, Miss Knox paused, and looked at me insinuatingly. Her eyes were greeny-grey, and very beguiling.

'Come on,' she said; 'they want you to start them!'

Pursued by visions of the just wrath of Lady Knox, I weakly followed Miss Sally to the farther end of the second field, from which point the race was to start. The course was not a serious one: two or three natural banks, a stone wall, and a couple of 'hurrls.' There were but four riders, including Flurry, who was seated composedly on Sultan, smoking a cigarette and talking confidentially to Slipper. Sultan, although something stricken in years and touched in the wind, was a brown horse who in his day had been a hunter of no mean repute; even now he occasionally carried Lady Knox in a sedate and gentlemanly manner, but it struck me that it was trying him rather high to take him from the pole of the 'bus after twelve miles on a hilly road, and hustle him over a country against a four-year-old. My acutest anxiety, however, was to start the race as quickly as possible, and to get back to the tent in time to establish an *alibi*; therefore I repressed my private sentiments, and, tying my handkerchief to a stick, determined that no time should be fashionably frittered away in false starts.

They got away somehow; I believe Sheehy's colt was facing the wrong way at the moment when I dropped the flag, but a friend turned him with a stick, and, with a cordial and timely whack, speeded him on his way on sufficiently level terms, and then somehow, instead of returning to the tent, I found myself with Miss Sally on the top of a tall narrow bank, in a precarious line of other spectators, with whom we toppled and swayed, and, in moments of acuter emotion, held on to each other in unaffected comradeship.

Flurry started well, and from our commanding position we could see him methodically riding at the first fence at a smart hunting canter, closely attended by James Canty's brother on a young black mare, and by an unknown youth on a big white horse. The hope of Sheehy's stable, a leggy chestnut, ridden by a cadet of the house of Sheehy, went away from the friend's stick like a rocket, and had already refused the first bank twice before old Sultan decorously changed feet on it and dropped down into the next field with tranquil precision. The white horse scrambled over it on his stomach, but landed safely, despite the fact that his rider clasped him round the neck during the process; the black mare and the chestnut shouldered one another over at the hole the white horse had left, and the whole party went away in a bunch and jumped the ensuing hurdle without disaster. Flurry continued to ride at the same steady hunting pace, accompanied respectfully by the white horse and by Jerry Canty on the black mare. Sheehy's colt had clearly the legs of the party, and did some showy galloping between the jumps, but as he refused to face the banks without a lead, the end of the first round found the field still a sociable party personally conducted by Mr Knox.

'That's a dam nice horse,' said one of my hangers-on, looking approvingly at Sultan as he passed us at the beginning of the second round, making a good deal of noise but apparently going at his

ease; 'you might depind your life on him, and he have the crabbed-
est jock in the globe of Ireland on him this minute.'

'Canty's mare's very sour,' said another; 'look at her now, baulk-
ing the bank! she's as cross as a bag of weasels.'

'Begob, I wouldn't say but she's a little sign lame,' resumed the
first; 'she was going light on one leg on the road a while ago.'

'I tell you what it is,' said Miss Sally, very seriously, in my ear,
'that chestnut of Sheehy's is settling down. I'm afraid he'll gallop
away from Sultan at the finish, and the wall won't stop him.
Flurry can't get another inch out of Sultan. He's riding him well,'
she ended in a critical voice, which yet was not quite like her own.
Perhaps I should not have noticed it but for the fact that the hand
that held my arm was trembling. As for me, I thought of Lady
Knox, and trembled too.

There now remained but one bank, the trampled remnant of the
furze hurdle, and the stone wall. The pace was beginning to
improve, and the other horses drew away from Sultan; they
charged the bank at full gallop, the black mare and the chestnut
flying it perilously, with a windmill flourish of legs and arms from
their riders, the white horse racing up to it with a gallantry that
deserted him at the critical moment, with the result that his rider
turned a somersault over his head and landed, amidst the roars of
the onlookers, sitting on the fence facing his horse's nose. With
creditable presence of mind he remained on the bank, towed the
horse over, scrambled on to his back again and started afresh.
Sultan, thirty yards to the bad, pounded doggedly on, and Flurry's
cane and heels remained idle; the old horse, obviously blown,
slowed cautiously coming in at the jump. Sally's grip tightened on
my arm, and the crowd yelled as Sultan, answering to a hint from
the spurs and a touch at his mouth, heaved himself on to the bank.
Nothing but sheer riding on Flurry's part got him safe off it, and
saved him from the consequences of a bad peck on landing; none
the less, he pulled himself together and went away down the hill
for the stone wall as stoutly as ever. The high-road skirted the last
two fields, and there was a gate in the roadside fence beside the
place where the stone wall met it at right angles. I had noticed
this gate, because during the first round Slipper had been sitting
on it, demonstrating with his usual fervour. Sheehy's colt was
leading, with his nose in the air, his rider's hands going like a

circular saw, and his temper, as a bystander remarked, 'up on end'; the black mare, half mad from spurring, was going hard at his heels, completely out of hand; the white horse was steering steadily for the wrong side of the flag, and Flurry, by dint of cutting corners and of saving every yard of ground, was close enough to keep his antagonists' heads over their shoulders, while their right arms rose and fell in unceasing flagellation.

'There'll be a smash when they come to the wall! If one falls they'll all go!' panted Sally. '! – Now! Flurry! Flurry! – '

What had happened was that the chestnut colt had suddenly perceived that the gate at right angles to the wall was standing wide open, and, swinging away from the jump, he had bolted headlong out on to the road, and along it at top speed for his home. After him fled Canty's black mare, and with her, carried away by the spirit of stampede, went the white horse.

Flurry stood up in his stirrups and gave a view-halloa as he cantered down to the wall. Sultan came at it with the send of the hill behind him, and jumped it with a skill that intensified, if that were possible, the volume of laughter and yells around us. By the time the black mare and the white horse had returned and ignominiously bundled over the wall to finish as best they might, Flurry was leading Sultan towards us.

'That blackguard, Slipper!' he said, grinning; 'every one'll say I told him to open the gate! But look here, I'm afraid we're in for trouble. Sultan's given himself a bad over-reach; you could never drive him home to-night. And I've just seen Norris lying blind drunk under a wall!'

Now Norris was Lady Knox's coachman. We stood aghast at this 'horror on horror's head,' the blood trickled down Sultan's heel, and the lather lay in flecks on his dripping, heaving sides, in irrefutable witness to the iniquity of Lady Knox's only daughter. Then Flurry said:

'Thank the Lord, here's the rain!'

At the moment I admit that I failed to see any cause for gratitude in this occurrence, but later on I appreciated Flurry's grasp of circumstances.

That appreciation was. I think, at its highest development about half an hour afterwards, when I, an unwilling conspirator (a part with which my acquaintance with Mr Knox had rendered me but too familiar) unfurled Mrs Cadogan's umbrella over Lady Knox's head, and hurried her through the rain from the tent to the 'bus, keeping it and my own person well between her and the horses. I got her in, with the rest of her bedraggled and exhausted party, and slammed the door.

'Remember, Major Yeates,' she said through the window, 'you are the *only* person here in whom I have any confidence. I don't wish *any* one else to touch the reins!' this with a glance towards Flurry, who was standing near.

'I'm afraid I'm only a moderate whip,' I said.

'My dear man,' replied Lady Knox testily, 'those horses could drive themselves!'

I slunk round to the front of the 'bus. Two horses, carefully rugged, were in it, with the inevitable Slipper at their heads.

'Slipper's going with you,' whispered Flurry, stepping up to me; 'she won't have me at any price. He'll throw the rugs over them when you get to the house, and if you hold the umbrella well over her she'll never see. I'll manage to get Sultan over somehow, when Norris is sober. That will be all right.'

I climbed to the box without answering, my soul being bitter within me, as is the soul of a man who has been persuaded by womankind against his judgment.

'Never again!' I said to myself, picking up the reins; 'let her marry him or Bernard Shute, or both of them if she likes, but I won't be roped into this kind of business again!'

Slipper drew the rugs from the horses, revealing on the near side Lady Knox's majestic carriage horse, and on the off, a thickset brown mare of about fifteen hands.

'What brute is this?' said I to Slipper, as he swarmed up beside me.

'I don't rightly know where Misther Flurry got her,' said Slipper, with one of his hiccoughing crows of laughter; 'give her the whip, Major, and' – here he broke into song:

> 'Howld to the shteel,
> Honamaundhiaoul; she'll run off like an eel!'

'If you don't shut your mouth, said I, with pent-up ferocity, 'I'll chuck you off the 'bus.'

Slipper was but slightly drunk, and, taking this delicate rebuke in good part, he relapsed into silence.

Wherever the brown mare came from, I can certify that it was not out of double harness. Though humble and anxious to oblige, she pulled away from the pole as if it were red hot, and at critical moments had a tendency to sit down. However, we squeezed without misadventure among the donkey carts and between the groups of people, and bumped at length in safety out on to the high-road.

Here I thought it no harm to take Slipper's advice, and I applied the whip to the brown mare, who seemed inclined to turn round. She immediately fell into an uncertain canter that no effort of mine could frustrate; I could only hope that Miss Sally would foster conversation inside the 'bus and create a distraction; but judging from my last view of the party, and of Lady Knox in particular, I thought she was not likely to be successful. Fortunately the rain was heavy and thick, and a rising west wind gave every promise of its continuance. I had little doubt but that I should catch cold, but I took it to my bosom with gratitude as I reflected how it was drumming on the roof of the 'bus and blurring the windows.

We had reached the foot of a hill, about a quarter of a mile from the racecourse; the Castle Knox horse addressed himself to it with dignified determination, but the mare showed a sudden and alarming tendency to jib.

'Belt her, Major!' vociferated Slipper, as she hung back from the pole chain, with the collar half-way up her ewe neck, 'and give it to the horse, too! He'll dhrag her!'

I was in the act of 'belting,' when a squealing whinny struck upon my ear, accompanied by a light pattering gallop on the road behind us; there was an answering roar from the brown mare, a roar, as I realised with a sudden drop of the heart, of outraged maternal feeling, and in another instant a pale, yellow foal sprinted up beside us, with shrill whickerings of joy. Had there at this moment been a boghole handy, I should have turned the 'bus into it without hesitation; as there was no accommodation of the kind, I laid the whip severely into everything I could reach, including the foal. The result was that we topped the hill at a gallop, three abreast, like a Russian troitska; it was like my usual luck that at this identical moment we should meet the police patrol, who saluted respectfully.

'That the divil may blisther Michael Moloney!' ejaculated Slipper, holding on to the rail; 'didn't I give him the foaleen and a halther on him to keep him! I'll howld you a pin 'twas the wife let him go, for she being vexed about the licence! Sure that one's a March foal, an' he'd run from here to Cork!'

There was no sign from my inside passengers, and I held on at a round pace, the mother and child galloping absurdly, the carriage horse pulling hard, but behaving like a gentleman. I wildly revolved plans of how I would make Slipper turn the foal in at the first gate we came to, of what I should say to Lady Knox supposing the worst happened and the foal accompanied us to her hall door, and of how I would have Flurry's blood at the earliest possible opportunity, and here the fateful sound of galloping behind us was again heard.

'It's impossible!' I said to myself; 'she can't have twins!'

The galloping came nearer, and Slipper looked back.

'Murdher alive!' he said in a stage whisper; 'Tom Sheehy's afther us on the butcher's pony!'

'What's that to me?' I said, dragging my team aside to let him pass; 'I suppose he's drunk, like everyone else!'

Then the voice of Tom Sheehy made itself heard.

'Shtop! Shtop thief!' he was bawling; 'give up my mare! How will I get me porther home!'


That was the closest shave I have ever had, and nothing could have saved the position but the torrential nature of the rain and the fact that Lady Knox had on a new bonnet. I explained to her at the door of the 'bus that Sheehy was drunk (which was the one unassailable feature of the case), and had come after his foal, which, with the fatuity of its kind, had escaped from a field and followed us. I did not mention to Lady Knox that when Mr Sheehy retreated, apologetically, dragging the foal after him in a halter belonging to one of her own carriage horses, he had a sovereign of mine in his pocket, and during the narration I avoided Miss Sally's eye as carefully as she avoided mine.

The only comments on the day's events that are worthy of record were that Philippa said to me that she had not been able to understand what the curious taste in the tea had been till Sally told her it was turf-smoke, and that Mrs Cadogan said to Philippa that night that 'the Major was that dhrinched that if he had a shirt between his skin and himself he could have wrung it,' and that Lady Knox said to a mutual friend that though Major Yeates had been extremely kind and obliging, he was an uncommonly bad whip.

# THE GOOD THING

## Colin Davy

'CREPELLO, a good thing!' exclaimed the small, wizened-faced man at the end of the bar. 'There ain't no such thing these days.' He spat accurately.

The spotty young man whose discourse had been thus interrupted turned a glance of disdain at the stranger. But something in the latter's appearance suggested more intimate association with racing stables than that gleaned from the pink, midday leaflet protruding from the youth's own pocket. So he tempered his sneer, and enquired: 'Wasn't two stone in hand good enough in your day, Dad?'

The little old man sucked his teeth. 'No it weren't,' he remarked shortly.

'I suppose in your day they 'oooked one up in the Gold Cup to win the seller at Windsor next day,' he suggested, winking at his mates.

'There were good things to bet on without nothing extravagant of that sort,' said the old man gazing meditatively into his empty glass. 'In those days, when the money was down, there were no ifs nor buts . . . No. Nor no short 'eads neither. They *did* win.'

The landlord winked encouragingly at the group, and tilted the gin bottle generously into the old man's glass. The recipient brightened remarkably, took a deep swig, and began: 'It's more than forty years ago . . . ?'

'Yes, Dad . . . ?'

'I was with Jack Quick wot trained at Puddlecombe near Wantage. He hadn't many patrons 'adn't Quick, and those he had seldom paid their bills. So, the establishment got the name of being a betting stable. That means that the trades-people knew not to come for their bills unless the stable's 'ad a touch. . . . We had a poor lot of 'osses, mostly selling platers, and one or two which at four and five years old were still waiting to win a maiden race. 'Owever, Quick by name and quick by nature, the boss usually had something ready when the bailiffs got too thick on the ground. . . .

'There were no 'igh-falutin' trade union ideas in those days about one lad doin' two 'osses. I often did three or four, and in bad times even five. Nor was there any rule about a fiver a winner. Usually one was on a good 'iding to nothing. . . . '

The speaker emptied his glass and saw it refilled with wistful eyes. After a pause, he went on gloomily: 'We 'ad one 'oss – one that I did – a big grey colt called Monastic Calm. Well named 'e was. By Glastonbury out of Evening 'ymn. 'E was that calm 'e was only fit to carry monks to matins. Lord Watercress had paid nine thousand for 'im as a yearling, and he'd hoped to win the Derby. Well, by the time 'e was rising five, the closest he'd got to classic honours was third in a selling race of four runners, and the winner disqualified. Monastic Calm! That described 'im. 'E wouldn't walk across the box to see if his manger was full. 'E 'ad to be fed where he stood out of a bucket, or 'e'd have starved 'isself to death. 'E'd stand for hours with his eyes shut, resting as many legs as possible with his lower lip hanging down like a sea-lion's. Can't think why young Watercress didn't sell 'im. He'd 'ave done well at the head of the Life Guards with a kettle drum on either side to keep 'im awake. Lord Watercress was young and an optimist. "All he needs is time," he'd say. His lordship was right. That's what he did need. Time. About five minutes to the furlong.

'Well, one day I was leaning against the grey 'oss's stable door, talking to Betty Quick the guv'nor's daughter. She was a nice bit of goods and no slower than her name implied, when the most extraordinary thing happened. The 'oss that had been standing like a bleeding statue ever since I'd called 'im in the morning, suddenly began to move. Very slowly he came towards us, poked his nose over the door and sniffed. Then suddenly quick as a monkey, 'e makes a grab and scuttles back into the far corner of his box.

' "Lawks!" screams Betty. " ''E's took the sausages!"

'Sure enough there was the 'oss with a string of Palethorpes hanging from his mouth and the queerest look in his eye you ever did see. There was no Monastic Calm about him. Proper baleful, that's what he looked. As if 'e challenged us to take even a link from him. Well, we watched those sausages disappear link by link like paper ribbon out of a conjurer's hat, but backwards on, if you know what I mean.'

The speaker watched his glass refilled with melancholy absorption, and continued: 'That night I noticed a change. When I dressed the 'oss down, he swished 'is tail twice and when I brought his feed he half-turned his head. But seeing no sausages, he dozed off again. But next day, he went so different – almost larkey, 'e was – that I could keep up with the yearlings cantering. Usually, I had to bash him all the way.

'After stables next day, I went to Betty and begged some scraps of meat from the kitchen – not much, but the knuckle end of a 'am, and some pork chops wot 'ad got tainted. He ate 'em bones and all, and when I went to him last thing, he turned right round and whinnied same as any other 'oss does at evening feed. And would you believe me? Next morning he went a fair treat upsides with old Bacchus, wot 'ad once won a forty-pound seller at Beverly!

'At first I thought of keeping this to myself, but the 'oss's improvement was so great and the price of meat so high I just had to tell the guv'nor. You should have seen his face when I told him. But when he'd seen the grey eat three pounds of catsmeat, a leg of lamb wot 'ad been spoiled by the sun, and seen 'im work next morning, he went away werry werry cogitatious.

'Later he takes me on one side and sez: "Nat, lad, we'll keep this to our two selves and 'oo knows, maybe get a nice touch out of this. You feed him 'is meat at nights when all the other lads is gone, and from now on you work the 'oss alone."

' "But 'ow are we to know how much he improves?" I asked.

' "Leave that to me," 'e sez. "I can always fix up a trial with one of me brother's from over at Boreham Down. We'll find out how he improves when the times comes."

'Well, I'd hate to think what it cost the guv' in legs of mutton and sides of beef, but he wasn't one to spare the golden eggs that might 'atch a goose. The best of everything wasn't too good for Monastic Calm after 'e'd clocked 'im over a mile once or twice. Of course I couldn't say what the time was, but I knew how me arms ached and how the wind whistled past, when the old sod got into top gear. It was more like riding the flying Scotsman than an 'oss.

'Well, after about two months we 'ad a secret trial with one of Quick's brother's 'osses. I didn't know what the weights were, but Monastic Calm beat the other quad by twenty lengths, and was never going more than half-speed neither.

'That night, I asked the guv'nor: "When do we run the grey? Ain't it time we got something for the butcher?"

'Mester Quick smiled and said: "We wait for Newmarket, and the butcher can wait too."

' "In a seller?" I sez.

' "Seller me foot," sez he. "He goes in the Cambridgeshire. 'E'll get about seven stone and will be a certainty."

'I suppose I said something about flying too high, but he cuts in quick and very supercilious, "Do you know what the 'oss was that you beat this morning?" he asks. "It was Bachelor. Bachelor, wot was second in the Eclipse! And you gave 'im a stone. Now go and give the grey 'is entrée and joint."

'Well, when I thought it over, I realised what that added up to. *We'd got the fastest horse in the world.* With seven stone in the Cambridgeshire, 'e'd be like a racing car against push-bicycles!

'A week before the race, I was sent off with the 'oss to a farm on the Suffolk side of Newmarket, where we lay low to avoid the touts. My orders were to hack him out in clothing in the afternoons when no one expected a horse to gallop, strip 'im quietly behind The Ditch, give 'im a breezer and off back to the farm before anyone twigged. I always finished the gallop not far from the Cambridgeshire winning post where another lad waited with a second set of clothing and a couple of loin chops for the colt as a sort of encourager. Comin' across the flat, the grey seemed to smell those chops, and . . . well, it were like flying. I often laughed to meself and thought of the crowd when they saw this unknown grey hoss 'undreds of yards in front of the others. I could hear them asking theirselves: "Wot's this perisher out in front?" It would be the sensation of a lifetime.

'The night before the race I went to the subscription rooms with Mr Quick to 'ear them call over the card. The guv'nor 'adn't backed him with a penny till then, and our 'oss was a hundred and fifty to one in some places and two-hundred to one in others. Mr Quick started very quietly in fifties and ponies, but 'e'd been busy, for by the time we came out Monastic Calm had hardened to thirty-threes.

'The guv'nor and I went to a quiet pub nearby to tot up what he stood to win. . . . '

The old man paused, drained his glass, and announced slowly: *'Mr Quick stood to win seventy-five thousand pounds, and I was to 'ave ten per cent.'*

The group in the bar stood in gaping silence. Then a dozen ready hands went out to refill the narrator's glass. But though he sipped his drink with relish, he seemed in no hurry to continue. His glance roved slowly and rather sadly from one to another whiskey advertisement decorating the wall.

As last, one spirit bolder than the rest broke in upon the old man's reverie.

'Did . . . did it win, Sir?' he asked.

The old man nodded. 'Aye. Monastic Calm won. Won by nearly a furlong.'

He drained his glass, reached for his cap, but yet the group knew the tale was not told.

'And the bookies paid up?' asked one youth, mopping his brow.

The old man shook his head. 'No,' he said. 'You see the jockey couldn't weigh in. So the horse was disqualified. It were this way. There was no little lad at the winning post with the loin chops as expected. And the 'oss was hungry. He threw the little lad wot rode 'im, and ate him. . . . ' He looked round gloomily and added: 'Boots and all.'

# THE LOSERS

## *Maurice Gee*

DINNER was over at the commercial hotel and the racing people were busy discussing prospects for the final day. The first day's racing had been interesting; some long shots had come home, and a few among the crowd in the lounge were conscious as they talked of fatter, heavier wallets hanging in their inside pockets. Of these the happiest was probably Lewis Betham who had, that day, been given several tips by trainers. The tips had been good ones, but it would not have mattered if they had been bad. The great thing was that trainers had come up and called him by his first name and told him what to back. He thought he had never been so happy, and he told his wife again how the best of these great moments had come about.

'He said to me: "Lew, that horse of mine, Torrid, should run a good one, might be worth a small bet." He's a cunning little rooster, but he's straight as they come, so I just said to him: "Thanks, Arnold" – I call him Arnold – and I gave him a wink. He knew the information wouldn't go any further. See? I didn't have to tell him. And then Jack O'Nell came up and said: "Do you know anything, Arnold?" and he said: "No, this is a tough one, Jack. They all seem to have a show." He's cunning all right. But he is straight, straight as a die. He'd never put you wrong. So I banged a fiver on its nose. Eleven pound it paid, eleven pound.'

Mrs Betham said: 'Yes, dear. Eleven pounds eleven and six.' She sipped her coffee and watched the people in the lounger. She was bored. Lew hadn't introduced her to anyone and she wished she could go out to the pictures, anywhere to get away from the ceaseless jabber of horse names. None of them meant anything to her. She realised how far apart she and Lew had grown. If someone came up and murmured Torrid in her ear she would just stare at him in amazement. But this whispering of names was the only meaning Lew seemed to demand from life these days. He had always dreamed of owning a horse and she had not opposed him. She had discovered too late he was entering a world with values of its own, a world with aristocracy and commoners, brahmans and untouchables. He, new brahman, was determined to observe all its proprieties. And of course he would receive its rewards.

Lew's horse, Bronze Idol, a two-year-old, was having its third start in the Juvenile Handicap tomorrow. It would be one of the favourites after running a fifth and a third. Lew was sure the horse would win and his trainer had told him to have a solid bet. He was tasting his triumph already. He excused himself and went into the house-bar to talk to Arnold. He wanted now to give a tip in return for the one he had got. Arnold would know the horse was going to win, but that was beside the point.

Mrs Betham watched him go, then looked round the lounge. This place, she thought, was the same as the other racing hotels she'd been in. There were the same pursy people saying the same things. There were the same faint smells of lino and hops, vinegar and disinfectant. And Phar Lap, glossy and immaculate, was on the wall between lesser Carbine and Kindergarten. The Queen, richly framed, watched them from another wall, with that faint unbending smile the poor girl had to wear. How her lips must ache.

Duties, thought Mrs Betham, we all have duties.

Hers, as a wife, was to accompany Lew on these trips. To wear the furs he bought her and be sweet and receptive and unexceptional. Surprising what a hard job that was at times. She yawned and looked for the clock, and found it at length behind her, over the camouflaged fireplace, over the polished leaves of the palm in the green-painted barrel. With straight dutiful hands it gave the time as ten past eight. She yawned again. Too late for the pictures, too early to go to bed. She prepared her mind for another hour of boredom.

There were a dozen or so men in the bar but only two women. Lew recognised one of these immediately: Mrs Benjamin, the owner, widow of a hotel man. She was sitting at a small table sipping a drink that appeared to be gin. The hand holding the glass

sparkled with rings. Between sips she talked in a loud voice to her
brother, Charlie Becket, who trained her horses. Arnold, wiry,
tanned, and deferential, was also at the table.

Arnold saw Lew and jerked his head. Lew went over, noticing
Mrs Benjamin's lips form his name to Charlie Becket as he
approached. When he had been introduced he sat down.

Mrs Benjamin said: 'You're the Betham who owns that little
colt, aren't you? What's the name of that horse, Charlie?'

'Bronze Idol,' said Charlie Becket. 'Should go well tomorrow.'

Lew nodded and narrowed his eyes. 'We've got a starter's
chance,' he said.

Arnold said: 'Well-bred colt. You've got the filly in the same
race, Mrs Benjamin.'

'Ah, my hobby,' cried Mrs Benjamin. 'I bred that filly myself.
If I can make something of her I'm never going to take advice
from anyone again.'

'She should go a good race,' said Arnold.

As they talked Lew watched Mrs Benjamin. She was over-
powdered, absurdly blue-rinsed; her nose was flat, with square box
nostrils, and her eyelids glistened as though coated with vaseline.
He'd seen all this before, and refused to see it. This was not what
he wanted. He wanted the legend. He remembered some of the
stories he'd heard about her. It was said she had a cocktail bar
built into the back of her car, and the mark of entry to her select
group was to be invited for a drink.

Perhaps, thought Lew, perhaps tomorrow. He found himself
wanting to mention the bar.

It was said she carried a wad of notes in her purse for charitable
purposes connected with racing. Nobody had ever seen the wad,
nobody had seen her pay out, but there were stories of failed
trainers mysteriously re-entering business, always after being
noticed in conversation with Mrs Benjamin. Lew did not believe
these stories, but he felt it was more important for them to exist
than for them to be true.

Mrs Benjamin said: 'And Bronze Idol is your first venture, Mr
Betham?'

Lew told her of his lifelong ambition to own a horse. He kept
his voice casual and tried to suggest that he was one of those who
would do well at racing without having to do well. He was trying
to make it a paying sport.

Charlie Becket twisted his mouth. He spoke about Bronze Idol and said the horse was very promising. Lew said it was still a bit green; tomorrow's race was in the nature of an 'educational gallop'. He saw Charlie Becket didn't believe him, and was flattered.

Mrs Benjamin interrupted the conversation to ask Charlie if he would like another drink. Lew understood that the question was really a request. Her own glass was empty while Charlie's was still half full. He was about to say: 'Let me, Mrs Benjamin,' and take her glass, when he realised it might be wiser to pretend he hadn't understood. He must not appear over-anxious. And his knowledge of women told him Mrs Benjamin was not of the type that liked to be easily read. Perhaps when she brought her request a little more into the open he might make the offer. . . .

But Charlie gulped his drink and stood up. He had a broad face, a broad white nose, and squinting eyes that looked everything over with cold appraisal – an expression, Lew thought, that should have been saved for the horses. Lew wondered if it was true that at training gallops Charlie always carried two stop-watches, one for other people, showing whatever time he wanted them to see, and one he looked at later on, all by himself. Of course, he thought, watching the eyes, of course it's true. I wish he was training my horse.

Charlie said: 'Don't feel like drinking right now. Come on, I'll take you for that drive.'

Mrs Benjamin had barely opened her mouth to protest when he added shortly: 'It was your idea, you know.'

She said: 'Oh, Charlie, why have you got such a good memory?' but she stood up and smiled at Lew and Arnold and said: 'Excuse us,' Charlie nodded and the pair left the bar. The eyes in the steam-follered fox head on Mrs Benjamin's shoulders glittered back almost sardonically.

Arnold sucked his lips into a tight smile, and nodded in a way that showed he was pleased.

'Charlie must be mad about something,' he said. 'He doesn't often turn on a performance like that in public.'

'So Charlie's the boss,' said Lew softly.

'Always has been. It just suits him to let her play up to things the way she does. All the horses she's got, they might just as well belong to him. Even this filly of hers – that'll only win when he wants it to.'

Lew nodded and tried to look as if he understood. It was a shock to have Mrs Benjamin, the legendary figure, cut down to this size. But he experienced also a thrill of pleasure that he was one of the few who knew how things really were. It meant he was accepted. He was one of those Charlie Becket didn't pretend to.

'Good thing too,' Arnold was saying. 'Most of these women get too big for their boots if they start doing well. And hard. My God, that one, she's sweet as pie on the surface but you scratch that and see what you find. She's got one idea, and that's money – grab hold of it, stack it away, that's how her mind works. Don't you believe these yarns about her giving any of it away. If there's one thing you can be sure of it's nothing gets out of that little black purse of hers once she's got it in.'

Lew nodded and said: 'I knew they were just yarns, of course.'

'There's been some fine women in the racing game,' said Arnold. 'But most of 'em go wrong somehow. Look' – he jerked his head – 'you take Connie Reynolds over there.'

Lew looked to a corner of the room where a young blonde woman with a heavy figure was arguing with a group of men.

'You've heard about Connie?'

Lew shook his head reluctantly.

'Christ, man, she's been banged by every jock from North Cape to the Bluff. And now, believe it or not, she's got herself engaged to Stanley John Edward Philpott. You've heard of him?'

'I've heard the name,' lied Lew.

'Stanley John Edward Philpott,' said Arnold, and he swept a hand, palm down, between them. For a moment Lew wondered what racing sign this was, then understood it was a personal one of Arnold's, meaning the man was no good.

'I could tell you a few stories about him. Could tell you some about Connie too.' Arnold smiled, and the smile deepened, and Lew leaned forward, breathing softly, waiting for the stories, feeling fulfilled and very, very happy.

At half past eight Connie Reynolds left the men in the house-bar corner and went into the lounge. She left abruptly after one of them had made an insinuating remark about her engagement. He said it wasn't fair to the rest of them to take herself out of circulation. As she went towards the door she felt she was behaving as

she'd always wanted to behave. She was simply walking out on
them. She glanced at the ring on her finger: pride and anger were
two of the luxuries she could now afford. And the freedom of not
having to please made her for a moment see Stan in the role of
champion and liberator, riding to slay the dragon and unchain the
maiden. But this image, the unreal figures springing on her from
the white delicately haunted innocence she had left long ago, forced
her into a hurried retreat, and, 'Maiden?' she said, shrugging and
giggling, 'that's a laugh.' And Stan as a knight on a white charger,
poor battered old Stanley, who had strength only to assert now
and then that one day he'd get his own back on all the bloody
poohbahs, just you wait and see if he didn't? No, nothing had
really changed, except that she was walking out on them, that and
the fact that she didn't care if she had drunk too much whiskey.
She didn't have to care any more.

Mrs Betham saw Connie come through the door and say something to herself and giggle.

The poor girl's drunk, she thought, and she looked round for
the dark tubby little man who'd been with her at dinner. There
weren't many people in the lounge. Most had gone out or into
the bar. She remembered that the man had gone upstairs with
friends some time ago, and she half rose and beckoned the girl.

'If you're looking for your husband,' said Mrs Betham, 'he's
gone upstairs.'

Connie stopped in front of her. 'He isn't my husband,' she said,
'he's my boy friend.'

'Fiancé,' she corrected. She sat down in a chair facing Mrs
Betham. She saw the woman smiling at her and thought she looked
kind.

'Do you believe in love?' asked Connie.

Mrs Betham could not decide whether the girl was serious. She
was a little drunk, obviously, but drunk people often talked of
things they managed to keep hidden at other times, the things that
really troubled them.

'You know, a man and a woman, to have an' to hold, an' all
that?'

'Yes, I do,' said Mrs Betham.

'Well, I was hoping you'd say no, 'cause I don't. An' I don't
think it's passed me by 'cause I've had my eyes wide open all the
time an' I haven't seen anything that looks the least bit like it.'

Mrs Betham thought of several clever things to say, but she didn't say any of them. 'Would you like me to try to find him for you?' she asked.

Connie said: 'No, he'll keep. And you can bet your life he's not worrying about what's happened to me. Still, I'm used to looking after myself. I shouldn't kid myself Stan's going to take over just because I got a ring on my finger.'

'You know, dear,' said Mrs Betham, 'these aren't the sort of things you should be saying to a stranger.'

'You aren't a stranger. You're the wife of the man who owns Bronze Idol. Stan told me. Stan's got a horse in the same race. Royal Return. You heard of Royal Return?'

Mrs Betham shook her head.

'Well, don't ask me if it's got a chance because it isn't forward enough. That's what I have been told to say.'

Mrs Betham laughed. 'And my instructions are to say that I don't know anything at all. Haven't we been well trained?'

Connie said: 'Yeah, but not as well as the horses. My God, I'd love to be groomed, just stroked an' patted an' brushed that way. Any man who treated me like that would have me for life. But I haven't got a chance. I'm just an old work horse, the sort that gets knocked around. The day'll come I'll be sold for lion's meat.'

'My dear, you sound very bitter.'

'You know why I'm getting married?' said Connie. She put a hand on Mrs Betham's knee. 'I'm getting married 'cause I'm tired an' I want a rest. Is that a good enough reason?'

'I'll find your fiancé,' said Mrs Betham. But she couldn't get up while the hand was on her knee.

'I want to know is that a good enough reason.'

Mrs Betham realised the girl was serious.

'Yes, dear,' she said, 'I think that's a very good reason.'

Connie thought for a moment, her mouth open and twisted to one side, eyes gazing at the Queen on the wall.

'And what's the way to be happy, then?' she asked.

'Why . . . to be happy,' said Mrs Betham, but she could find no answer. 'I suppose each one's got to put the other first,' she said lamely.

'No,' said Connie, her eyes bright and questioning, 'I don't mean him, I mean me, the way for me to be happy.'

Mrs Betham knew she should say: My dear, I think you'd better not get married at all, but instead she said, with sudden sharpness: 'You've got to make sure he needs you more than you need him. That's the only way I know.'

She forgot Connie and thought of herself and Lew. After twenty-five years the roles had been reversed. Now she didn't need him any more and so she couldn't be hurt. But over the years he had grown to need her, she was the faithful wife, part of his sense of rightness. Without her his world would crumble. And she thought, so I'm still a prisoner really, just the way I always was. But now it doesn't hurt, and it doesn't mean anything either. It's just one of the things that is.

She turned back to Connie. The girl was almost in tears.

'Well, then,' said Connie, 'it's all wrong. It isn't Stan who needs me it's me who needs him, because I'm tired and I've got to stop, just stop, you see, and be still and let things go past me for a while. And Stan had to have some money to buy the horse, so I gave it to him and he's got to marry me.'

Mrs Betham tried to speak, but the girl said fiercely: 'It doesn't matter if he needs me. That isn't important at all.'

'No, of course, dear,' said Mrs Betham, trying to soothe her. 'As long as you both put each other first. That's the main thing.'

But Connie jumped up and ran from the room. Mrs Betham wondered if she should follow, then decided against it. She couldn't think of any advice to give if she did catch the girl. She could only tell the truth again, as she knew it. She wasn't the sweet fairy-godmother type to heal with a sunny smile.

After a while she took a magazine from the rack under the coffee-table and opened it at random. *Plump Correspondent Puts In Cheery Word For The Not So Slim*, she read.

She smiled wryly.

Not So Slim. Why couldn't that be the most serious affliction? A world made happy by dieting and menthoids.

She put the magazine aside and looked round the room. The glossy horses posed, the slim Queen smiled down, and over the fireplace the clock said that at last it was late enough to go to bed.

She yawned and went up the stairs, thinking about Connie, and the impossibility of ever helping anybody.

Stan Philpott was playing poker in the room of Jeff Milden, an ex-bookie and small-business man who had failed to survive tax investigations and a heavy fine. He now worked in a factory, where several sly gambling ventures had shown disappointingly small returns, a fact he put down to working-class prejudice against an ex-employer. The truth was that, irrespective of class, nobody he had ever known had really liked him. He was aware of this only in a vague uncomprehending way, and tonight he was directing most of his energy to finding other reasons for his guests' preoccupation. He supposed Joe Elliot the trainer was worried about money or his horses, whereas Joe was really worried about having a stable boy who blushed and giggled whenever he was reprimanded and cried when threatened with being sent home. He supposed Stan Philpott was worried about money and Royal Return. In this he was right. The tremendous complex of preparation, bravado, fear, assessment of chance and luck, which had driven Stan frantic for weeks past had reduced itself on the eve of the event to an urgent knowledge of necessity: Royal Return must win tomorrow or he was finished. It was as simple as that. He, Stanley John Edward Philpott, was finished.

Fingering his cards he told himself that if the horse didn't win there was only one way left to get some money, and that was a way he could never take. He tried to read in the hand he held a sign that he should never even have to consider it. The hand was poor; he threw it aside and watched the others bet.

'Can't seem to get one tonight,' he muttered, and Jeff Milden, pulling in winnings with one hand, pushed the cards towards him with the other, saying:

'Come on, Stan. Stop worrying about that donkey of yours. Deal yourself a good one.'

Stan treated this as an invitation to talk. As he shuffled the cards he said: 'You know, it's that bloody thing of Becket's I'm scared of.' So that he might talk about Royal Return he had told the others to back the horse tomorrow, but had suggested enough uncertainty about winning to make sure they wouldn't.

Joe Elliot shook his head and said with an air of sad wisdom: 'Don't hope for too much, Stan.'

'If there's one bastard who could beat me it's Becket. He's got it in for me.' Stan continued to shuffle though Jeff Milden was showing impatience.

'I'm one up on Becket, and I don't reckon he's going to rest till he gets it back on me.'

'Christ, Stan, that happened years ago,' said Jeff. He snapped his fingers for the cards. But Joe was tired of playing. He asked to hear the story.

Stan smiled, recalling his victory, then began with practised brevity: 'Was when I was riding over the sticks. Becket was just beginning to make his way then. He had a pretty good hurdler called Traveller's Joy. I used to ride it in all its starts so I knew when it was right. We waited, see, we got everything just like we wanted it, an' I said to Becket, right, this is it. So he pulls me aside in that sneaky way he's got an' says, I've got twenty on for you. So then it's up to me, and sure enough I kick that thing home. And then do you think I can find Becket? I chased him all over the bloody course. After a while I give up, and I take a tumble to what's happening. I'm getting the bum's rush. And sure enough next time this horse starts there's another jock up. So I get cunning, see. I think out a little scheme to put Mr Becket where he belongs. I know he thinks the horse is going to win again, an' I think so too, so I decide to do something about it. Becket's got some kid up, and that's a mistake he wouldn't make now, so just before the race I go round and make myself known to this kid, an' I say, Listen, kid, I've ridden this horse lots of times an' I know how he likes to be rode, an' I tell this kid he's got to be held in at the jumps. Take him in tight, I say, he's got to be steady, an' the kid thinks I'm being decent an' he says, Gee, thanks, Mr Philpott, or words to that effect. Well, this horse Traveller's Joy is a real jumper, he likes to stretch right out, so at the first fence the kid takes him in on a tight rein and gets jerked clean over the bloody horse's head, an I look round an' see Becket standing there with his face all red an' I spit on the ground an' say, That's for you, bastard, an' he looks at me, an' I reckon he'll be asking that kid some pretty pertinent questions when he gets hold of him.'

'When the kid gets out of hospital,' said Jeff. 'Come on, deal 'em round.'

Joe Elliot said nothing. Stan hadn't enjoyed the story, either. Surprisingly he had lost heart for it as he went along and the climax hadn't been convincing. He said, in a puzzled voice: 'That bloody Becket.'

The telling of the story hadn't changed Becket; he'd stood through it hard and aloof, clothed in success; and Stan saw that the stories a hundred Philpotts could tell wouldn't change a thing about him, wouldn't draw them up or him down in any way that mattered. There was no way to attack him.

Stan thought, It's only the poor bastards who don't like themselves much that you can get at. A man's only piddling in his own boot if he tries with Becket and the rest of them poohbahs.

He was so shaken by this that he wanted to get off alone somewhere so that he could cry out or swear or beat the wall, break something to prove himself real. He stood up and left the room. There even Joe Elliot's silence, the familiarity of a has-been like Milden, were working for Charlie Becket.

He slammed the door behind him and went along the passage. He was angry that his feet made no sound on the carpet, and when he came to his room he slammed that door too.

'Stan?' said a voice from the bed. It was a wet husky voice with a little ridge of panic in it, and for a second Stan didn't recognise it.

'Connie,' he said, and turned on the light.

She was lying on the bed fully clothed except for her shoes. One shoe was on the floor, the other balanced on the edge of the coverlet. This was so typical of her, of what he called her sloppiness, the way she let her money, her time, even her feelings dribble away, the way she dressed and undressed, and spoke and ate, that he broke into a rage. Becket, grey-suited and binoculared, seemed to stand beside him reproaching him with this blowzy fifth-hand woman. He entered a grey dizzing whirl made up of all he had never won and never achieved, a past of loss and failure, of small grimy winnings, a past of cheap beds and dirty sheets and bad food, of cards, smoky rooms, overflowing ashtrays, of women you could only want when you were drunk, of scabby horses, pulled horses, falls, broken bones, stewards' committees and lies, a past of borrowing and forgetting to pay back, of bludging and cheating and doping, a past of asserting your worth and greeting your winnings with a bull's roar so that you could believe in them, a past of noise and dirt and slipping lower and lower until a frayed collar and a three-day growth and a fifth-hand woman were part of you you weren't even conscious of. All these ran out in words he had never known he could use and broke against the hard withdrawn figure of Becket and made the woman on the bed curl and shrink and turn sobbing into the blankets until she was just tangled yellow hair and a shaking back. And these, the hair and back, were all Stan saw as he freed himself at length from the grey clinging fragments of his past.

He went slowly to the bed.

'Connie?'

He sat down and put a hand on her shoulder.

'Connie, I'm sorry. I didn't mean it.'

He sat stroking her shoulder. In a few moments she was quiet.

He turned out the light and lay down with her. His feet knocked her balancing shoe to the floor. She gave a small start that brought her body more firmly against his. After a while she said: 'Stan?'

'Yes, Connie?'

She turned suddenly and they lay close together, holding each other.

'Tell me it's going to be all right.'

'It'll be all right. Don't worry about it.'

'Can we get married soon, Stan?'

'Don't you worry. We'll get married. Stanley's got it all figured out.'

It was the first time, he realised, that he'd ever been with her and talked quietly, held her like this and not wanted her. He felt her going to sleep, and soon he heard her gentle snoring; and this sound, that she always refused to believe she made, brought him even closer to her, made him realise how helpless she was.

Yes, he thought, yes, it'll be all right. As long as the horse wins. It'll be all right. He stroked her hair as she slept, then carefully drew away and found his coat and laid it over her softly so that she wouldn't wake.

## II

Charlie Becket walked from the saddling paddock to the jockeys' room. By the time he was there he had the instructions clear in his mind. The filly looked good, but she wasn't quite ready yet – and there was too much money on her. A poor race, a run home in the ruck, would lengthen her price for the next start. He'd get good money off her, but not today.

He beckoned the jockey and spoke to him in the corridor. The little man nodded thoughtfully then went back into the room to smoke. The instructions were simple. He'd ridden work on the horse and knew her well. She always went wide at the turn. He wasn't to check her; let her dive out, pretend to fight her, make her look green. It was a simple job – if you were a good jockey, a top jockey. He smiled and drew deeply on the cigarette and thought about how much he'd tell Becket to get on the big race for him. There was a sure win there.

Charlie went back to the stand and smiled as he climbed the steps. Betty was looking at him anxiously, like a grandmother fox in her furs. She was waiting to be told what to bet. She must bet on her dear little filly. Twenty quid he'd tell her. It would teach her a lesson to lose.

He took the money and went to the tote. Bronze Idol was surprisingly long. A tenner each way would net him sixty. And a little bit on Philpott's horse. There was sly work going on there. He placed the bets and went to stand beside the judge's box. He liked to be alone. A quarter hour without Betty twitching at his sleeve was something to be valued.

At the saddling paddock Stan had Royal Return ready. The horse seemed jaded and was slightly shin-sore. He shouldn't even be in work with the tracks so hard, but Stan told himself not to worry. He aimed his habitual punch of affection at the horse's ribs and murmured: 'It's over to you, you goori.' Royal Return responded by ambling in a circle. Stan placed his mouth beside its ear and pretended to whisper. The smell of the dope had gone. He grinned as though at his clowning and led the horse past Connie on the fence and into the birdcage. Everything was as right as he could make it. It was over to Lady Luck now. And as he walked Royal Return round and round and saw the white silks of the jockeys moving in the corridor he began to sweat. This formal part of the business had always made him nervous. He felt shabby on the green lawn, and was made to realise how much he had lost, how much he had to win back, and he tried not to think of the things he still had to lose. It was over to Lady Luck – she owed him for a lifetime of losses.

Connie had come to the birdcage fence and was watching the horses circle. Presently the first jockeys came out and mounted, and she wondered how they managed to look so serious. Perhaps just getting into those colours and looking neat and clean made the difference. One of the first things she'd learned about men was

that they were horribly vain. But knowing things like that didn't
seem to help women – or rather, not her sort of woman. She'd
read stories about the siren type who could charm men to them
and play them like harps, and she'd tried to be the siren type
herself but it hadn't worked. It had failed so badly that now it was
all she could do to hold even Stan who, as far as she knew, had
never been wanted by another woman, anyway. He looked rather
grimy out there among the glossy horses and bright little jockeys.
He didn't compare very well with all those steward and owners
and trainers under the members stand verandah, with Mr Betham
for instance. Betham was rather red-faced, but very handsome in
his suit and Stetson and fancy shoes, very prosperous and dis-
tinguished looking. She'd tried to catch men like that and once or
twice had actually thought she'd succeeded. But she couldn't hold
them and soon she discovered that they'd caught her. They'd tossed
her back like an eel from a slimy creek.

She wondered what it was that made the difference. Was it
clothes, or money, or just not having to worry about so much?
She looked from Betham to Stan. Perhaps somehow all three of
those put together. But Stan at least was real, you knew where
the real part of him began and where it ended. That was something
you'd probably never find out about Betham.

She watched as Stan talked to his jockey and helped him mount.
Then Stan went off somewhere and the horse was on its own.
Everything was naked and simple now. The future was that horse
out there and a little Maori jockey in red and white silk. This was
somehow a point, an end, the top of a hill or something like that,
but there was no way of seeing how you'd got to it and no way
of going back. You couldn't even see how you'd started on the
way. Perhaps it had begun back there at school. You liked some
things and you didn't like others. You did a hundred thousand
little things and you didn't do the hundred thousand others you
might have done. Then some time later you understood that you'd
really been making a great big simple choice. What was her choice?
Slut, racecourse bag. Once she'd thought she might be a model.
But all the little things she'd done had made her a slut. She'd
wanted so much to enjoy herself.

There should be some way of letting people know what they
were doing. It was all so serious. Every little thing done was so
serious.

A voice beside her said: 'They're really rather beautiful, aren't they?'

She turned and saw Mrs Betham there. Mrs Betham nodded admiringly at the horses.

'Yes,' said Connie.

Watching the horses in the birdcage was the only thing Mrs Betham enjoyed at the races. They were so clean and so polished looking, so sleek and yet so powerful. They seemed to dominate the men, and she wondered how the jockeys ever found courage to climb on their backs. Most of the jockeys were only boys. Yet they sat there so unconcernedly – some of them even chewed gum. There was a Maori boy on number eleven who looked like a trained chimpanzee, but the jockey on her husband's horse was quite old and looked rather tired. She felt sorry for him and wondered how on earth he'd survive if the horse fell over. He looked consumptive; the purple and orange colours didn't suit him at all.

'Which one is yours dear?' she asked Connie.

Connie pointed to the one with the Maori on and Mrs Betham said: 'He looks rather nice.' But the horse that had really taken her fancy was a little black one. It moved daintily, prancing sideways, then going backwards with tiny mincing steps. She was annoyed that the effect was spoiled by the dull moon-faced jockey sitting hunched on its back. The horse was definitely superior. She would have liked to turn it loose in the hills and see it gallop away along the skyline.

*Odalisque*, she read, *bl. f. Owner Mrs E. Benjamin. Trainer C. F. Becket.* She was pleased it was a filly (smiled that she hadn't noticed) and that a woman owned it, and she made a mental note to look up odalisque in the dictionary when she got home.

The first horses went out for their preliminaries and a bell began to ring over at the totalisator. The horses came back down the track, some galloping, others just cantering. Mrs Betham thought again there was something really graceful and exciting about it all. The worms in the apple were the people. There were queues of them still stretched out at the totalisator scrabbling away at their money.

Connie said she was going round to the hill and Mrs Betham asked if she could come too. Lew would want to be with the trainer for this race. They went round the back of the stand, past the refreshment tents and the smelly bar where men were gulping down their last drinks. Mrs Betham saw the man who was Connie's fiancé come out and hurry into the crowd wiping his mouth. Before she could point him out he had disappeared in front of taller people. She realized then how short he was; and he seemed some shades darker too, but perhaps that was due to his old-fashioned navy-blue suit.

The stream of people moved on and they moved with it until they found a place halfway down the hill. The horses were at the five furlong start when they arrived. The race would soon begin.

'I hope one of us wins,' said Mrs Betham. She was finding it embarrassing to be with Connie. She couldn't get the girl to talk. She decided that if there were things on her mind it would be kinder to keep quiet. She tried to concentrate on the horses, but couldn't pick any of them out, and she knew she'd have to listen to the course announcer to find out what happened. And she'd have to listen carefully. It was one of those short races that was over almost as soon as it started.

'Don't you wish you had binoculars?' she remarked wistfully, thinking of Lew's expensive pair. There was no reply, and she turned, rather annoyed now, and saw that Connie was staring away down an alley in the crowd. At the end of it was the man in the navy suit, her fiancé. Mrs Betham could see that their eyes were meeting.

'Your finacé,' she said. 'Why doesn't he come up?'

The man seemed to be trying to say something, though he was too far away for them to hear; he smiled, with a small twist of his mouth, and lifted his fingers in a V sign, Churchill's way, rather pathetically she thought. Then he moved to one side so they couldn't see him any more.

'He should have come up,' said Mrs Betham.

Connie began to stare at the horses again. Her face seemed thinner and more bony. 'Get them started,' she said. She moved a few steps away.

Mrs Betham shrugged and told herself not to be angry. Connie was perhaps not so ungracious as she seemed – the race must mean a lot to her. For that reason she hoped Royal Return would win, if Lew's horse didn't.

No, she thought, no, I hope it beats Lew's horse. They probably need the money more than we do.

The announcer's voice blared into her thoughts. 'The field is lining up for the start of the Juvenile Handicap.' He mentioned the horses that were giving trouble. One of them was Royal Return. But soon they were all in line and she saw the heave of brown and heard the crowd rumble as they started. She still couldn't pick out any of the horses.

'Bronze Idol has made a good beginning and so has Odalisque.' Then there was a list of names with Royal Return in the middle. She wondered how the announcer picked them out. She couldn't see any horse clearly. They were all melted together, and their legs flickering under the rail made them look like a centipede.

'As they come round past the three furlong peg it's Bronze Idol a length clear of Samba with Odalisque next on the rails on the inside of Conformist. A length back to Song and Dance getting a trail, a length to Sir Bonny.'

The next time he went through them she counted and found that Royal Return was eighth. Bronze Idol was still a length clear of the field. Lew would be getting excited.

At the turn it was the same except that she was pleased to hear Royal Return had ranged up on the outside of Conformist. Then the horses came into the straight and they seemed to explode. They spread out right across it. She thought this was normal, but the announcer was excited and said Odalisque had run wide and had carried out two or three others and Bronze Idol was holding on a length clear of Samba. She didn't hear Royal Return's name. But she was excited herself now. She could see Bronze Idol looking really beautiful, heaving along with his head out straight and his tail flowing and his body slippery with sunlight as the muscles moved; the little consumptive jockey was crouched very low on his back, not using the whip. They were past too quickly for her. She would have loved to see them going on like that for ever.

Above the roar of the crowd the announcer said Bronze Idol was winning as he liked. She was pleased for Lew's sake, and, she admitted, a little bit for her own too. It had been very exciting.

Then she remembered Royal Return. It hadn't been mentioned after the corner. The girl would be disappointed.

She looked round to find her. But Connie hadn't waited for the finish. She had seen Royal Return go out at the straight entrance, and had turned and gone back through the crowd. She had broken past the red paralysed faces of people staring stupidly away at something they didn't know was already over.


## III


Mrs Benjamin wanted to stay the night at the Commercial Hotel but Charlie Becket insisted on going home. Finally, after he had threatened to leave her behind, she agreed, and a few minutes before nine o'clock they left town and set off along the Auckland highway. It was a fine night, mild and cloudless. The stars were very bright.

They drove for some time in silence, then Mrs Benjamin began to complain about the meeting. There hadn't been anyone interesting there. All her friends were dying or losing interest.

'Common thing with old people,' said Charlie, hoping to quiet her.

But she seized on the statement and began to worry it with persistent whining energy and he knew she was working to the complaint that nobody cared about her any more. He broke abruptly into her talk, saying: 'That filly isn't right yet. You've been making me push her too fast.'

She grasped this subject eagerly. 'Oh, Charlie, I know she'll be all right. I've never seen a horse I liked better.'

'She over-reaches,' said Charlie. 'Cut herself one day, you see.'

'But I can't afford to lose twenty pounds on her,' she continued. 'Why did you tell me she was going to win?'

'Because I thought she was,' said Charlie. 'It's not my fault if the jockey can't ride her. I'll get someone different next time.' He smiled, remembering how perfectly Armstrong had let her go on the corner. A good jockey, a good man to have, even if he was expensive.

Mrs Benjamin sighed.

'She looked as if she was going to go down, pushing those big horses right out. She's so tiny.'

Charlie said: 'Yeah, funny thing happened about that too.'

He told her how after the race, when he'd been talking to Betham, Philpott had come up and accused him of sabotaging Royal Return.

'I told him I'd hardly do that when I had a few quid on it

myself, and that seemed to make him worse. I've never seen anyone sweat so much or look so mad. He'd have stuck a knife into me if he'd had one. He's got a kink I reckon. He'll end up in the nuthouse.'

'What happened?' said Mrs Benjamin.

'He followed me all over the course until I had to tell him to clear out or I'd call a cop.'

'What did he do?'

'He cleared out. They're all the same these broken-down jocks. Yellow. No guts. That's why they don't last.'

'But he was a good jockey once.'

'Plenty of good jockeys. They're a dime a dozen. Plenty of good horses too. What I'm interested in is good prices.'

'Sometimes you're just too hard, Charlie.'

Charlie said: 'We're not here to make friends.' It was his favourite saying and it never failed to please him. He drove on smiling, and Mrs Benjamin lay back stiffly in her corner and tried to sleep.

After a time she said wearily: 'It was a boring meeting. I didn't meet anyone I liked.'

Charlie grunted.

A little later she said: 'That Betham man is rather nice.'

'Got a good horse,' said Charlie.

'It's a pity his wife's such a mousy thing.'

'Anyway,' she said, 'I took him out for a drink.'

'You drink too much,' said Charlie.

They wound down a long hill. The lights ran off down gullies and over creeks and paddocks. Charlie fought the car, making it squeal in a way that pleased him.

They came to a level section of road. It ran for a mile without a curve and then went sharply left. Just round the corner the headlamps picked out two cars and a group of people standing at the back of a horse-float. The tail of the float was down and men were clustered in its mouth, white and yellow in a glare of light.

Charlie drove past slowly.

'Horse is probably down,' he said.

Then, as Mrs Benjamin said: 'Let's stop, Charlie,' he saw that the float was coupled to a big pre-war Oldsmobile.

'Philpott,' he said. He increased speed.

'But, Charlie, I want to see what's happened.'

Charlie didn't answer. He changed into top gear. Soon the speed-ometer reached sixty again.

'There are plenty of people there to help. Joe Elliot was there. He'll know what to do.'

'Charlie, why can't you do what I want to, just for once?'

But again Charlie didn't answer. A hundred yards ahead the lights had picked up the figure of a woman walking at the side of the road. She was going their way but she didn't look round as they approached or make any signal. The car sped past.

'It's Connie. Connie Reynolds. Stop, Charlie.' Mrs Benjamin was peering back.

'Charlie, *stop*.'

'Charl*ie-ie*.'

'I don't feel like it,' he said. The speedometer kept level at sixty.

For a while Mrs Benjamin sulked in her corner. She didn't see why she couldn't know what was happening. Then she grew morbid. She was old – she wondered how many more pleasures she was to be allowed. Perhaps she couldn't afford to lose this one.

Charlie said: 'For God's sake don't start the waterworks.'

Mrs Benjamin had not been going to cry but she allowed herself two or three tears and held her handkerchief to her eyes. Then she rearranged herself fussily in her seat, grumbled a little about its hardness, and watched the road in an effort to stay awake. Her frequent desire to sleep had worried her lately. But this time she found reason for it in the motion of the car. She closed her eyes and let her mouth loosen comfortably. Her body sagged a little and she felt a settling lurch in her bowels. Her hands turned in her lap until the palms faced upwards.

She slept, as heavily as a child, and soon Charlie Becket put out a hand and tipped her against the door. He did not want her falling over him as he drove.

Connie had not found Stan until two races after the Juvenile Handi-cap. She knew at once he'd been drinking, but believed him when he said he wouldn't drink any more. He was determined to win back everything and he asked for money. She gave him the few pounds she had, keeping only enough for petrol to get home on. The hotel bills could be paid by cheque and though the cheque would bounce that was a worry for another day. Now the only thing that mattered was to keep Stan from doing anything crazy. He went off and she sat down shakily on a seat. She had never seen him looking so bad. His face was always blue-bristled by mid-afternoon, but now the skin under the bristles seemed more yellow than white, and his eyes were blood-shot, the lids scraped looking and salty. She wanted desperately to help him; and she wondered what was wrong with her, as a woman, that the only way she could help was by giving him money.

After the sixth race he came to her again. He had won a little, enough to bet more solidly with. But after the seventh race he did not come. That would mean he had lost. She went to sit in the car. From there she heard the announcer describe the last race. A horse called Manalive won. She had never heard Stan speak of it, and it paid only a few pounds.

Most of the traffic had gone by the time he came. He told her he'd won twenty pounds on a place bet in the eighth. They drove out of the course without picking up the float. He said there was a card game he wanted to get to. His voice was rough and urgent, and impersonal, not directed at her.

'But, Stan,' cried Connie, 'you can't win enough on a card game.' She didn't know what she meant by enough, but the word frightened her, it seemed so full of things that might happen, it uncovered years that might go any way at all.

'I can win something,' said Stan savagely. 'I can win enough so I won't have to . . . ' He too used the word and then didn't finish the sentence: she was more frightened; it was almost as if she had to open a door knowing there might be something terrible behind it. She wanted to put everything farther off.

'Stan, don't let's talk about it. Just drive.'

The card game was in a shabby house down by the harbour. She could see the sad battered hulk of a scow sunk lower than the wharf it was moored to, and over beyond a spit of land three sleek launches in front of a white-sand beach. It seemed they were only lazing, it seemed they could fly away out of the harbour at any moment they chose.

She waited two hours without any tea. The launches slowly faded into the dusk. Then Stan came.

He had lost.

He made her go to a restaurant and went to get the horse. He was gone for a long time. When he came back she tried to buy him some food but he said he wasn't hungry. He wanted to get on the road.

They were some miles out of town when she remembered their bags at the Hotel. He said quickly: 'We can't go back for them now.'

She argued. They were hardly out of town. It would take only a minute.

'We can't go back.' He shouted, and behind the anger in his voice there was despair, a drawing out of the 'can't' so that she knew he had done something that was frightening him.

'Stan, you haven't . . . ?' But he began again before she could finish the question.

'What are you talking about? What do you mean, haven't? I just say we're too far out of town and you start thinking all sorts of things.'

She knew then he had done something back there. For a moment she even wondered if anyone was chasing them, and she looked at the petrol gauge. But the gauge showed the tank was almost full. That, in its simplicity, shocked her terribly, and she said under her breath: Stan, what's happened, what's happened? Stan never bought petrol. It was one of the things he always had to be reminded of. Yet today, after that race, he had remembered.

Now as they drove on she grew more aware of the float, and she thought, That's the trouble, that's what causes all the trouble, we're tied to these horses and we can't get away. We're like servants or slaves.

Why couldn't Stan get another job? Why did he have to do things they had to run away from? Why couldn't he go out to work every day, to an ordinary job, like other men? Everything was so complicated. Why couldn't it be simple, as clean and white as that beach and those launches?

The float dragged heavily, lifting the front of the car in a way that gave her almost a feeling of lightheadedness. In this slight dizziness she knew she must speak of the marriage. She must have that chance, the chance for something different even if she couldn't make it just the quiet and rest she wanted.

She said, hesitating: 'Stan, do you – remember last night?'

He broke out again.

'I said I'd marry you, didn't I? What more do you want me to say? I won't break my promise. That's one of the things I don't do.'

'Stan, why can't you – I mean, you could sell the horse, and then get a job.'

'Sell the horse,' he said, and now he spoke softly, as though not thinking of what he was saying.

'He ran a good race today. He was going well until the turn and that wasn't his fault. Somebody would buy him.'

'He's a mongrel,' said Stan. 'He was so full of dope he could hardly breathe. Without it he wouldn't have got to the barrier.'

His hands were light on the wheel so he could feel it move and jump. The float was swaying as they wound down a long hill.

Connie began to speak again, but she stopped when she realised he wasn't taking any notice. He seemed to be listening. And then, from the way he was driving, she saw he was aware of the float.

'Is something wrong, Stan?'

'What do you mean, wrong?'

He turned on her irritably.

'Back there, in the float.'

'What could be wrong? God damn it you say some stupid things.'

The car sagged heavily into the road at the foot of the hill and she heard a faint whinnying scream from the horse, and then a scraping sound that lasted only a second. She looked at Stan quickly.

'Excitable – excitable horse. Doesn't like bumps,' Stan jerked out, and he tried to smile at her.

They came to a straight level stretch of road and he began to drive faster. His hands were white on the wheel. He was sweating, and the float was rattling louder than it ever had before.

'Stan, have you done something to the horse? Is he down?'

Then Stan seemed to go crazy. He began to sway the car over the road; the float lurched and dragged, and the horse screamed again.

'Mongrel, bloody mongrel,' he groaned. He ran the car halfway over the broken edge of the road. It bucked and jolted along; stones rattled against the mudguards and thumped on the chassis and on the bottom of the float.

'Mongrel,' he shouted.

Connie was screaming at him and tearing at his arms, almost

running the car off the road. Then she turned from him and opened her door. Grass and bracken whipped on the metal. She looked back but could see only the yellow half-lit face of the float, so close it seemed to overhang and threaten.

'Stan, for God's sake stop.'

There was no sound from the horse.

'Stan,' she screamed. She tugged at his arm again and the car jumped to the middle of the road. The open door beat once, like a broken wing.

'Stan.' She fell against him. She was crying, uselessly beating his shoulder with her fist.

At last they came to a corner and he slowed to take it. He said, the first word coming on the rush of a long-held breath: 'All right, we'll stop, but nothing's wrong. Excitable, that's all. Just might have got himself down.'

She had time only to half realise the weakness of his pretence before the car stopped and she was out and back at the float. He followed slowly.

The horse was moaning.

'Christ,' said Stan, but his voice was flat. He pulled her away from the locks and lowered the ramp.

Royal Return was down. At first she could not make out how he was lying. Then she saw that his chest was on the floor and his body was twisted left and right from it, the hind quarters turned one way and raised so she could see a leg that dug spasmodically at the straw (like a chicken's, she thought, and the unnatural likeness struck a sort of terror into her), head and neck turned the other, the neck forced by the wall to an erectness that had dug a great pit in the horse's shoulders. One eye was towards her, but not seeing – it was held in a desperate steadiness just above agony.

'Get the torch,' said Stan.

'Oh God.' Connie moved away from him. 'God. Stan. You *did* it.'

'Get the torch,' he repeated dully.

She stopped at the roadside grass. 'You *did* it.'

'Connie, I . . . '

'You *did*, Stan.'

'Connie, it was for you. Don't you see?'

She turned abruptly at that and stumbled down the road.

'Connie, don't go away.'

She made no answer.

'Connie.'

Soon she was out of sight.

After a while Stan went to the car himself and got the torch. He went down on his knees and looked underneath the float; and stood up immediately, leaving the torch on the ground. He moved to the roadside and sat down in grass with his feet in a gutter. Soon he began to retch. He didn't notice that another car had stopped and other people were climbing into the float, but he heard the horse scream, and he felt himself travelling back with terrible urgency to times and places where there had not been even the smallest beginnings of things like this. He was riding back to salute the judge after his first win, a tiny apprentice in gold and green on a chestnut colt with a white blaze. It was a sunny day and people were clapping.

But then Joe Elliot and another man pulled him to his feet and started asking questions. All he could answer, with his face in his hands, was: 'I'm sick, I'm sick.'

They threw him back into the grass.


The Bethams left the hotel shortly after Mrs Benjamin and Charlie Becket. Mrs Betham wondered if Lew had taken so long over his last drink in order to drive back to Auckland behind them. His pleasures, it seemed, were becoming increasingly simple; but in spite of that she had to admit they seemed to satisfy him as nothing had done before – as she herself had never done: he spoke of Bronze Idol with an enthusiasm he had never displayed for her. In thinking this she was frightened. She did not want her memories attacked, she did not want them involved in this business at all. The present must not be allowed to war on the past. That must be kept intact. She wondered then what this past really was. Just a few short years after all – the slump years, when they had lived on porridge and rice and turnips in a tin shed that filled with smoke from a fire that couldn't warm it. How could those be the happy years? And yet she thought of them as a sort of Golden Age. Lew and she had been together in a way that could never be broken, not letting the outside touch them at all. Or was it, she wondered, just that memory ran the good things together, creating a closeness that had never really existed? It had all happened so long ago. Yet in spite of her doubts those years would continue to live.

It was a sort of Golden Age, she thought, and now's the depression, when we've got everything we want.

She began to study Lew. He was concentrating on his driving, trying to catch Charlie Becket.

Perhaps the immortals are equipped with faster cars, she thought. Or perhaps their cars have wings and can fly while ours remain earthbound. Her amusement was brief. She seemed suddenly to be driving with someone she knew only slightly. The face was familiar, but the intentness was created by an ambition she could never understand.

Lew seemed to sense her mood. 'What are you so quiet about?' he said.

She could tell by his voice he expected her to complain about something.

I should, she thought, but it wouldn't do any good.

'Nothing,' she said.

'Haven't you enjoyed yourself?'

'Yes,' she said.

'Well, what is it then? You don't seem very excited. Don't you realise some people own dozens of horses before they get a winner?'

'Yes, dear. And you've done it first time. That's very clever of you.'

The sarcasm had come in spite of her. She had now to listen to a lecture about her lack of wifely enthusiasm, her inability to enjoy herself as other women did.

'I don't understand you,' he finished. 'I do everything I can to make you happy.'

She had many answers to that but he had heard them all and not been impressed. So she sat watching the dark bush, trying to see into it, imagining some primitive settlement deep in there, a place where life was simple and people had time to know and like each other. But the headlamps never rested on anything for long. Her mind couldn't settle. Lew was driving too fast. There was a car going down the hill ahead of them, disappearing round a new corner every time they caught sight of it. He was trying to get closer to see if it was Charlie Becket's.

On the flat at the foot of the hill they saw it wasn't and Lew seemed to lose heart. He drove more slowly.

'I think I'll stop and have a whiskey,' he said.

Just then they went round a corner and saw what looked to be an accident. Two cars were pulled up behind a horse-float and a third was in front of it. There were some men at the mouth of the float and two inside. They couldn't see the horse.

Lew went past slowly and pulled in at the front of the line. He told Mrs Betham to wait where she was and went back to the float. He was gone for perhaps five minutes.

Mrs Betham would have liked to see what was happening, but she thought if the horse was sick or hurt she'd only be in the way. Besides, she hated to seem curious. But she did notice two rather strange things: this was horse business and Charlie Becket hadn't stopped, and back beside the float a man was sitting in the grass. He was very still. At first she thought he was a small tree or a clump of bracken. Then the shape became clearer. he was bent forward with his arms across his knees, his face in the arms. Nobody was taking any notice of him, although the way he was sitting made him appear lonely and in need of comfort. She felt she should go along and see if there was anything she could do.

When Lew came back she said: 'Who's that man sitting in the grass?'

'Philpott,' he said. It was not so much an answer to her question as something he was saying to himself. Then he swore, using a word he'd never used in front of her before.

'What's happened, Lew?' she asked nervously.

Lew was pouring himself a whiskey. When he'd drunk it he looked at her and said: 'He's just butchered his horse.'

'Butchered it. You mean he's killed it?'

He shook his head and she saw his eyes fill with tears. 'It's not dead yet,' he said. 'They've gone to get a gun to shoot it.'

She couldn't understand, but she listened as Lew told her what had happened. Philpott had loosened the boards at the front of the float so the horse's legs had broken through when the car hit a bump.

'They must have been trailing along the road for miles. They're almost torn off. Just hanging in tatters. You can see bits of bone.'

Lew poured himself another drink. His hands were shaking and whiskey slopped on his trousers.

Mrs Betham was saying to herself: But that's awful, how could he, how could a person do a thing like that? – but she couldn't say it aloud. Nothing was adequate as she pictured the tattered legs and the pieces of bone.

'But, Lew . . . ' she said.

'He did it for the insurance,' said Lew. 'You knew horses were insured, didn't you?'

'There are people who could do a thing like that for money!'she said.

'For money.' Lew threw the bottle into the glove-box.

'I hope he gets ten years,' he said. 'If I was the judge I'd order a flogging.'

'What about the girl?' said Mrs Betham. 'Was she in it?'

'His girl? Connie Reynolds? No, she wasn't there. How do you know her?'

'I saw her on the racecourse today,' said Mrs Betham.

Lew grunted. His mind was still on the horse. Mrs Betham, too, was unable to keep her mind from returning to the horrible picture he had painted. She had had a moment's relief when she heard that Connie wasn't involved, but then she turned and looked again at the figure in the grass. It was motionless, in a hunched cowering attitude.

It's too late for him to be sorry, she thought. And her loathing increased. But strangely it changed so that it was not so much for him as for what had been done. He seemed now to exist outside the act. The act was unimaginable, but he was there, part of the horror he had brought into existence, the only part of it she could really see.

She knew that soon she would feel sorry for him, and she told herself it wasn't right to have that much pity. It was dangerous to forgive too much. There must be things that could never be forgiven, and surely this . . .

The tattered legs and pieces of bone . . .

No, that could never be forgiven.

Lew had started the car and they were moving again. He drove without talking, and she was glad, though she expected him to break out at any minute. Her mind was calmer now, and she was trying to convince herself a person couldn't do a thing like that for money. There must be other reasons.

No, she thought, it's not just the money. That's too simple. It's everything money means. You can't blame a person for failing to survive that. And yet you can't forgive. Here I am trying to forgive.

But as she thought of the horse with its legs torn off, and the man sitting on the grass, both seemed equally terrible mutilations, the one as pitiable as the other.

'There's his girl now,' said Lew. He didn't slow down and they flashed by almost before Mrs Betham saw her.

'Stop, Lew. We'll pick her up.'

'After what happened back there?' said Lew.

But she argued with him and made him stop and back up to the girl. He was angry, but knew she was determined to have her way. He'd showed his disapproval by not looking round or speaking as Connie got into the back seat.

Then, as he drove on and heard his wife explaining that they knew what had happened and heard the girl break into long scratching sobs, he was seized with an almost physical revulsion. He felt he wanted to be sick. The girl and the crying, and Philpott and the horse, were a sort of disease; he felt unclean having her in the car. There must be ways of avoiding things like this, ways of getting about so that you never saw them.

God, why can't things be perfect, he thought.

He heard the girl say: 'I don't know what to do. I don't know.'

'Then wait,' said his wife. 'Just don't do anything. You'll find out what's right.'

A little later Connie said: 'I want to go back, but I *can't*.'

'Just wait,' said the wife. 'Don't think of anything.'

He recognised her 'soothing' voice. It made him jealous when she used it for anyone but him, and he stabbed savagely with his foot to dip for an oncoming car.

The girl said, still crying: 'This is the first time probably he's ever really needed me – and I can't go.'

'Shh,' said Mrs Betham.

But Connie had not been talking to her, and hadn't listened. In a few moments she stopped crying.

'He said he did it for me,' she whispered. She gave a little moan.

'Shh. Don't think,' said Mrs Betham.

'So really – really . . . ' She stopped and seemed to talk to herself, and almost cry again.

'So really – it's as much my fault as his.'

'No. Don't even begin to think that,' said Mrs Betham. She

tried to take Connie's hand but the back of the seat made it awkward for her and Connie made no move to help. So she rested her arm along the seat-back with her fingers brushing the sleeve of Lew's coat, and smiled kindly at the girl, wishing there was something she could give her, something she could do: the dead paws of the fur, dangling over her arm, were no more useless than she was.

Later, when they thought she was sleeping, Connie leaned forward and said 'Stop, please I want to get out.'

Lew stopped quickly. His wife leaned back and put a hand on Connie's arm. 'What are you going to do?'

'I don't know,' said Connie.

She opened the door, got out clumsily, closed it, and came to Mrs Betham's window to say something. Lew couldn't hear for the noise of the engine, and didn't want to hear. He thought her face was yellow and ugly; he wanted to get away.

The car began to move again; Mrs Betham said nothing. She watched until the girl was lost in the darkness. Then she leaned against her door with her cheek against the cold window.

Lew let a little time pass. He said: 'You want to save the Good Samaritan act for somebody worth while. I could tell you stories about that girl.'

'I don't want to hear,' said Mrs Betham.

He shrugged and drove on. He was happy now that Connie was gone.

Soon he saw a tail-light shining in the darkness ahead, and he increased speed, wondering if at last he had caught up with Charlie Becket.

# THE ORACLE

## A. B. (Banjo) Paterson

No tram ever goes to Randwick races without him; he is always fat, hairy, and assertive; he is generally one of a party, and takes the centre of the stage all the time – collects and hands over the fares, adjusts the change, chaffs the conductor, crushes the thin, apologetic stranger next him into a pulp, and talks to the whole compartment as if they had asked for his opinion.

He knows all the trainers and owners, or takes care to give the impression that he does. He slowly and pompously hauls out his race-book, and one of his satellites opens the ball by saying, in a deferential way,

'What do you like for the 'urdles, Charley?'

The Oracle looks at the book and breathes heavily; no one else ventures to speak.

'Well,' he says, at last, 'of course there's only one in it – if he's wanted. But that's it – will they spin him? I don't think they will. They's only a lot o'cuddies, any 'ow.'

No one likes to expose his own ignorance by asking which horse he refers to as the 'only one in it'; and the Oracle goes on to deal out some more wisdom in a loud voice.

'Billy K – told me' (he probably hardly knows Billy K – by sight) 'Billy K – told me that that bay 'orse ran the best mile-an'-a-half ever done on Randwick yesterday; but I don't give him a chance, for all that; that's the worst of these trainers. They don't know when their horses are well – half of 'em.'

Then a voice comes from behind him. It is that of the thin man, who is crushed out of sight by the bulk of the Oracle.

'I think,' says the thin man, 'that that horse of Flannery's ought to run well in the Handicap.'

The Oracle can't stand this sort of thing at all. He gives a snort, wheels half-round and looks at the speaker. Then he turns back to the compartment full of people, and says, 'No ope.'

The thin man makes a last effort. 'Well, they backed him last night, anyhow.'

'Who backed im?' says the Oracle.

'In Tattersall's,' says the thin man.

'I'm sure,' says the Oracle; and the thin man collapses.

On arrival at the course, the Oracle is in great form. Attended by his string of satellites, he plods from stall to stall staring at the horses. Their names are printed in big letters on the stalls, but the Oracle doesn't let that stop his display of knowledge.

''Ere's Blue Fire,' he says, stopping at that animal's stall, and swinging his race-book. 'Good old Blue Fire!' he goes on loudly, as a little court collects. 'Jimmy B – ' (mentioning a popular jockey) 'told me he couldn't have lost on Saturday week if he had only been ridden different. I had a good stake on him, too, that day. Lor', the races that has been chucked away on this horse. They will not ride him right.'

A trainer who is standing by, civilly interposes. 'This isn't Blue Fire,' he says. 'Blue Fire's out walking about. This is a two-year-old filly that's in the stall – '

'Well, I can see that, can't I,' says the Oracle, crushingly. 'You don't suppose I thought Blue Fire was a mare, did you?' and he moves off hurriedly.

'Now, look here, you chaps,' he says to his followers at last. 'You wait here. I want to go and see a few of the talent, and it don't do to have a crowd with you. There's Jimmy M – over there now' (pointing to a leading trainer). 'I'll get hold of him in a minute. He couldn't tell me anything with so many about. Just you wait here.'

He crushes into a crowd that has gathered round the favourite's stall, and overhears one hard-faced racing man say to another, 'What do you like?' to which the other answers, 'Well, either this or Royal Scot. I think I'll put a bit on Royal Scot.' This is enough for the Oracle. He doesn't know either of the men from Adam, or either of the horses from the great original pachyderm, but the information will do to go on with. He rejoins his followers, and looks very mysterious.

'Well, did you hear anything?' they say.

The Oracle talks low and confidentially.

'The crowd that have got the favourite tell me they're not afraid of anything but Royal Scot,' he says. 'I think we'd better put a bit on both.'

'What did the Royal Scot crowd say?' asks an admirer deferentially.

'Oh, they're going to try and win. I saw the stable commissioner, and he told me they were going to put a hundred on him. Of course, you needn't say I told you, 'cause I promised him I wouldn't tell.' And the satellites beam with admiration of the Oracle, and think what a privilege it is to go to the races with such a knowing man.

They contribute their mites to the general fund, some putting in a pound, others half a sovereign, and the Oracle takes it into the ring to invest, half on the favourite and half on Royal Scot. He finds that the favourite is at two to one, and Royal Scot at threes, eight to one being offered against anything else. As he ploughs through the ring, a Whisperer (one of those broken-down followers of the turf who get their living in various mysterious ways, but partly by giving 'tips' to backers) pulls his sleeve.

'What are you backing?' he says.

'Favourite and Royal Scot,' says the Oracle.

'Put a pound on Bendemeer,' says the tipster. 'It's a certainty. Meet me here if it comes off, and I'll tell you something for the next race. Don't miss it now. Get on quick!'

The Oracle is humble enough before the hanger-on of the turf. A bookmaker roars 'ten to one Bendemeer;' he suddenly fishes out a sovereign of his own – and he hasn't money to spare, for all his knowingness – and puts it on Bendemeer. His friends' money he puts on the favourite and Royal Scot as arranged. Then they all go round to watch the race.

The horses are at the post; a distant cluster of crowded animals with little dots of colour on their backs. Green, blue, yellow, purple, French grey, and old gold, they change about in a bewildering manner, and though the Oracle has a cheap pair of glasses, he can't make out where Bendemeer has got to. Royal Scot and the favourite he has lost interest in, and secretly hopes that they will be left at the post or break their necks; but he does not confide his sentiment to his companions.

They're off! The long line of colours across the track becomes a shapeless clump and then draws out into a long string. 'What's that in front?' yells someone at the rails. 'Oh, that thing of Hart's,' says someone else. But the Oracle hears them not; he is looking in the mass of colour for a purple cap and grey jacket, with black armbands. He cannot see it anywhere, and the confused and confusing mass swings round the turn into the straight.

Then there is a babel of voices, and suddenly a shout of 'Bendemeer! Bendemeer!' and the Oracle, without knowing which is Bendemeer, takes up the cry feverishly. 'Bendemeer! Bendemeer!' he yells, waggling his glasses about, trying to see where the animal is.

'Where's Royal Scot, Charley? Where's Royal Scot?' screams one of his friends, in agony. "Ow's he doin'?'

'No 'ope!' says the Oracle, with fiendish glee. 'Bendemeer! Bendemeer!'

The horses are at the Leger stand now, whips are out, and three horses seem to be nearly abreast; in fact, to the Oracle there seem to be a dozen nearly abreast. Then a big chestnut sticks his head in front of the others, and a small man at the Oracle's side emits a deafening series of yells right by the Oracle's ear:

'Go on, Jimmy! Rub it into him! Belt him! It's a cake-walk! A cake-walk!' The big chestnut, in a dogged sort of way, seems to stick his body clear of his opponents, and passes the post a winner by a length. The Oracle doesn't know what has won, but fumbles with his book. The number on the saddle-cloth catches his eye – No. 7; he looks hurriedly down the page. No. 7 – Royal Scot. Second is No. 24 – Bendemeer. Favourite nowhere.

Hardly has he realized it, before his friends are cheering and clapping him on the back. 'By George, Charley, it takes you to pick 'em,' 'Come and 'ave a wet!' 'You 'ad a quid on, didn't you, Charley?' The Oracle feels very sick at having missed the winner, but he dies game. 'Yes, rather; I had a quid on,' he says. 'And,' (here he nerves himself to smile) 'I had a saver on the second, too.'

His comrades gasp with astonishment. 'D'you hear that, eh? Charley backed first and second. That's pickin' 'em if you like.' They have a wet, and pour fulsome adulation on the Oracle when he collects their money.

After the Oracle has collected the winnings for his friends he meets the Whisperer again.

'It didn't win?' he says to the Whisperer in inquiring tones.

'Didn't win,' says the Whisperer, who has determined to brazen the matter out. 'How could he win? Did you see the way he was ridden? That horse was stiffened just after I seen you, and he never tried a yard. Did you see the way he was pulled and hauled about at the turn? It'd make a man sick. What was the stipendiary stewards doing, I wonder?'

This fills the Oracle with a new idea. All that he remembers of the race at the turn was a jumble of colours, a kaleidoscope of horses and riders hanging on to the horses' necks. But it wouldn't do to admit that he didn't see everything, and didn't know everything; so he plunges in boldly.

'O' course I saw it,' he says. 'And a blind man could see it. They ought to rub him out.'

'Course they ought,' says the Whisperer. 'But, look here, put two quid on Tell-tale; you'll get it all back!'

The Oracle does put on 'two quid', and doesn't get it all back. Neither does he see any more of this race than he did of the last one – in fact, he cheers wildly when the wrong horse is coming in. But when the public begin to hoot he hoots as loudly as anybody – louder if anything; and all the way home in the tram he lays down the law about stiff running, and wants to know what the stipendiaries are doing.

If you go into any barber's shop, you could hear him at it, and he flourishes in suburban railway carriages; but he has a tremendous local reputation, having picked first and second in the Handicap, and it would be a bold man who would venture to question the Oracle's knowledge of racing and all matters relating to it.